STUFF TO SPY FOR

STUFF TO SPY FOR

A NOVEL

DON BRUNS

Oceanview Publishing

IPSWICH, MASSACHUSETTS

ISBN-13: 978-1-933515-22-9

Published in the United States by Oceanview Publishing,
Ipswich, Massachusetts
www.oceanviewpub.com

2 4 6 8 10 9 7 5 3 1

PRINTED IN THE UNITED STATES OF AMERICA

This book is dedicated to Jody Stacy, who introduced me to the world of spying. Don't ever get on Jody's bad side!

ACKNOWLEDGMENTS

To my wife, Linda, who always reads the first version. Thanks to Bob and Pat Gussin from Oceanview who give me the reason to write. Thank you to Maryglenn McCombs who is the greatest publicist in the business, to Mary Stanton and Claudia Bishop who are my good friends in this crazy business, to Sue Grafton who made sure I had a career as a writer, to my good friend, author Stuart M. Kaminsky, who championed this series, and to "Miami" Tom Biddle who always shares my research adventures. What a time we've had. To Mike Trump, my Chicago connection, and to all the others who've answered numerous questions and solved numerous problems along the way. Thanks.

DB
Sarasota, Florida
November 2009

STUFF TO SPY FOR

PROLOGUE

I'd always heard that when you die your entire life passes before you. You see all the people you knew, all of your relatives, alive and dead. In a flash you see your friends from high school and college, and I'm pretty sure that would include all of your girl-friends. My mother once told me that you would see all the good things and bad things that you'd done with your life, and she warned me that I'd better have a bunch of good things to look at.

I don't know if it happens for some people or not. I don't know if they have a flash of that roller coaster at Busch Gardens in the eighth grade, or if they relive that gross wet kiss on the cheek from Aunt Sylvie at Uncle Harold's funeral. Maybe they see the first time they stole from their little sister or lied to their father. Maybe they flash on that moment when a sinkhole almost swallowed them. I can't speak for anyone else.

All I know is, when I died, my life didn't pass in front me.

CHAPTER ONE

Sarah Crumbly graduated from high school one year behind James and me. She was voted "most likely to succeed," and I was one of her fans. We'd gone out a couple of times, to a movie and a burger joint, and I thought she rocked. Cheerleader perfect, with legs that I dreamed about, but since she was an overachiever, I got left by the curb. I always thought about what might have happened with Sarah. And then I found her, about eight years later, and in a matter of days, I realized I was lucky the relationship had never gone any further.

I'm Skip Moore, and I'm basically an underachiever. I graduated, barely, from college, and I'm working for a security company in Carol City, Florida. Carol City is a rundown, poverty stricken urban community that has nothing to secure. So, you can imagine that the prospects are slim.

But the call came in from Synco Systems, and when I showed up there last Tuesday, Sarah met me at the front desk.

"Sarah?"

"My God. Skip?"

I stared at her for several seconds. Golden hair cut just under her cute ears and that picture-perfect figure right below her cute face.

"Skip, you're my security guy? You?"

"I am."

"This is a surprise. I really should just show you around the building and tell you what we're looking for, but I'd like to catch up."

And right away, knowing that Em was expecting me for dinner tonight, knowing that Emily and I had worked out an arrangement that we would be somewhat exclusive, knowing that a permanent relationship was what I longed for, knowing that if Em found out she would kill me, I asked Sarah if she would be interested in having dinner.

"I would."

"I'm serious."

She looked me right in the eyes, giving me an impish smile. "Skip, so am I."

Damn. If she'd even hesitated, I would have remained true, but she didn't. She didn't hesitate a second.

Twenty minutes later she'd given me the rough layout. I'd followed her around like a puppy dog, her short skirt swishing over her perfect thighs, the high, shiny black heels highlighting her balancing act. And I'd tried to pay attention to business. The company wanted us to tear out their old security system and put a state-of-the-art system in place.

"One of our newest clients is demanding that we upgrade our security system. That's why you're here."

"Well, you've got a smart client." I had to agree with anyone who was putting a paycheck in my pocket.

"This client has something to do with the U.S. government, but I'm not sure exactly what."

Obviously, Sarah wasn't in on everything regarding the company.

Synco Systems — she was emphatic that it was pronounced Sin-co, not Sink-o — was a software company that designed protection systems for computer networks. It seems that every time someone developed a protection system for business networks, somebody else found a way to hack into that system. So it seemed to Sarah, and to me, that Synco Systems was in no danger of going out of business any time soon.

And, it seemed that way to my roommate and best friend, James.

"Skip, that's what I'm talking about." We were sitting on the tiny slab of stained concrete that passed for a patio behind our pitiful apartment. James swallowed a mouthful of beer and waved his brown bottle in the air. "Man, that's textbook smarts. Start a company that can never become obsolete. I mean, somebody hacks your system — well, you have to design a new system. And you know they'll hack that system eventually. And the next, and the next. So you just keep coming up with new systems, and you never, ever go out of business."

I'd seen it with my own eyes. "Pretty technical stuff, James. If they buy our security system for their building, it'll be the biggest sale I've ever made. Maybe the biggest sale in this part of the state. Seriously. And she thinks the demand is coming from someone associated with the United States government. So I'd say the odds are pretty good we get the job."

James lit a cigarette and blew a stream of yellow smoke across the way to the row of stucco gray apartments about fifteen feet from ours. It was a lovely view. We stared into their back bedroom windows and they could stare into ours. We got to see their overfilled garbage cans and they got to see ours. And to the right was a muddy ditch, about eight units down. I often told people we had a "water view." We didn't exactly live in squalor. I think squalor was a few steps up from how we lived.

"We'd be tearing out the old system and installing a bunch of stations and there would be motion detectors, sound sensors, door and window monitors, a camera monitor at minimum."

"How much, Skip?"

"How much is it going to cost them?"

"Yeah."

"Well, I'm going to do an estimate on the number of sensors that we'd install, then Michael—"

"Michael the ass?"

"The same. My boss. He'll come out and check my work, and—"

"An estimate, son. Give this boy a bone. How much?"

"Tearing out the old system, installation of our new one, plus the first year of the contract, seventy-five thousand dollars."

James took another swallow and belched. "And you get how much of that, amigo?"

I didn't have any figuring to do. I'd pretty much been thinking about it since two o'clock in the afternoon. Pretty much been considering it for four solid hours. Pretty much spending it for the last three. That was after I'd gotten over the shock of realizing this could actually happen. "A little over eleven thousand dollars."

"Almost half of what you made all of last year, pard. Am I right?"

"You are."

"Truck only cost twelve thousand."

James was speaking of his $12,000 investment in a used box truck. We'd gone into the moving business with that truck and almost gotten ourselves killed. Then, we'd turned the truck into a small kitchen, selling food to the believers at a salvation crusade put on by the Reverend Preston Cashdollar. And again, we'd

5

almost gotten ourselves killed. He was talking about *that* truck. "What are you getting at, James?"

"Not getting at anything, brother. Just noting. If we ever decided to get a fleet of trucks, you could almost —"

"No."

"I'm just saying —"

He is always *saying*. "No box truck." Maybe retire one of the college loans, pay the one-month back rent we still owed, and maybe buy a case of imported beer. The cheap stuff we'd been buying at Gas and Grocery, the rickety little carryout we go to in Carol City, was starting to get a little rank.

"Skip, I want you to think about it. We always talked about a fleet of trucks and —"

"*You* talked about a fleet of trucks, James."

He threw up his hands. "Okay, amigo. But don't discount it."

"James, I don't have the sale yet. Synco Systems is interested. That's all there is at this moment."

"Are they shopping it around?"

There was the rub. If they were just getting quotes, I'd actually have to sell. I'd have to go through the script book and make an argument for my company. That's when my job became tedious.

I had forgotten to ask her. I was so surprised that Sarah was my contact, I'd forgotten to ask. It's supposed to be a standard question when we visit a business. "Are you shopping for a system anywhere else? Can I ask where? Oh, XYZ? That's a fine company. Can I show you why our system makes more sense? You see, we offer terms, and we can install in one week and— and —" and on and on. It's all in the sales manual that I've only skimmed once in a while. It's really quite lame.

"I'm thinkin', pardner, you meeting up with Sarah. What are the chances? It's got to be more than just coincidence. Maybe it's the Lord's will."

"I don't think he had anything to do with it." James had taken to throwing the phrase around ever since we worked the reverend Preston Cashdollar's revival tent meeting several months ago. James wasn't a religious guy, so it had sarcastic overtones.

"Seriously, Skip. Maybe this was meant to be."

I'd been thinking the same thing. Something really good comes into your life, like me seeing Sarah again, and it's followed by something else that's really good, like maybe selling a $75,000 security system. And on top of that, they say good things come in threes. I was anxious to see what the next thing would be. I found out, and it looked great. But, as I mentioned before, it backfired. It actually got me killed.

CHAPTER TWO

I didn't tell James about dinner. I actually lied to him and told him I had to meet with Michael and go over figures to quote the job for Synco Systems. And I didn't tell Em about dinner. I lied to her as well. It didn't feel right, even though I was sure nothing was going to happen between Sarah and me, but I lied nevertheless.

And I lied to Sarah. When she asked me if I was seeing any-one, when she asked me if I'd ever been serious with anyone, and when she asked me if I'd ever considered being a father. I answered no to every question. I can't explain why I denied the truth. But I did. I lied to her, and those innocent white lies came back to haunt me in a way I never would have dreamed of.

It was at this time, when she asked me those questions, I realized she was either very interested in my life, or she was lead-ing up to a story about her own life. You know how it is when you want to introduce a topic about yourself, so you start asking the other person if they've ever thought about or considered some-thing, then you turn it around and talk about yourself? Well, it turned out, she needed to spill the story of her life. Just as well. My life sucks. Always has, probably always will.

"I'm very serious about someone, Skip."

We were sitting on the patio of Barton G's restaurant, having the Garden Sea Bass with pickled ginger and a variety of vegetables, including the flash-fried asparagus. It was more than I could afford but what the hell. With a little luck, I was going to pocket eleven thousand dollars in a very short period of time, and eventually I could afford this fancy place. For a brief time.

"It didn't start off that way."

I nodded. This was my second glass of wine, and I was feeling a little tipsy already. I could drink six beers without much effect, but I was trying to impress Sarah, and wine seemed more sophisticated. The problem was a couple glasses of wine could knock me out.

"We met through a . . ." she hesitated, "a dating service." She folded her hands in front of her. Her golden hair hung in ringlets around her face, and I briefly glanced down at her low-cut blouse.

"A lot of people use dating services. This was an Internet dating service?" She needed a service? Every guy in the world would fall down and worship this girl.

She hesitated, searching my face with her big blue eyes. "It wasn't quite like that."

"What was it like?" I held a finger up and motioned to our waiter. "Do you have Blue Moon beer?" He rolled his eyes, then glanced at Sarah's cleavage. Well, it was there for the viewing.

"I suppose the gentleman wants an orange slice?"

"No, thank you." I shook my head. You always put an orange slice on a Blue Moon, and I really liked having an orange slice, but I didn't like this guy's attitude. I showed him.

Sarah pushed her vegetables around the plate with her fork, never looking at me. "I'm telling you this, Skip, because you may do work for our company."

I couldn't figure out why her love life would affect my business.

"This guy was—is—married."

"You knew?" I was hoping her answer was no.

"It didn't matter."

"What didn't matter?"

"Whether he was married."

"Sarah, you're losing me."

She hesitated, picking up a spear of the crispy asparagus, biting off the head. There was something very sensual about the act. Sensual, and scary at the same time. "It's not important, okay. The thing is, I'm seeing him."

"And how does this affect me?"

"Sandler is the president of our company."

"Wow."

"I know, I know. If you're going to date, you may as well start at the top."

"Sarah, how does this affect my job?"

"I'm your contact, Skip. You and I will be working very closely together. If Sandy likes you, you'll get the job and everything will go smoothly."

"If he doesn't like me?"

"He'll like you."

"Then it's all good."

"He'll like you because you're my new boyfriend."

Man, I had stepped into it. She asked if I was seeing anyone. She asked if I was serious about someone and if I'd ever considered being a father. And now this? Talk about an awkward moment.

"Sarah, we went out a couple of times, but—"

"Sandy's wife thinks he's having an affair."

"And?" She'd just told me he was. With her. And now she wanted me to be her boyfriend?

"She's not certain. If she finds out for sure, she'll destroy him."

"Look, Sarah, I really want this job. I need this job, but what am I getting into?"

Sarah reached across the white linen-covered table and grasped my hand. "Carol Conroy's father owns Synco Systems. So it becomes a real problem." She squeezed my fingers tightly.

"Your beer, sir." An orange slice was stuck in the opening of the bottle. I said nothing. The waiter lingered, taking another look.

"Sarah. You're making no sense. I'd really like to help you here, but —"

"Carol Conroy is Sandy's wife. If she can prove that he's having an affair, she'll have her father fire him. She'll destroy Sandy's career. Can't you see that?"

I couldn't see anything. I had no idea where this was going, but that eleven thousand dollar commission was looking less and less attractive.

"Skip, I'll make it very simple for you. I need a boyfriend. I need someone who, at least for now, appears to be my significant other. If you can do that, if you can keep Carol Conroy from suspecting that I'm having an affair with her husband, you've got the job. Sandy will hire you tomorrow. And there will even be a bonus for you. Now, how's that?"

A bonus? My ears perked up. Maybe pretending to be her boyfriend wasn't so bad. Of course, I'd have to figure out how to present this to Em. God, Em would never understand this, much less agree to it. "What happens when the job is done? You can't keep trotting me out the rest of your life."

"Sandy is in line for a huge bonus. So big he can start his own company. So big, he may never have to work again. So big, Skip, that Sandy and I can do just about anything we want to do. Go anywhere we want to go. Once he gets the bonus, he can walk out on his wife." She finally released my hands, and a big smile

11

covered her cute face. "Skip, we're looking at property in the south of France. Can you imagine that? The south of France."

I couldn't.

She took a deep breath and settled back into her chair. Sipping her cosmopolitan, she looked directly into my eyes. "You and I will have a pretend relationship, Skip. And it's only for a couple of months at the most. And you aren't seeing anyone, so what do you say?"

I had no idea what to say. I took a swallow of Blue Moon beer, trying to buy a little time.

"There's a bonus, Skip. How does ten thousand dollars sound?"

I choked on the beer, spitting it all over the table.

CHAPTER THREE

"And there's no sex?" Clearly James was disappointed.

I'd come clean on the dinner with Sarah. Of course, he wanted to know every detail.

"Come on, James. Would I even be interested?"

James looked at me, shaking his head.

"Hey, man, keep your eyes on the road."

He slowly shifted his gaze to the road ahead of us. The rickety box truck chugged along, occasionally coughing and spewing puffs of black, brown, and gray smoke. The old girl burned oil, and we'd never had enough money to fix the problem. The problem being, the truck was old, and if we were going to use a truck as a way to produce income, we needed a new truck. In our current fiscal crisis, even a newer truck would suffice.

"A make-believe girlfriend. It's very strange, amigo." James pursed his lips, and affected a frown on his face. He squinted his eyes as if he was assessing the situation. I wished I'd never mentioned it.

"Actually, it's a make-believe boyfriend, James. She's the one who has to pretend. Pretend that I'm her boyfriend until this Sandy character gets his big paycheck. Then, it's off to France, or wherever they're going. It's all just a joke." He'd beat it to death. I know exactly how his mind works.

"This paycheck—"

"Must be a monster. She said he'd never have to work again. They could do anything they wanted."

"Man. Can you imagine how much that would be?"

"Two million or more?"

James laughed. "Try ten or more. These people live in a different world, compadre."

"True." How could someone imagine ten million? How could someone spend ten million?

We'd stopped at Pep Boys and bought a case of oil, then stopped at Gas and Grocery and picked up a case of Yuengling long necks. Much better than the stuff at home. James had an open bottle tucked beside his worn cloth seat and he checked the rearview mirror to make sure there were no cops following us.

"James, I haven't agreed to do the deal." The bonus was very tempting. But there was Em.

He took a long, deep swallow of beer, this time keeping his eyes on the road. "But you will get the job, pally. It's the Lord's will." James's sarcasm was shining through.

"All you have to do is pretend you like the girl and you make an eleven thousand dollar profit. It can't be that hard, Skip. Think this through."

I hadn't told him about the bonus. Man, he would go crazy if he knew. And I knew that sooner or later I'd spill it. I always did. James, love him or hate him, was my best friend, and sooner or later you tell your best friend everything.

Unless you're sleeping with his wife. And that thought got me thinking about Sarah, sleeping with somebody else's husband, and that got me thinking about playing make-believe with Sarah, and what Emily would say about that. And then I thought maybe I wouldn't tell Em. Just not mention it. I wasn't really cheating on her. I wasn't really having any physical contact. I mean, how much trouble would that be? A couple of months — keep it low key, and then I get the bonus, the commission, and no one has to know anything.

"So tell me again. She meets this guy online?"

"Some sort of a dating service."

"Sarah shouldn't need a dating service. Is she still built like a brick —"

"She's built, James. Very sexy. And she dresses in really high heels, a tight dress and a plunging neckline. I mean, it was the complete package."

He pulled into our parking lot and parked the truck in front of our shabby apartment. A rusted-out Ford pickup truck was pulled in at an angle next to my old Chevy, and Jim Jobs's *Odd Jobs* Chrysler van was on the other side with its hideous orange and red sign. *Jim Jobs's Odd Jobs/ No matter what the job, Jim Jobs can do it.* We'd never explored the veracity of the statement.

"Think about what it would have been like if she dressed like that in high school."

"I don't want to think about it. She never would have gone out with me at all." She would have been propositioned by every good-looking senior guy in our graduating class, and probably by every guy in her class as well.

"Skip," he stepped from the truck, avoiding the loose running board. He'd twisted his ankle twice on that dangerous piece of aluminum. Someday I was going to get a hacksaw and just cut the damned thing off. "Skip, I love you like a brother —"

"But?"

"But you were never in her league."

I smiled and got out of the truck. "Tell me, James. Am I in Em's league?"

15

"You got me there, pard. No one is in her league. Your snotty little rich bitch? Just ask her."

He was right, but it didn't seem to matter to Em. She seemed to "get" me, and I was very happy about the relationship.

I put the case of oil behind the passenger seat, in the narrow closet of the truck. James took the case of beer inside. By the time I hit the front door, he'd popped the cap on his second bottle.

"Internet dating services."

"A dating service. You could use one, James. It's been a dry spell the last several months, hasn't it?"

"Screw you."

He sat down at the computer and booted it up, sipping on his beer. Actually, I'd picked up the tab on the case. It was my beer. Very seldom did James have enough liquid capital to buy the brown stuff.

"Internet dating services. If I just Google dating services, and put in her name, maybe I could —"

"She's found the guy, James. I'm sure she's not still listed."

"Yeah, but sometimes these people keep their profile up for a while." He stared at the screen, running his fingers over the keyboard. "You know, in case it doesn't work out." Click, click, click.

I wondered if Em had a profile on a dating service. I'd never even considered it.

"And his name was?"

"Sandy Conroy. Or try Sandler. And I'm positive he'd put his name up on there so his wife could find it and destroy the poor S.O.B."

"No need to get sarcastic, pardner."

"Think about it, James. It just wouldn't be a sound idea. The guy would not advertise his own name, saying he was looking for an affair. He's a big-time business executive. He didn't get to be president by being stupid. Got it?"

16

"You never know, Skip."

"Whatever." There was no way he could figure this one out.

His fingers flew over the keys. I went into the kitchen and opened a beer. Yuenglings. They brewed it up in Tampa, so James's reasoning was it had to be fresh. Bud was brewed up there too, but when I had a couple of bucks, he opted for Yuengling.

"We should have started an Internet dating service, Skip. Could have made a killing."

"Do you understand anything at all about setting up computer systems?"

"No."

"Do you understand anything about women?"

"Now that you mention it —" his eyes were laser focused on the screen.

"So, it's better left to the computer geeks."

"Point well taken." He kept stroking the keyboard, and as I sipped the lukewarm beer I could see images racing across the screen.

"If I take the job, we'd have installers come in and tear out the old system. Then, they'd do all the wiring, with the motion detectors and everything."

"Uh-huh." He was leaning into the computer screen, studying the pictures.

"James, you're not going to find her."

"So, there will be installers?"

"A job this big, we'll need a couple of supervisors. A couple of people who get to know the layout of the building and will be able to work with the installers, getting answers for their questions, assisting the operation and stuff like that."

"Uh-huh. Gofers, right?"

"Any chance you can get a week off from Cap'n Crab?"

"What?"

Cap'n Crab was the seafood shack where James worked. He

cooked the crab. A far cry from his dream when he attended culinary school. But my security company was a far cry from my dreams when I attended business school at Samuel and Davidson University. James and I were still trying to find the American Dream. I was starting to think maybe, just maybe, I'd found a piece of it. "Can you get a week off?"

"Why?"

"James, I just told you. We need some supervisors."

He glanced up from our computer, with it's $40-a-month access fee that I usually ended up paying. "Me? A supervisor?"

"I was thinking."

"How much does it pay?"

"Got to be more than you get boiling crab. And you won't come home smelling like shellfish."

"How much, amigo?"

"Twelve an hour. Eight hours a day. One hour for lunch."

He gave me a big smile.

"Makes you happy, eh?"

"No. I'll do your supervisor job, Skip, but that's not why I'm happy."

"What then?"

"Remember the movie *Ten*?"

"The little guy who played in *Arthur*? Dudley somebody?"

"No, a Belgian movie, came out about 2002."

Usual obscure movie from James. While I watched most of the movies with him, I didn't remember all of them. "What about it, James?"

"There's a line in there. Two ladies are talking. One says, 'You are wholesalers, we are retailers.'"

The movie didn't ring a bell. James saw a lot of films and remembered a lot of quotes. To be honest, I didn't have the interest in remembering everything about those movies. Sure, I saw the movies with him, but memorizing movie quotes happened to be a somewhat useless talent. I didn't want to be reminded. "Get to the point, James."

"I've got Sarah's picture." He nodded an exaggerated head bob and pointed at the screen.

"How did you find that?" On top of being a movie quote buff, James was also a whiz on Google and Yahoo.

"You just keep plugging in words, pard."

"Give me a break. You found her?"

"Words like, Miami, date, executive, services. Stuff like that."

When I needed information, James was always on top of it. "Sarah? She still has a profile?"

"No, Alexandra has a profile."

"Alexandra?"

"Look."

I took a swallow of beer and leaned over the screen. There she was, smiling back at me. There were face shots, upper-body shots, full-figure shots, and some casual shots of her in tight jeans and a halter top. God, she looked good. Sleek, tan, showing off a lot of smooth skin.

"Says here her name is Alexandra, Skip."

She'd been a little cagey when I asked her about the dating service. And, when I'd asked if she knew Sandy was married, she said something like, "It wasn't important."

So she didn't want anyone to know who she was. That's no big deal."

"You're right. She didn't want anyone to know who she was. Why do you think that is?"

"Don't know, James." With my roommate it was like playing Twenty Questions. He wanted to play it out to its conclusion.

"I'll tell you, friend. This isn't a dating service."

"Then get to the point and tell me what it is."

"The Empire Club."

"Empire Club?" I took another swallow of my Yuengling, waiting for James to finally spit it out.

"It's an escort service, Skip. The prostitute says to the house-wife, "You're in the wholesale business, we're in the retail busi-ness.' Your Sarah is a high-class prostitute. A hooker."

CHAPTER FOUR

"Sarah, you remember James?"

She did. "James," she reached out and took his hand. His eyes were wide and slightly out of his head. He was thinking about this hot Sarah, and the Sarah he used to know, and the Sarah now who was for hire. I only hoped he'd just shut up and do his job. Knowing James—

"Sarah, James is going to be one of our supervisors. As I told you and Mr. Walter, there will be seven guys who are doing the installation. It shouldn't take over five days, and we will be as unobtrusive as possible."

She gave me a sly smile. "Skip, does he know?"

He did. Em didn't. "Yeah." He knew I was the pretend boyfriend. He didn't know anything else. At least he couldn't prove it. And even if he could, he'd better keep his damned mouth shut.

"Sarah, if I was Skip, I'd play any kind of role just to be around you. You're even better looking than when you were in high school. And I thought you were hot back then."

She giggled. "Thank you, James. This," she spread her

perfectly manicured hands out, as if to emphasize the massive lobby of the building, "this is only temporary. I told Skip, probably a month. Sandy and I are out of here. Out of this crappy community, out of this state, maybe out of this country. But you can't say anything, James. I'm really relying on you two to keep this confidential. Just between us, okay?"

Sarah the looker. Sarah the hooker. I can't describe the feeling, but it was kind of cool and kind of creepy to know that I'd dated a girl who had become a high-class prostitute. A hooker. I mean, as a kid — maybe in junior high — we used to talk about hookers. Girls who made money having sex. There were jokes, stories, rumors, and legends about hookers. And now, I was the pretend-boyfriend of one. Too strange for words. God, I wanted to ask her all kinds of questions, but I knew if I let her know what I knew, it would all be over.

"Ralph will be by in a little while to walk you guys through the building. He wants everything to go as smooth as possible." She pointed at the entrance door to the company's inner sanctum.

Ralph Walters was Sandy Conroy's right-hand man. As VP of the company, he pretty much ran things as he saw fit, and he'd let me know he was in charge from the second I'd met him.

"Nothing happens in here that I don't know about. Got that Mr. Moore? Nothing at all."

First words out of his mouth, swear to God. I'd just been offered twenty grand, so I wasn't in a position to argue. "I won't do a thing without consulting you, Mr. Walters." My mother wasn't stupid. She wasn't a great mother, but she taught me to be nice to people who signed my paycheck.

"We'll get along fine then." The short, balding man gave me a curt nod, glanced at his watch, and walked away.

And now James was about to meet the second in command. I just hoped he'd use his charm, and not revert to the smartass he could easily be. "Twelve bucks an hour, James. Just suck it up and agree with whatever the man says."

Ralph Walters had been with the company for ten years. He told me that he'd been born to work at Synco Systems. "Let me tell you something, young man. The first thirty years of my life were simply preparation. This company is the final result."

I'd nodded, not wanting to say anything to jeopardize the financial situation. Nothing to jeopardize what would amount to over $20,000 in my pocket. I know, believe me, I know there are more important issues than money. I haven't found them yet, but I've been told by so many people, I have to believe it.

We sat in the expansive lobby, studying the artwork on the walls. Abstract paintings, appearing to be originals, with flashes of bright colors, bold strokes of pastel colors, and solid scrapes done with palette knives. Em had explained those things to me on a tour of her parents' mansion. I couldn't appreciate the talent, but I had the feeling that they were expensive pieces.

"She's hot, amigo."

"James, you know and I know. But you can't let on. I'm serious, man. You tend to wear your feelings on your sleeves. Don't."

"She's hot, Skip. You don't want to bring Em into this, trust me."

"No." I agreed with him. The minutes became an hour. The hour dragged on twenty more minutes.

"Guys, I am so sorry." Sarah stuck her pretty head into the lobby, like a nurse in a doctor's office. "I'm going to find out what's taking him so long."

"If he's in his office, why don't we just come on back with you?" James, being the pushy son of a bitch that he can be.

She hesitated. "Okay."

"Sarah. We don't have to."

"It's okay."

We stood up and followed her lead. Through the lobby

doors, down the hall into a large room with computer stations, workbenches, and several dozen employees, all quietly working at their stations. Some ran small machines at the workbenches, but most were glued to their computer screens. I swear you could hear a pin drop. Five offices opened into the room from the far wall. Each office was numbered.

Sarah paused, turned and looked at us, and smiled. Bright white teeth, perfect in every dimension. Whatever she made in her escort life, she spent wisely. On cosmetic dentistry to start with.

She knocked on door number five. Knocked again, then louder the third time.

"Must have stepped out."

"Should we come back? Later this week?"

"Skip. We set the appointment. He'll be here."

She knocked again. Nothing.

"Here." James, the pushy S.O.B, reached beyond her and pushed on the office door. It swung inward smoothly, showcasing three-quarters of the spacious room. I looked over his shoulder and could see the massive oak desk, the floor-to-ceiling book-shelves, some more art that I had no interest in, and two visible skylights that bathed the room in early morning light.

"Mr. Walters?" Sarah gave James a dirty look.

James just smiled. "The door was open. It must have been the Lord's will."

It probably wasn't the smoothest thing to open someone's office door. But James didn't have an office, and he was good at sticking his nose into other people's business, so it didn't seem that strange to him.

"Mr. Walters?" More timid this time. Sarah reached for the doorknob to close the door, but once again James barged up to the doorway. He stepped into the office as Sarah whispered loud-ly, "Stop it. You can't just—" she followed him in two steps behind.

"James, it's time to go." I'd just gotten the job and I didn't want to lose it already.

"Pretty nice office. Guy must be pulling down some serious jack."

"James, please." She nervously looked around the office.

I stepped in. Not to see if Mr. Walters really was there or not, but to escort my good friend out. "James, I've met Ralph Walters. He's a no-nonsense kind of guy, and he's going to be pissed off if he finds us in his office. I can't afford to lose this job, and neither can you."

"Yeah," he hesitated, obviously taken with the surroundings. I could tell he was picturing himself working in a fancy office like this. James was always dreaming about hitting the big time.

"James. Let's go."

"Okay, we're out of here, pally." James gave it one last look, turned, and exited. I was close behind. Sarah followed, backing out and starting to pull the door shut. I saw her stumble and stop.

"Oh, my God." Her eyes were riveted on Walters's desk.

"What?" She spun around, and in that hushed whisper she said, "Somebody's feet are under his desk."

"Where?"

"Under the desk."

James and I both turned and looked. Sure enough, the soles of someone's shoes, socks, and the cuffs of brown trousers were visible under the desk.

I looked at James, and he shrugged his shoulders. In his own hushed voice he said, "Maybe the guy takes naps there? Or maybe, just maybe," he glanced at Sarah, "he has a mistress and they meet under the desk."

She rolled her eyes. "Mr. Walters?"

No answer.

Finally James did what James does best. He barged back into the office and walked behind the desk, involving us again in a truly messy situation. I should never have involved the son of a bitch.

"Holy crap, Skip. Come here." He grabbed the edge of the big oaken desk.

Sarah took several steps in his direction.

"Sarah, I don't think you want to see this."

The two of us reached the rear of the desk at the same time. Ralph Walters's body had slid from the desk chair and was on the floor, his legs protruding from the front of the desk. In his right hand was a blue steel revolver and the left side of his head was blown away, remains of brain, bone, and blood spattering the veneer of the desk drawers.

CHAPTER FIVE

I've seen dead bodies before. I could never get used to that. But what about a coroner or a funeral director? Someone who dealt with dead bodies every day? They must have a cast-iron stomach and nerves of steel. Me? I ended up shaking and thinking I was going to be sick. I suppose I should have put my arm around Sarah and comforted her. Some pretend boyfriend I turned out to be.

So we waited while the police did their investigation. They interviewed each of us separately.

"You broke into the office?"

"Um, the door was open and my friend sort of pushed it."

"You didn't notice anything unusual when you entered?"

"Not the first time."

"You mean you went back a second time?"

"Well, when we saw the feet."

"The feet?"

"Under the desk."

I don't think any of us were really suspects, but they asked us a lot of questions. It wasn't too bad. We checked with each other afterward and we'd all told the same story. It had happened so fast, we didn't have time to make one up.

"How bad would things have to be?" James sipped his coffee. The three of us were sitting in the break room, sterile white tiled walls on four sides, and a stainless refrigerator, microwave, and coffee maker.

"Bad." I couldn't fathom the feeling. What the hell would cause me to take my own life?

"Ralph was — well, I haven't been here that long, but he was like the rock. I mean, he loved this place and he loved his job. And I think he had an idea that Sandy might be moving on, so he was in line to take over." Sarah's color had come back to her face, and she was on her second cup of high-voltage coffee.

I couldn't drink the mud brown liquid. My stomach was still churning, and I kept seeing that head covered in blood. "Guys, girls," Em hated being called a guy, "this man must have had some serious problems."

"Well, as the song says, suicide is painless."

I nodded. "*Mash*. Donald Sutherland, Sally Kellerman, Elliot Gould. Nineteen —"

"Seventy." James stirred his coffee with his finger. "Before we were born, amigo."

Sarah looked back and forth at us, trying to figure out where the conversation had gone south. It always did.

A man with graying hair stuck his head in the door. From the shoulders up I could see a loosened tie, a stiff collared shirt, and tanned face with just the slightest hint of a five o'clock shadow. I took a quick guess. Sandler Conroy.

"Sarah. Can I see you for a moment?"

She gave me a quick look, almost like a girlfriend would give her boyfriend before going off with another man. Or maybe it was just my imagination. She stood up and walked out to greet him. We could hear her heels click down the hallway.

We were both quiet for a moment, the only two people in the room. I could hear a very small buzz and traced it to a clock that hung above the sink.

"Skip, we've stepped into it before, but —"

"But."

We didn't talk for several minutes. James sipped his coffee, and I pretty much stared at the table. I was trying to work out everything that had happened in the last week.

"There's still a good side to this, my friend."

I didn't say anything.

"Look, you're still making good money. I mean, this shouldn't shut down the installation. Am I right?"

"You're right, James."

"So we've got that going for us."

Us? It was always us. James had been my best friend since grade school and we shared about everything. Even Ginger Stevens in the seventh grade. Of course, I think she pretty much kissed every guy in 7A.

"You think that was her guy?"

"Sandler Conroy? Yeah, I'd bet. He's got to be a little shook up right now."

"Yeah. And you?"

"I don't know what to make of it."

"Nothing. Don't make anything of it, pard."

"This thing with Sarah. I mean, I can get past the part that she's a high-class hooker, but —"

"No you can't."

"You're right. I can't. It's very weird."

"Very."

"James, how does a girl, a woman, how does she decide to do that?"

"Skip, let's say you meet some great looking girl at a bar."

"I know where this is going."

29

"Humor me."

I humored him too much as it was.

"You buy her a couple of drinks, offer to take her out for a nice dinner, and you end up at your place. Or, her place."

"It's still not the same thing, James."

"It's a one-night stand, amigo. And you paid for it."

"But a woman? How does she make the conscious decision to do this for a living?" I just couldn't picture it.

James cleared his throat and stood up. He walked to the doorway and peered out into the hall. "No one around." He turned and came back inside, put his hands on the back of his chair and stared intently at me. "This little scenario I cooked up. It was a one-night stand for both of you. She didn't fall in love with you, you didn't fall in love with her. It was sex, Skip. Sex."

"And?"

"And she starts thinking. Maybe there's more than just a couple of cosmos and a steak dinner in this little game. She gets dollar signs in her eyes, Skip. She thinks, maybe, just maybe, I can fall into a compromising situation and do better than a couple of drinks and dinner."

"Oh, come on."

"Come on? That's the way it happens. You know it does. It's like the old question, why does a dog lick his privates? Because he can! The woman finally figures out she can make some serious money charging for it. You're just mad because you can't do it. Excuse me, compadre, but you are just an ordinary, halfway good-looking guy." He stepped back from the chair and gave me a hard look. "I'm giving you the benefit of the doubt, amigo. Listen. It ain't gonna happen for you. But, if you could have one-night stands and get paid five hundred, a thousand dollars, wouldn't you do it? If you could have sex whenever you wanted and get paid big bucks, you'd do it. We'd all do it. Every man on the planet. What's the difference, Skip?"

30

I couldn't tell him. Because maybe there wasn't any difference. Except I'd never picked up a girl at a bar, bought her two cosmos, taken her out for an elegant steak dinner, and fallen into bed with her. Nice dream, but it had never happened. Not to me anyway. That never seemed to be the Lord's or anyone else's will. But it seemed pretty real to James. Maybe there was something about my friend I didn't know.

"But this pretend boyfriend stuff. I mean, that's pretty strange." It was. I was feeling used, but paid well at the same time. Taking a bonus for being a pretend lover. I had this fleeting thought. Did that make me a male prostitute?

James shook his head and walked to the sink, pouring himself another cup of the bitter brew. "Everything about this is strange. What does she want you to do?"

"Walk her to her car after work."

"That's it?"

"A couple nights a week I'm supposed to park my car outside of her condo, just in case Carol Conroy drives by."

"So far this sounds pretty innocent."

Yeah. It was innocent. I wasn't a male prostitute. I didn't want to think of what I was. I just wanted the bonus. Ten grand. Pretty sweet.

"So that's it? Park the car outside her place?"

"Hey, James, it's not like I'm going to be sleeping with her. And we're not going to the movies or holding hands. After all, she does have a boyfriend."

"Ah, yes. The head honcho. The much talked about, seldom seen, Sandy."

I could hear the heels clicking in the hall. "Cool it."

She walked back into the room, Sandler Conroy nowhere in sight. "Sandy says he's sorry you had to see what happened."

James nodded. "He's sorry?"

"He feels bad that you guys were here to see it. That's all."

31

"What else?"

I could see tears welling in her eyes. "There is nothing else. Okay? The installation will start Wednesday and whatever you need, get in touch with me."

She turned and hurried out of the room. I could hear gentle sobbing as she walked away.

"She and Sandy must have had words." James pointed in the direction she'd gone.

"It would seem."

"Something a good boyfriend would have picked up on."

"Drop it, James."

He didn't say another word as we left the building. If he had, I might have decked him.

CHAPTER SIX

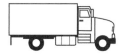

At seven the next morning I was in Michael's office. Michael, director of Jaystone Security's Carol City office. The lowest of the low, and a far cry from the splendor of Ralph Walters's office. Michael's tiny, closet-sized office was drab, sparsely furnished, and dreary. No artwork on the walls, cheap wallpaper that was peeling in the corners, a gray metal desk, and a ratty cloth office chair that showed major signs of wear. But at least he had an office. I, on the other hand, got to file my paperwork in the room that doubled as the reception area. As if we had customers who walked in and needed to be recepted. As if. Worn, soiled carpeting, a build-it-yourself desk that was falling apart, a big computer that was built during the Dark Ages, and a desk chair with wheels that had frozen probably ten years ago.

"A suicide?"

"You saw it on the news, Michael."

"But, Skip. You found the body. That can't be good." He sat behind his tiny desk and shuddered.

"For me. For the company, for the situation it means nothing. Don't worry about it."

"Well, as long as we still have the order." Mr. Bottom Line. As long as we still had the order. Maybe the company was going to buy him a new desk chair with the profits.

"We do. We still have the order." I prayed we did. I needed that order worse than Michael did.

"Skip, you have one supervisor for the project."

"James Lessor."

"Yeah, yeah." He frowned. He'd met James and obviously didn't think much of him. "I'm not entirely happy with that choice, but I guess we'll deal with it." Michael shuffled papers on his desk. "But we need two. The contract calls for two. It's a bull-shit position. Any ideas of who could do it?"

"You've got the installers?"

He nodded. "We need a second supervisor. It's a gopher position, Skip. You've been on these jobs before."

Actually, I hadn't. The few sales I made were mostly residential. Selling safety and security to people who had very little to secure. And when I did sell to businesses, they usually needed one or two door detectors and maybe a window sensor. Hardly any reason for a supervisor.

Michael looked past me, shaking his head. "What did it look like?"

"What did what look like?"

"The suicide."

"You don't want to know." I couldn't get the image out of my mind. The gory, blood-stained desk and carpet and the side of the man's head with a hole in it.

"No. I don't." He looked back at me. "We need another supervisor. Simple stuff, really."

"I can do it. I'll be the second supervisor."

"No. You're in charge of the project."

"But I could—"

"No, Skip. Regulations call for two supervisors, and one person in charge of the project."

"So what's my title?"

"Person in charge of the project." Michael shrugged his shoulders.

Great title. I squinted my eyes and gave him a questioning look. So if I could figure a way to also be supervisor, I could make an additional twelve bucks an hour.

"And, no. You can't be both."

The son of a bitch was on to me.

"My title is really Person in Charge of the Project?"

"Sure. Why not?"

I shook my head. "I might know someone."

He looked up from his gunmetal desk in his tiny cubicle office. "That would help. As person in charge, it's going to be your job to find that someone. And if they screw up, as I feel certain your roommate will, it's going to fall on your shoulders."

The guy was a prick. "This man I've got in mind, he has his own business. He's obviously good at management, and I think he'd work well in this environment."

"Bring him by tomorrow, okay? I'm going to need to at least meet him."

I was faking it. I had a vague idea, but who knew? The guy might be legit, he might be a fake.

"Michael, I'll have him here tomorrow morning. You'll be in till noon?" He had a habit of scooting by eleven thirty. You'd never see him the rest of the day.

"Um, yeah. You get him here no later than noon, okay?"

"Sure."

I didn't know what time he woke up, but I was going to pound on Jim Jobs's door tonight until he finally answered. There was no way this job was going to get away from me because of a missing supervisor. I didn't know Jim Jobs well, but for what this position called for, anyone could do it.

Hell, I'd hired James hadn't I?

CHAPTER SEVEN

Sure, I should have contacted someone I knew. This was a job that was paying me a fortune, and I should have approached it with a little more responsibility. However, in my defense, I am not a responsible person. In my short life, I've come to accept that fact. I think I'm stuck in an immature, irresponsible lifestyle, and I have to be content with that. As it turned out, I wish I'd looked elsewhere.

I knocked three times, and finally he opened the door.

"Huh?" Spoken like someone who had just been wakened from a deep sleep. At two in the afternoon.

"Jim Jobs?"

"Huh?"

"I'm sorry. I'm Skip Moore, two doors down? Apartment 12 E?"

He just stared at me, scratching himself through the white Hanes Jockeys.

"You do odd jobs, am I right?"

He seemed to be a little more clear. "I do." His thick head of hair was spiked all over his small head and his face sported a two-day, three-day, maybe a four-day growth. Various shades of brown and gray.

"Well, I've got an odd job."

He squinted, scratched himself again, and nodded. "Can you give me just a minute? I think I need to make myself presentable, this bein' a business deal and all."

"Sure."

He came back a minute later, dirty T-shirt and a pair of khaki cargo shorts. The shirt was gray, but appeared to have been white originally. I was relieved that he'd dressed, until he scratched himself again.

"People usually call me on the phone."

I could understand why.

"In fact," he now scratched his chin, "this is the first time anybody ever came to my door asking about a job."

I thought about using the phone the next time I wanted to contact him.

"What is this job?"

I noticed he'd used water to try and smooth down the unruly hair. He hadn't been successful. "Different than anything you've done before."

"I've done a lot of jobs."

"Trust me, Jim. It is Jim, right?"

Jim Jobs shook his head back and forth. "No. Name's Albert. Albert Jobs. But you can call me Jim. Everyone does."

I considered going somewhere else for my hire.

"Now, what is this job?"

Get it out of the way. Bust his chops and move on to someone who would be good at it. "It's this way, Albert . . . Jim. I need someone for just a week who can work in security. We're installing a system for a company, and this position would be for someone who runs information back and forth between the installation teams." It was complicated, and I really didn't want to get into the details.

"I used to work for two companies that do exactly that." Jim Jobs smiled at me, two front teeth totally missing.

"Do exactly what?"

"Install security systems. And I helped set the whole thing up. Worked with the crew, told them where to install motion detectors, sound detectors —"

"You did this?"

"I did. Is that why you're calling on me?"

I had no choice. I gave Albert the job.

"You did what?"

"Em, you have no idea what it's like to live without any money."

"Oh, jeez, Skip. Don't start with that."

"Then where do I start? This job is going to pay me more than I made all of last year, Em. It's not like I'm sleeping with her." Although if I had enough money—

She shook her head and bit into another bite of cornbread. We were lunching at Esther's, on Twenty-seventh in Carol City, where they serve biscuits and gravy, sausage, baked chicken, and this fabulous peach cobbler. I'd decided to make a clean confession.

"You always play the money card."

"Em, I love you. You know that. And I'm always amazed that you reciprocate, but there is a money issue."

"It's not important to me." She pursed her lips and closed her beautiful blue eyes for several seconds.

"Because you have a lot of money and I don't have any." My father had abandoned the family when I was very young, and my mother, younger sister, and I lived off welfare for about as long as I can remember. Em's father owned a huge construction company, and he'd made a boatload of money off the wealthy homeowners in the richest districts of Miami.

"Just because I work for my father—"

The argument came up once in a while. About every other day.

"So what exactly are your obligations?"

"I pretend we're dating. Sarah and I. At the job site. And, I park my car in front of her condo three nights a week."

"You don't park *yourself* at her condo?"

"Come on, Em."

"This lasts how long?" I could see her softening, the fire leaving her eyes, and her fist opening into a five-fingered hand.

"Until we're done."

"Which is when?"

We'd be done in four or five days. The Sarah thing should be done at the end of the month. "Three, four weeks tops. Em, I'm not interested in her. It just seemed so innocent, and—"

"You're helping Sarah destroy a marriage. You're helping her break up this Sandler Conroy and his wife. Am I right?"

"Well, I think the marriage—"

"Am I right?"

"Yes." How could I argue that point.

"How did she ever get involved with this guy?"

I said I was making a clean confession. That isn't exactly true. I was leaving out a certain part of the story. I figured that Em would buy most of the story. The hooker part, I wasn't so sure about. "Dating service. Once she found out he was married, it was too late. She was hooked."

"Skip," she looked into my eyes, and I knew she was going to agree, "you fall into some of the strangest situations."

"Em. Let me finally break even. I'm going to make over twenty thousand dollars. Do you realize that I've never had that much money at one time in my life?"

She nodded. This beautiful, sexy woman who probably made over $100,000 a year, she got it. She couldn't argue with me. I knew it.

"So I've got to pretend that you're dating someone else?"

"No. It's a couple, three weeks, Em. That's all. And it stays inside the company."

We both still had a full plate of food. I thought that confiding in Em would make me feel better. Instead, a partial confession only made me feel worse. I could feel a burning in my stomach, and I couldn't touch another bite of food.

"I'm not happy about it, Skip."

"I didn't expect you would be."

"What if I told you I'd leave you because of this?"

"Would you?"

She sipped on her glass of water.

One of the servers stepped out from behind the buffet counter and headed toward the restroom. He turned to look at Em. A lot of guys do. As he turned and stared, he slid on a spot of grease and fell hard on the tile floor. Em never even noticed, and I immediately thought to myself, a lot of people had taken a fall for Emily. She just shrugged it off.

"Well, would you? Leave me?"

The server picked himself up, made a point of looking the other way, and continued toward the restroom.

"I should."

"Don't."

She slid out of the booth and stood up. "I won't."

I let out the breath that I'd been holding.

"But this stays at Synco Systems, right?"

"It does." My cell phone rang, "Born in the U.S.A." blaring from the little black box.

"Hello."

"Skip Moore?"

41

I couldn't place the voice, and I didn't recognize the phone number.

"Yes?"

"You represent the company that is installing a security system at Synco Systems?"

"I do." I smiled. I was the point man for big jobs.

"And you're dating Sarah Crumbly?"

I glanced up at Em, standing there, waiting for me to come out of the yellow vinyl booth and walk her to her car.

"Well—"

"I need to talk to you. As soon as possible."

The female on the other end sounded very businesslike.

"And you are?"

She hesitated. "I'm Carol Conroy. My husband is Sandler Conroy, president of Synco Systems, and I think you need to know some things about the death of Ralph Walters."

CHAPTER EIGHT

"Monte Carlo. Have you ever been there?"

I hadn't been out of the state of Florida. Travel had been pretty much out of the question. My mother didn't have any money and neither did I. I dreamed about traveling, and I knew where Monte Carlo was. I saw it on a Discovery Channel show one day.

Sarah looked into my eyes, and I felt a cold shiver. I looked away. I kept repeating to myself, *hooker. She's a hooker.*

"I won like two thousand euros in the Casino. It was so cool. I mean, much more class than Vegas, you know?"

I had no clue.

"It's this beautiful old building with ornate chandeliers and thick carpet. And just like in that James Bond movie, *Casino Royal*, guys wear suits and tuxedos and a lot of the women have formal dresses." There was a faraway look in her eyes. "Sandy promised me we'd go back once this project is done."

Casino Royal was filmed on Paradise Island in the Bahamas. But I didn't tell her that. And, as far as ever going to Monte

Carlo, or the Bahamas for that matter, well, I couldn't even imagine.

"And Cannes, Skip. Sparkling blue waters, quaint stucco buildings with orange tile roofs that descend like stair steps down to the ocean. During the film festival. Oh, my God, I met Adrian Grenier from *Entourage,* and we saw Angelina and Brad, and Daniel Craig. And, Skip," her eyes got big, "we sat front row to see U2, and then went backstage. I mean —"

It was almost more than I wanted to hear. Em had never done half of those things, and she could afford them.

"I met Bono. Bono, Skip. He kissed my hand."

Now it was getting tiresome.

"And Sandy leased a yacht that went on forever. I don't know how big it was, but you could sunbathe totally nude on the deck and nobody batted an eye."

What? I would bat an eye. Among other things. Who talked like this? Who experienced this kind of lifestyle?

I cleared my throat. "You did?"

She flashed me a shy smile. "Uh-huh."

I tried to picture that.

"Honest to God, Skip, I never thought I'd do anything like that. And then he asked if I'd like to work here at Synco Systems. Well, you can imagine it would have been very hard to say no."

Duh. We were sipping coffee in the break room. I'd taken Jim Jobs through the building, and, surprisingly, he'd understood everything. He'd even made some suggestions regarding placement of some of our hardware. He'd left in what James affectionately called the Jim Jobs mobile. Now, Sarah and I were talking. Our first "date," and I kept thinking how happy Em would be.

"Have you ever met Carol?"

I didn't know what to say. I had an appointment with

Sandler's wife in a couple of hours, but I didn't feel it was a good idea to tell Sandler's girlfriend. And I wasn't about to tell *my* girlfriend. The whole thing was so sordid.

"No."

"I have. Several times. I was invited to a cocktail party at their house just last week."

"You visited their house?"

"She's a bitch."

"He told you that."

"She's with him for status. That's all. And I think she keeps an eye on Sandy for her daddy."

And Sarah was with Sandler for the money.

"Anyway, it will soon be over. Once Sandy gets the money, he's promised me we're out of here."

She was a year younger than James, Em, and me. And her financial future seemed to be set. Maybe James had been right. If I'd been born a good-looking blonde girl, I might have sold my body and my soul to be in her shoes. Then again, maybe not.

"By the way, can you park your car in front of my condo tonight?"

"Sure." James was going to pick me up and drive me back to our dingy apartment.

"Sandy seems to think his wife is suspicious of me."

Suspicious? From what Sarah had told me, Carol Conroy could have enough evidence to kick Sandler out for good.

She slowly stood up, letting me admire her figure in a short red dress that pulled tight at her chest. "God, I hope he gets his paycheck soon."

I hoped I got mine soon. What had started out to be a really good opportunity was fast becoming a nightmare.

"Then, I'll see you tonight." She paused for a moment. "Well, I'll see your car. She gave me that soft smile. Sarah reached down and touched my hand giving it a gentle squeeze.

"One more thing." I hesitated. I hated this part of the sale, especially when I knew the client. "The contract calls for fifty percent up front and —"

"Skip. Are you afraid you won't get paid?" She let go of my hand and gave me a quizzical look.

"No, no. But Michael, the boss, plays by the rules." I figured if they didn't pay half up front Michael would still authorize the installation. There was no way he was going to lose a sale this big.

"I'll get you the check before you start the job. Which," she looked at her gold Rolex watch, "should be in two days. Right?"

I nodded.

"We're anxious to get started on a new project, Skip, and I know that Sandy wants the security system functional before we go into production."

"You never did tell me what this big project is."

Sarah put an index finger to her lips. "I'm not supposed to tell anyone. I'm not even supposed to know."

All kinds of secrets going on at Synco Systems.

"But it has something to do with the Department of Defense. I'm pretty sure that's who it is. Pretty sure."

"The federal government?" I pushed my chair back and stood up. The top of her golden head barely reached my shoulder.

"You can't tell anyone."

"No."

"They're putting in a new computer network program and we've come up with a system that is fool proof. Ralph," she hesitated, a catch in her voice, "Ralph told me just yesterday, that there was no way anyone could hack this system."

I wasn't allowed to tell anyone that our job involved the Department of Defense. I wasn't supposed to mention the fact that I was Sarah's pretend boyfriend, and I certainly couldn't tell

Sarah that I knew she was a prostitute. And, oh yeah, I wasn't going to tell anyone that Carol Conroy wanted to talk to me about Ralph Walters's suicide. And I was this guy who wasn't any good at keeping secrets.

CHAPTER NINE

The Red Derby was a tiny bar that was crammed into a little stucco strip of four buildings on Biscayne Bay Boulevard. The lounge sported a neon red derby hat that flashed outside the door, and I wondered how a bar like this got its name. Did the owner wear a red derby? Did anyone wear a red derby? I'd never even seen anybody wear a derby in my entire life.

I parked down a couple of spaces from the dirty white front of the building and walked up, past a small barbershop, studying the yellow stains where the cracked sidewalk met the stucco. I didn't even want to think what those stains might be. What was Carol Conroy thinking about when she called a meeting in a place like this? The Red Derby wasn't even a place that James and I would usually go, and we'd go just about anywhere that served cold beer.

Inside, the odor hit me fast. The smell of stale beer that had soaked into the carpet, the cigarette smoke that had permeated the heavy curtains, the curtains that hung in shreds from the window, and a sour smell that I couldn't quite place. A lone drinker with long hair and jeans and a T-shirt sat at the bar, hunched over his shot and beer. The bartender stood behind his vinyl bar and wiped the counter with a towel. I squinted in the dim light and could make out five tables and five booths. A neon beer sign hung above one booth advertising Strohs beer, and I was pretty sure that beer wasn't even made any more.

There was no sign of Carol Conroy.

"Skip Moore?"

I spun around and could make out the shadow of her face and figure. Tiny, about five foot, and dark brown hair freely framing her pretty face. She looked all of twenty-five years old. I hadn't uttered a word.

"Are you Mr. Moore?"

"Um, yeah." How lame.

"I'm Carol Conroy. I called you and —"

"I know."

"There's a booth over there."

She fully expected to meet here and tell her story right here. I'd expected to go to someplace a little more upscale. We walked to the booth and sat.

"Bud, Bud Light, Miller, Miller Light." The rotund, balding bartender looked around the room, never making eye contact, bored with the entire process.

We ordered two Bud Lights, and I waited. Mrs. Conroy played with the napkin the bartender had placed in front of her, folding it, unfolding it, and occasionally looking up at me. The bartender finally brought the beers, a smart-aleck smile on his pudgy face. I'm sure he thought we were two illicit lovers, before or after a session at a cheap hotel. This certainly wasn't a place for business meetings.

"You're in the security business."

"I am." I took a long swallow of beer. Warm and definitely past its prime.

"You're setting up a security system for my father's company?" She'd pulled a yellow pencil from her purse and was tapping the eraser on the table.

"We'll be installing a complete security system for Synco Systems. State-of-the-art motion detectors, smoke detectors, door monitors, window monitors —"

"Mr. Moore —"

"Please, call me Skip." I took another sip from the bottle. It wasn't as bad this time. By the end of the bottle it would be just fine.

She paused for a moment, considering my request. "I can't do that. Calling you Skip is just a little too informal. Mr. Moore, you know that my husband is president of Synco Systems."

"Yes ma'am." So it was Mrs. Conroy and Mr. Moore. Very businesslike.

"And Ralph Walters was vice president of operations, in line to take over the company if something should happen to my husband."

I wanted her to get to the point. I seriously didn't care about the hierarchy of her company. She was like Em. A rich bitch who already had hers, and probably didn't get that I was way down the pecking order. But I quietly waited. I was in line to make over twenty grand, and if it meant dealing with these people for a couple more days, I could do it. I could do anything, almost anything, for twenty grand.

"Mr. Moore, I talked to Ralph Walters's wife." She closed her eyes for a moment. "His widow." Another long pause.

"And —"

Mrs. Conroy pointed the tip of her pencil at me like the barrel of a gun. "And she is convinced that her husband's death was not a suicide."

It was my turn to pause. I'd been first on the scene, and when a man has a gun in his hand, and his brains are spattered over his desk, I didn't know what else to call it but suicide.

"Did you hear me?"

I took another swallow of beer and saw she hadn't touched hers. "Yes ma'am. Ma'am, I was there."

"I know."

"It certainly appeared to be a suicide."

She paused, giving me a long look. "Mr. Moore, are you a detective?"

"No, ma'am."

"Have you witnessed a suicide before?"

"Um, no."

Carol Conroy pursed her lips and shook her head.

"Maria Walters doesn't think it was a suicide, and neither do I."

I finished my beer. "Why are you telling *me* this?"

"Because you're in security."

I looked into her brown eyes. "Mrs. Conroy, as you just pointed out, I'm not a policeman. I'm not a detective. I'm just a security salesman."

The lady moved her bottle of beer over to my side of the pitted booth. "Have mine." I looked down and saw someone had carved the word "muerte" in the vinyl. I was pretty sure the word was Spanish for death.

"What makes you think someone killed Mr. Walters?"

She took a deep breath. "Ever since Synco Systems took on this new project, there have been strange things going on. I'm not supposed to tell anyone this, but the project does involve the United States government. Enough said."

I just kept listening.

"Did Sarah tell you about Tony Quatman?"

I shook my head. The name didn't ring a bell.

"He is the designer of the system. This new computer system that's supposed to prohibit any hackers from breaking in."

"Okay."

"A week after Synco signed a contract with the government, Tony resigned. Didn't give a reason. He just wrote a note and walked out." She made a flourish with her right hand, brandishing the yellow pencil as if she was writing the note herself.

"And why is that a problem?"

"Tony was to get a very nice bonus when the project was completed."

I understood. I was to get a very nice bonus when I'd finished playing Sarah's boyfriend. And thinking about that made me feel kind of sleazy, sitting here talking to Sandler Conroy's wife while Conroy was probably boinking his prostitute girlfriend. My pretend girlfriend. This whole thing was so sordid.

"He walked out. No bonus. Now does that make any sense to you? You're a businessman, Mr. Moore. Would you walk out on a bonus?"

"Mrs. Conroy—"

"No one has seen or heard from him since."

I shrugged my shoulders.

"His secretary, Julia Bayford, she didn't show up the next day, and we've heard nothing from her or her husband."

"People move. People change plans."

"I want you to look into it."

"What?"

"You're a security guy." She let that hang, as if I should jump at the chance to use my vast experience in selling security systems to help solve a possible murder and disappearance.

"As I said, I sell security systems. That's it."

"Listen to me. You're going to have full access to the building. You're brand new to the company and you can look places that no one else has looked. If you stumble onto something you shouldn't see, you just tell them that you were doing security work."

I nearly swallowed the entire second beer.

52

"Mr. Moore, I believe Ralph was murdered. I believe that someone either forced Tony Quatman out, or they killed him. I believe Julia Bayford —"

"I can't do this. I wouldn't have a clue what to look for. I have no idea why these people are disappearing, and to be honest, Mrs. Conroy, I don't care. I just want to do my job, get paid, and leave. Look, I really need this job. I can't take a chance of screwing this up."

She shook her head, pulling her hair back from her face. In the dark bar I saw the dark side of the pretty lady. Her lipstick was a little more red than I'd first noticed. Her eyes a little dark with the makeup. Maybe a little too much blush on her cheekbones. "Mr. Moore, if I'm right, and Ralph Walters was murdered, if Tony Quatman was murdered, I believe someone else is going to be killed as well. Believe me when I say I'd like to prevent that at all costs."

"Who would —" The bartender stood by the table. He took us both by surprise, and I wondered what he thought if he'd heard the conversation.

"Another beer?" I shook my head no. Three in mid-afternoon was pushing it a little bit. I had to drive back to Carol City.

"What do you propose?"

"I propose that you do security work for me. I'll give you ideas of what to look for and you basically become my spy."

"Mrs. Conroy, I could lose my job."

"You work for me. My father owns the company. My husband is the president." These rich bitches.

"I work for you?"

"And I pay you on top of your salary, your bonus —" If she only knew.

"And how much am I being paid, Mrs. Conroy?"

"Ten thousand dollars, Mr. Moore."

My mouth must have dropped wide open.

"And, another five thousand if you find any solid information."

This was crazy. I wanted to call Em and James and tell them the news. It was official. I was going to be rich.

"So, do we have a deal?"

"You're going to tell me what to look for?"

"I am."

"You're going to give me an idea of where to look?"

"I am."

"Mrs. Conroy, are you sure I'm the right person for this job?"

"You're the logical person for this job."

"Because?"

"You're in the right place at the right time."

Working a deal with Sandler Conroy's mistress; working a deal with Sandler Conroy's wife. I needed the money. There's no other logical explanation why I would have put myself in such a screwed-up position. It was greed, pure and simple. There is no other answer.

"Then we've got a deal." I reached across the booth to shake her hand, but she'd laid the pencil on the table and put both hands in her lap. The lady was very cold. Sarah's comment about "bitch" came to mind.

She slid from the booth, stood up, and dropped a twenty on the vinyl top. "I want you to start immediately. As I said, it's a matter of life and death." She walked to the doorway, never even looking to see if I was keeping pace. "I'm very worried about my safety. And, I'm worried about my father's company."

I grabbed the pencil and shoved it in my pocket, walking quickly to catch up. "You have a right to that. Are you close to your father?" It was none of my business, but I thought I'd ask.

Carol Conroy paused, studying my question. Finally she turned around. "Not especially. But that's not the issue is it?"

"So you're close to your father's company."

The lady smirked. "Mr. Moore, I'm hiring you to do a job. I'm not interested in your philosophy."

When we walked outside, she squinted in the late afternoon sun.

"Mrs. Conroy, let me walk you to your car." I followed her eyes, up the street from where I'd parked.

"What is he doing?" Carol Conroy shouted, pointing up the street, and I looked. An Asian man with a ball cap pulled low knelt by a Lexus half a block from us.

"I don't know. It appears he's —"

"That's my car." Her sharp tone was almost accusing. "Stop him." She spun around, and her eyes burned into mine.

I took off running, assuming I'd figure out what to do when I reached the man. My first assignment and I'd just started the job seconds ago.

He saw me or heard me and leaped to his feet as a gray Honda Civic in the next block burned rubber, beating me to the man and stopping right in front of the Lexus. The short Asian guy stepped into the street, yanked the passenger door open, and jumped into the Honda as the driver pulled back into the street, the door swinging wildly. For a moment I thought he might fall out, but he managed to grab the handle and pull the door shut. I stopped by her car, breathing hard, watching the other car disappear. Half a block and my chest and lungs were on fire. I was beat. What kind of condition was I in? Too many beers, pizzas, burgers, and no exercise. I had to do something about this. Especially if I was going to be in this type of business. I already knew Mrs. C. was going to be pissed.

She was walking in measured strides, shaking her head. When she got to the Lexus she gave me an annoyed look. "Too bad you didn't move a little faster."

"Excuse me?" I was still trying to catch my breath and I could feel my heart racing. I could have had a heart attack, and she was telling me I was too slow?

"Did you get a good look at him?"

"Not a good look. His ball cap was pulled down in front. But I might recognize him if I saw him again."

She pursed her lips, staring in the direction of the departed Honda. "I didn't get close enough to see. Mr. Moore, I told you this might be a matter of life and death."

It was a matter of $15,000. I had to tell myself it was all about the money. "I assume you're worried about your husband? With Ralph Walters being killed, Mr. Conroy is possibly a target?"

"Sandler?" She laughed, a harsh, nasty, sarcastic type of laugh. "Please, Mr. Moore. I could give a rat's ass about my husband." Pretty harsh words from such a petite young woman.

"Then who do you think might be the next victim?"

She looked down the street again, biting her bottom lip. "Me, Mr. Moore. I believe I'm next in line to be killed."

CHAPTER TEN

I parked my dirty tan 2000 Chevy Cavalier in the parking lot outside Sarah's condo building. When I'd left Carol Conroy at the Red Derby I'd made sure she saw me get into the little car, so if she did drive by Sarah's condo, checking on her husband, she'd notice my crappy little piece of junk. I thought about going up and telling Sarah that I was fulfilling my obligation, but I wasn't sure what I'd find. Maybe Sandler Conroy himself. The deal was to park the car overnight, and that's what I did.

James had followed me to the complex. I got in the truck and he sat there, staring at the building.

"Opera."

"What?"

"Name of the building. High-end condo for Sarah the hooker. She must have made some serious jack hooking."

"James, every time I see her I think about that. But she got me the job. That's a good thing."

"Yeah. And she's also put you in a position."

"There's that, too."

"Seems to me, amigo, that you should get hazard pay."

I didn't say anything for a while. Hazard pay. I was getting it. James didn't know I was getting it.

Finally, James pulled out of the lot. "We're not getting any younger, Skip. If we're going to make a mark, it's about time we do that."

"James—"

"And we're never going to make our mark working for someone else."

"James." It was his obsession. Make a million by the time we were thirty. Or before.

He reached down beside the driver's seat into a small bucket on the floor and pulled out a pack of cigarettes. Putting one in his mouth, he lit it with a match, bending the match with one hand and one finger, striking it with his thumb. "Tell me I'm wrong, Skip."

"About the hazard pay."

"Hazard pay?"

"You mentioned hazard pay."

James took a long drag on his cigarette, letting the smoke drift from his mouth out the window into the warm Miami evening. "I don't mean to be the materialistic weasel of this group, but do you think we'll get hazard pay out of this?" He turned to me and smiled.

It took me a moment. "*Armageddon*?"

"Ah, the man knows his movies."

"Good quote."

"Good movie." He slouched back in his seat and stepped on the gas. The truck moved a little faster. Not much.

"James, she offered me hazard pay."

"Oh?" He looked at me with a frown on his face.

"Yeah. I'm being paid for the job."

"Gigolo."

"Ten grand."

He was silent for a moment. "A well-paid gigolo. Why didn't you tell me this?"

"I'm telling you now."

"And I get the feeling there may be more to this."

"Hey, ten grand, James. That's damned good hazard pay."

"You weren't going to tell me."

I could tell his feelings were hurt. "Listen. I'm getting paid. And there is more to this."

He was holding the cigarette with one hand, steering and tapping his fingers on the steering wheel with his other. "So spill."

"I may have bitten off more than I can chew."

"We're reversing roles here?"

"What's that supposed to mean?"

"I tend to be the one who goes out on a limb. Our relation-ship —" he took another mouth full of smoke, "it depends on me being the adventurous one. You are the voice of reason, amigo."

"Usually."

"So we're reversing roles."

I shrugged my shoulders. A Cadillac Escalade entered the highway, and James slowed down to let it ease into traffic. Before he died, James's father dreamed of driving a Cadillac, and James always showed a lot of respect for any of their vehicles. He swore he'd own a Cadillac or two or three before he was thirty.

"What sparked this moment of adventure?"

I had the answer ready for him. "Greed."

My partner was quiet for a minute, maybe two. He never took his eyes off the road as we hit highway 95 and cruised along, past the concrete and stucco buildings, the myriad entrances and exits, the cement walls that rose on the side of the highway, shel-tering the residential communities from the noise of traffic.

Finally I had to speak. "I'm not going to tell you I'm sorry. I mean, we're not married, man. And even married couples don't share everything."

He didn't say a word.

"All right. Here's the rest of the story."

James glanced at me, his eyes wide and bright. My buddy from fourth grade. My best friend. Ready for another quest. I needed him. Right now. "I had a meeting with Carol Conroy this afternoon."

"What?"

"Sandler Conroy's wife."

"Oh, man, you didn't tell her about —"

"Never came up."

"Then pray tell, what was this meeting about?"

"She wants to hire me."

"Skip, you're already hired. You've got two jobs at Synco Systems. Setting up the security system and pretending to be Sarah's boyfriend. I mean, what the hell else is there?"

"I accepted a third position."

"Pard! What are you doing?"

And I told him. I told him how Carol Conroy thought that Walters's death may not have been suicide. I told him about Tony Quatman and his secretary. I told him that she didn't feel close to her father, and she didn't seem to care about her husband. Actually said that she didn't give a rat's ass about Sandler Conroy. And finally I told him that Mrs. Conroy thought she might be in line to be murdered.

We swung off the highway by the Miami Dolphin stadium and headed to our apartment complex.

"You still haven't told me how much."

"After all that, and you want to know how much? Aren't you worried about a woman who thinks she's going to be murdered?"

James tossed his cigarette out the window, the sparks scattering brightly in the air. "Maybe I should be more worried that she trusts you to prevent the murder. I'm not sure I'd even trust you when it comes to that."

"I told you. I may have gone too far."

"How much?"

"That depends."

"On what?"

"Have you noticed that I have no idea what I'm looking for? She didn't give me a clue what I should expect."

He was quiet again.

"Okay. She didn't give me a clue as to what *we* should expect."

James gave me a wry smile. "Whatever the lady wants us to look for, that's what we'll look for. It sounds like she's going to make it up as she goes."

"I had my first assignment today."

"You're just gung-ho about making all this money, compadre. I'm proud of you."

"James, someone was messing around with her Lexus."

"Lexus?" His eyes were bright. The fact that someone was messing around wasn't important. The fact that the lady owned an expensive luxury car—well—

"Lexus. It looked like maybe he was doing something to the tires."

"And?"

"I tried to chase him down, but somebody picked him up in a Honda Civic."

"What did he look like?"

"Short, Asian, maybe in his thirties, but I didn't get that close."

"Skip?"

"What?"

"How much?"

"James, I'm not sure this is a good idea. Something else I didn't mention."

My partner shook his head. "How much have you kept from me, amigo? If you don't want me involved, just say so."

"Quit feeling sorry for yourself. I'm telling you now, aren't I?"

"So spill."

"Sarah said this involved a contract with the federal government."

"This guy who invented the security system for the computers. Tony Quatman. He invented this for the government?"

"Department of Defense."

"Heavy stuff."

"Yeah."

We were both quiet as James drove. This was way over our heads. Way.

"And he's disappeared?"

"Gone. No trace."

"His secretary?"

"Gone."

"Mmmm."

"That's it? Mmmm?"

"How much?"

"I don't think it's a good idea, James."

"How much?"

I reached into my pocket, pulled out Carol Conroy's yellow pencil, and wrote the figure on a discarded candy wrapper between our seats. I turned the figure toward James. The dashboard lights were bright enough for him to see the numbers.

"Ten thousand dollars? Dude."

"If we do the job. And she's throwing in another five thousand if we get any hard information."

"Fifteen grand?"

"Fifteen grand." I studied the pencil. Printed on the side in bold black letters were the words TINY TOTS ACADEMY.

"Listen to me, compadre. It's not a good idea."

I couldn't believe it. James, of all people, was saying it wasn't a good idea. "So now you're the voice of reason?"

"It's not a good idea, Skip. For fifteen grand? It's a great idea."

CHAPTER ELEVEN

Early the next morning James drove me back to my car. I made about five sales calls, till early afternoon. My heart wasn't in it. Hell, my heart was never in it. I was like a machine, walking into a home and trying to convince these residents of Carol City that they needed a security system. A lot of these people were unemployed and those that actually worked for a living didn't make as much as I did. We live in a pretty depressed area.

My thoughts were all about Synco Systems. Why couldn't I find one of those companies about once a week? Once a month? Once every six months?

The last couple I met with actually lived in an apartment two blocks from where James and I slept. They were both home in the middle of the afternoon so it was obvious they didn't have day jobs. And then the two admitted they were about ready to be thrown out of their living quarters and the only reason they'd signed up for an interview was that they wanted to win the free cruise to the Bahamas that Michael was advertising. The winner had to pay a security deposit, food deposit, sailing deposit, and all taxes and tips. Then, voilà, the trip was free.

"So, if we buy this system —"

I stared at the big guy, locking eyes with him. "Look, Mr. Whitman, you don't need this system."

Mrs. Whitman, an overweight lady who pushed the limits on the waistband of her jeans, spoke up. "But if we put a down payment on the system, what are our odds? What kind of a chance do we get on winning the Bahama cruise?"

I couldn't do it. I figured they'd call Michael and tell him how bad my social skills were, but it didn't matter. I shoved my sales manuals, the book, and flyers into my case and stood up.

"You don't need this. Your chance of winning a free trip are zip, and even if you did, it would cost you more than it's worth. Seriously, you don't need a security system. Take the money and pay an extra month's rent on your apartment." I walked out of their humble abode and didn't look back.

I drove the Cavalier home and walked into our little corner of the universe. James was hunched over the kitchen table, staring at the computer screen.

"Hey, Skip, do you remember Jody Stacy?"

"Jody? Macho Jody?"

"Yeah. From high school into the Marines." James sipped one of my Yeungling beers.

"What brings his name up?"

"He went into the Marines, got out a couple of years ago, and was a cop up in Delray Beach."

The idea of someone we graduated with saving our country, then enforcing the law was beyond me. I wasn't old enough to know which end was up. How did people like Jody Stacy have enough presence to save the world? "James, are we going to do this with everybody we graduated with?"

"What?"

"Go through their backgrounds?"

"No."

"Good. Because if you're going to explore the history of two hundred fifty kids—"

"Stay with me compadre. Jody owns his own business."

"Well, good for him." James was always interested in people who owned their own businesses. Especially people he knew. "I never knew him that well, and I really don't care."

"Ahhh. I think you'll find this interesting, pard. Jody owns an investigation company."

"Investigating what?"

"Whatever needs investigating. If you think your office is being bugged by a competitor, Jody is your guy. If you think that your spouse is cheating on you, Jody is your guy. If you think your business partner is stealing you blind, Jody is your guy."

I dropped my sales case on the floor, pulled off the old worn green tie that was looped around my neck, and tossed my faded blue sport coat on one of the two kitchen chairs. Em would have scolded me for having no fashion sense today. And probably for not hanging up my coat.

"Good for Jody."

"Good for us."

"Oh, yeah?"

"Not only does Jody do his own investigations, but he sells stuff."

I flopped down on the stained couch, thinking about closing my eyes for about fifteen minutes. I was tired, grumpy. The cold beer bottle dropped down beside me.

"Drink it, amigo. You'll feel better." He stood above me, waiting until I pulled a swallow or two from the bottle.

I twisted the top off and took a long drink. James was right. I felt better. "All right, I'll bite. What kind of stuff does Jody sell?"

"Spy stuff, Skip."

"What the heck is spy stuff?"

"Have another sip."

I did.

"I made some printouts."

Which meant he'd used toner and paper. With our limited budget, we usually avoided printing.

"Check it out, Skip." He handed me the first sheet. There was a simple picture of a metal box with GPS-4 printed beside it.

"GPS box. You stick it to the gas tank of a car with magnets, and you can trace the vehicle on your computer. Sit right here at the table, or," I looked up and his eyes were lit up like Christmas lights, "or from a laptop in the back of the truck."

"What are you talking about?"

"Check this out, Skip."

The next sheet of paper featured a laser-beam machine.

"You point this at a window, pard."

"And?"

"You can pick up any conversation. Bedroom talk, secret meetings —"

"Help me, James. What are we going to do with this stuff?"

"Have another sip, amigo."

I took a long swallow. James wasn't the only one who could drain a bottle of beer in three gulps. "Okay, now tell me."

"We're going into the spy business."

"Oh, no."

"Skip. You've already been hired."

"James. Dude. We were asked to keep our eyes open. That's it."

He walked around the couch and I heard him open the refrigerator door. Two more beers. James plopped down on the couch beside me. "Check this out, Skip." He handed me a picture of a sprinkler head for a sprinkler system.

"Two hundred bucks for a —"

"Camera. Yeah. It's a great little camera. Look." Another printout showed a household smoke detector. The price—$171.

"Another camera?"

"And this." A desk-sized picture frame with a digital temperature readout and a digital clock.

"A camera?"

"Mrs. Conroy said to keep your eyes open."

"James —"

"These are our eyes. They'll be easy to install. I mean, you guys are installing security stuff. A couple more things like this won't even be noticed."

"You're crazy."

"Let's talk to Jody."

"Let's not."

"You're making some good money on this gig, compadre. Invest a little in some equipment, and it makes the job easier. We're working for the owner's daughter. She'd probably think this stuff was a good idea." There was a little hint of pleading in his voice. I've heard it since we were both ten years old. "Come on Skip. It takes money to make money."

"But we're not going to tell her about this stuff." I took a pull on the new bottle of beer. Never make important decisions when drinking. How many people have learned that lesson over time?

"She'd love it." He took a swallow.

"James, she's also the president's wife. And the conversation I had with her led me to believe that she's not too fond of her husband. And with the Sarah situation—Sarah pretending to be my girlfriend, and being Sandler Conroy's lover or whore or whatever —"

"Okay. I know it's a little messed up."

"A little?"

"All I'm asking is that you consider it, Skip."

"James —" I was intrigued. I wasn't going to okay it, but I was intrigued. Ever since I was a little kid and used to read the Hardy Boys mysteries, I'd had a real fascination with detectives and spy stuff. And I loved to watch the old James Bond movies with Sean Connery and watch Q and all the gadgets he used to invent.

"We don't need all of this stuff just to keep an eye out."

"Think big, Skip. It's not just this job. We could do this, dude. We could get our P.I. licenses and do this spy thing on the side. Maybe turn it into a full-time business."

"Do you ever listen to yourself? You're a lunatic. We know nothing about being P.I.s." I loved the idea.

"We'll work with Jody. Skip, pardner, you just got offered fifteen thousand dollars to do a job that will last two or three days. If you could get, maybe twenty of those jobs a year, we'd make —"

James had studied to be a chef. His ability to do math in his head, or anywhere else for that matter, left a lot to be desired. Three hundred thousand dollars, James."

"No kidding."

"No kidding."

"Spy stuff, Skip. And we can use the truck. People will think it's a service truck, but we can stock it with the spy stuff."

"You're crazy. Do you remember the Bond movie where Q was showing Bond some missiles that shot from the headlights on his car?"

"Come on, man. You're talking to the king of movie quotes. Q looks at Bond and says, 'Need I remind you, 007, you're licensed to kill, not to break traffic laws.'" His British accent was almost perfect.

"I'm telling you, James, this is not a good idea."

"Skip, can we talk to Jody? It's your gig, I know. But I think you're missing the boat if you don't at least —"

"We'll talk to him." It was a mistake. I knew it. I always know it. I figured if I lived long enough, I'd eventually learn not to listen to James Lessor. As it happened, as I pointed out at the beginning of this story, I didn't. I didn't live long enough.

CHAPTER TWELVE

Em was amazed. Not good amazed

"You constantly surprise me, Skip." Her eyes shifted to the water, where South Beach lay past Star Island and Palm Island. Twenty-three stories up, sitting on her balcony, we watched the sun bouncing off the green saltwater, glinting off of the boats in the marina below.

"I don't want to be predictable."

"You're not."

"You don't like surprises?" I'd read in *Men's Health* or some guy magazine that girls like surprises. And, they like men who are full of surprises. *Men's Health* seemed to know what they were talking about. I mentioned this to her.

"There are girls who like bad boys too. I don't happen to be one of them." I guess this was a good thing to know.

I changed the subject. "Do you think James has a bad-boy image?" I'd always wondered what attraction James had to women. They always seemed very intrigued by him.

She rolled her eyes. "James is an idiot. He has an idiot image. Wanting to be a spy?"

"Em, I can't let James take the rap for that." The causeway traffic that went to South Beach was slowed down. Half the vehicles going over and coming back were white box trucks, servicing the wealthy residents of the islands, and the fancy hotels and restaurants that catered to the flocks of tourists who visited for the sun, the sand, and the crazy nightlife. Em could watch it anytime she wanted. And, she could visit South Beach anytime she saw fit. She had the location. She had the means.

"It's always James. When you get in trouble and —"

"Hey. I explained it to you. Carol Conroy is willing to pay a minimum of ten thousand dollars if I just keep my eyes open."

"Skip, have you considered why people, and especially attractive women, are suddenly throwing money at you?" Her eyes were wide and she had this surreal smile on her face.

Considered it? I was consumed with it. Selling my services for cash. Now it was more than just Sarah doing it. I cleared my throat. "I hadn't really thought about it like that."

"Bull. You expect me to believe that?" Em took a sip of her mojito, never making eye contact. Wearing shorts and a halter top, her feet were up on a wicker footstool, and I admired her smooth, tan legs. We'd spent the last hour inside with nothing on, but she looked great, clothes or no clothes.

Inside I could hear her printer chattering away. She worked at home most of the time, helping daddy run his construction business. The slip in the housing market hadn't affected the old man much. He worked for the upper-upper end of the rich and famous, and those people never seem to suffer an economic downturn.

Finally she spoke. "And this thing with Sarah? She's not coming on to you at all?"

I finished my bottle of Heineken, Em's treat. "Are you kidding? Like I told James, she's out of my —" I'd already said most of it.

"Oh?" She spun around and looked at me with a frown. I wasn't scoring points here at all. Em got up and walked to the railing. "But I m not?"

"What I meant was —"

"I heard you, Skip. She's out of your league. Which must mean you think she's really hot, and," she paused, "I'm not."

"If it makes you feel any better —"

She looked away. "It probably won't."

"James says you're out of my league as well. I tend to agree with him."

I could see the corners of her mouth start to turn up. I hadn't told Em about the hooker connection. The escort. The prostitute angle. I was afraid she'd go ballistic.

"Skip, why are you even telling me about all of this?"

"Because you're my girlfriend."

"Oh yeah? But you're taking money to be someone else's boyfriend."

"Pretend, Em. Pretend."

"But what do you want? From me?"

"Your advice."

"Oh. Well then, let me give it to you. Don't do any of this. Stop. Right now. Get out while you can. And blow off your loony roommate."

"Your support?" I certainly didn't want *that* advice.

"Do you want to do this?"

"I want the money, Em."

She didn't look at me, just stood by the railing gazing into the distance. "Then you've got my support."

"Really?"

She kept looking out at the cruise ships that anchor just beyond the causeway. I'd thought about the faraway places they go. The Caribbean, Alaska, Europe, places I could only dream of. And now, it seemed extremely important to be able to afford to take Em on one of these ships. First-class accommodations. Could you do that for $10,000?

Em walked back over and picked up her drink, the pale mint leaves floating in the clear liquid. "Really. If it's important to you, it's important to me."

She'd raised her concerns, told me how she felt, and realized I was dead serious about proceeding. "Em, I—"

"Skip. Up front. I'm not happy about Sarah Crumbly. I want to make that perfectly clear. Not happy at all."

I had a lump in my throat. "I understand. But it's not a deal breaker, right?"

"No. It should be."

We were both quiet. It was as if a line had been erased. I saw more box trucks driving over the causeway. Plumbers, caterers, pool service trucks, carpenters, but no spy trucks. None that I could see.

Finally she broke the silence. "So when do we visit Jody and see some of this spy equipment?"

CHAPTER THIRTEEN

I couldn't sleep that night. We were to start the big project with Synco Systems day after next, and I was keyed up. Way too many things were going on in my life, and they were all tied up with the job. I tossed and turned, working the sheets into a knot, fading in and out, sweating while I had bouts with the heat and humidity. Finally I climbed out of bed and walked out to our living room, the dingy little rectangle of carpeted space that held one chair, one small couch, a coffee table, lamp, and TV.

James was snoring on the sofa and Conan was signing off on our small screen. I pulled on a pair of torn, faded jeans that I'd thrown over the chair and unlatched the door. Why we even lock it I have no idea.

Outside the moon was shining over the stadium across the way and our pathetic parking lot was dimly lit with fading bulbs from the two pole lights that *hadn't* been broken by thrown rocks. James's truck was parked directly in front of our apartment. Even in the faint light, the basketball-sized flaking orange rust spots stood out along the bottom of the cab. Jim Job's van was parked two doors down, and my Cavalier was three doors down.

Someone had parked a gray Honda Accord in my spot beside James when I came home so I parked my car down the way where no one lived. The strange gray Honda was still there, the tires nuzzled up against the sidewalk. I should have put up a sign. Parking Spot Property of Skip Moore.

Shirtless and barefoot, I walked into the parking lot and gazed around the shabby, rundown complex. I shared the dream that James had, and the dream that Em lived. Enough money so that I didn't have to worry about where the next buck or hundred bucks or thousand dollars were coming from. Enough money that I could leave this crappy apartment, leave Carol City, maybe even leave Florida and get a start somewhere else. Enough money that I could take Em on a cruise. I shared the *dream*. Not the reality.

Deep down I knew that this job wasn't going to get that done. The money issue was still just a dream. But I started seeing the big picture, something James has been looking at for some time. There's more to life than a twenty- or thirty-thousand-dollar-a-year job. And that's a good thing. Especially with the price of gas. Putting yourself out there, I mean just exploring everything that comes your way, could have all kinds of monetary benefits. James wanted the truck idea to work. So maybe his spymobile wasn't a bad idea.

My eyes adjusted to the dim light, and when I turned back to look at the apartments on our row, I noticed the iron gates that fronted several doors. I figured that it couldn't be too difficult to pry the gates open and break into those apartments. It's just that, like our place, there would be nothing worth stealing. I made a mental note to talk to those people and try to sell them a security system. Should have thought of that a year ago. Wasn't it P. T. Barnum who said, "There's a sucker born every minute"? It was probably true.

The movement caught my eye. Three doors down. Subtle motion, something close to the ground. A cat. Dog. Maybe a snake, or possibly a rat. I stared and didn't see any motion this time. Snakes and rats lived in palm trees and orange trees, and there were five scraggly palms planted around the perimeter of the parking lot. I was scared to death of snakes and rats.

A cloud drifted over the moon and the lights from the parking lot barely cut through the nighttime gloom. I slowly walked toward my car, hoping there was no broken glass in the lot to cut my bare feet. No glass, and God, please don't let there be a snake. Or a rat.

Soft steps. I should have worn shoes.

Something had moved. Now everything was quiet. The hot, muggy, Carol City night was oppressive. Our small room air conditioner in the apartment didn't do much except make a lot of noise, but it cut a little of the humidity. Outside, the moisture clung to me like a net.

I stared at the spot where I'd seen the rapid movement. Probably a neighbor's cat. There were a lot of them in the complex.

As I got close to my car I said it under my breath. "Anybody there?"

Silence.

I was a little louder next time. "Anybody there?"

I stepped up onto the sidewalk and walked down toward James's vehicle. Jesus. Now there was a flash of movement under the bed of his run-down truck. I believed it might be my imagination. A movement under my car? A movement under James's truck? I stopped still, waiting for something else to happen.

There it was again. Bigger than a rat, bigger than a cat. I could feel the humidity and the perspiration on my face and arms. Now I wished I'd stayed inside and just tried to go back to sleep. Something was between me and the door to my apartment. Something, or somebody. It had to be just an animal or a figment of my imagination. If I yelled and it was just a large dog, I'd wake people up and be embarrassed. If I—it moved again and I could hear some scurrying.

"Who's there? Come out where I can see you." I was surprised at the volume of my voice. "Move. Now."

The cloud moved off the moon's smiling face and the parking lot was brighter. Cracks and holes. Large pieces of asphalt were missing like a jigsaw puzzle and the holes were large enough to swallow a car. Well, maybe a small motor scooter.

"Who's out there?"

What could they do to me?

I stepped closer, my eyes aching from staring. Nothing. Now I was about ten feet from the truck, and I thought about waking James. Open the door and ask him to get his lazy ass off the couch, wake up from his deep sleep, and help me out. And then I thought about how pitiful that might be.

I knelt down on the blacktop and peered under the truck. Now I couldn't make out anything. I stood up and backed my way up the small stoop in front of our door. I froze right there, trying to blend in with the cheap stucco wall.

A night bird called with a mournful howl. Maybe a loon. No motion. I waited about two minutes, the sweat beading on my face and running down my bare chest. When the bird was quiet, there was a deathly stillness in the early morning air. Finally, I turned and went back into our apartment.

"Amigo, where were you?" James was sitting up, watching some car commercial where girls in bikinis were dancing around the dealership. *Now* he wakes up.

"I took a walk. Thought I saw something in the parking lot."

"There is something out there." His voice was low and sinister.

"You saw it, too?"

"Yeah. Cars. Trucks. Vans. That's what parking lots are for."

"Funny."

An engine started nearby, kicking over on the first turn of the key. I hesitated, then stepped back outside. The car parked next to James's truck, the one in my spot, was gone.

CHAPTER FOURTEEN

"It's a GPS." The gray block was a little bigger than a brick. "You put a plastic binder on it, like this, with the magnets attached." Jody was wrapping the plastic binder around the gray contraption lying on his countertop.

"One on each end, right?" James was so excited I expected to see drool run down his chin.

"Right, James. These magnets are really strong."

"And to install it?" Em was skeptical. We stood in a tight group as Jody put on his show.

He smiled at her. Maybe a little flirting. Em is a good-looking girl, and Jody is a good-looking guy. "You reach under the car, set it on top of the gas tank, and you're good to go."

"It's that simple?" James had a glassy-eyed look, with a big smile on his face.

"You still have to load the software onto your computer. Desktop, like this, or a laptop. You can be portable if need be. Once that's done, you can check the location of that vehicle twenty-four-seven."

"Anywhere, right?" James had told me we could use a laptop in the almighty truck.

"Anywhere." Jody walked behind the counter and flipped on a countertop monitor. "Here. Emily, why don't you come over here where you can see —"

I wondered what about James and me? Since we were setting this all up, it would be nice if we could see too.

"Now, here's a map of South Florida, and here are the seven cars I'm tracking today." He pointed to the screen, and we all crowded in.

Seven dots appeared on the roads, four apparently moving on highways and byways. Three were stationary.

"This one," he pointed to the third car up on the map, "she's supposed to be at the mall."

Em nodded. "That's not a mall?"

"Most definitely not."

James chimed in. "Maybe a drugstore? Laundromat?"

Jody laughed out loud. "This isn't guesswork, my friend."

"No?"

"No. This is," he paused scrolling down a subscreen on his monitor, "this is 2867 Briar Lane. Just north of Miami."

"And?"

"Home to Mr. Fernando López."

We all watched, marveling at the technology.

"Guys," he smiled, looking into Em's eyes, "this is nothing. I mean, this is easy stuff."

Em watched the computer, ignoring Jody's probing eyes.

"So this López, he's what?"

"The guy my client's wife is supposedly screwing around with."

Outside the showroom people were walking down the sidewalk. The town of Delray Beach was hot, in the low nineties, and through the large windows I could see men with sleeves rolled up and ties loosened. A couple of women walked by in sundresses, but the window wasn't low enough to see their legs.

"Wow." James wasn't paying any attention to the sights outside. He was staring at the stationary number three car. "You monitor this lady all the time?"

"I can. But her husband has the same software. He can watch her wherever she goes. It's part of the package. You can join in the action." Jody laughed, a low, throaty chuckle.

I stepped back and looked around the room. Gadgets of every kind. I'm sure Jody would have been upset to hear me refer to them as gadgets, but that's what they appeared to be. Hidden cameras, motion detectors, secret audio devices, and an assortment of items that defied description.

"What kind of spy work are you doing?"

He looked straight at me. I couldn't tell him. I didn't have any right to confide in him. The job I was doing was strictly confidential. I couldn't possibly tell him anything about the delicate position I was in. If I told him anything, I could put myself and my friends in serious jeopardy. I wasn't about to do that.

"The daughter of the owner of the company Skip's working for thinks she might be the target of a murderer. Skip's installing a security system for this company called Synco Systems, and they're designing a software program for the United States Department of Defense. There have been some strange things happening at this company."

Of course, with a loud-mouthed roommate I didn't have to say a word.

I saw Em shoot James a very dirty look, complete with frown, slanted eyebrows, and a squint. I'm sure she was thinking about her statement that James had an idiot image. I couldn't argue with that.

"Fill me in, guys." Jody came around from the back of the

counter. "I'd be happy to take the case, but if you want to do it, I can make some serious recommendations regarding the equipment you may need. We've got state-of-the art equipment here. State-of-the-art."

"Jody, despite what James may have told you, we don't have a clue what this woman wants. She told me that she would give me instructions when the time came."

Jody walked to the center of the showroom and pointed to the ceiling. "Those are sprinkler heads."

They were.

"That one, that one, and not that one." The third was the same as the other two.

"And what is that third head?" Em looked puzzled.

"A camera."

"No." Em was amazed.

"Come here." He put his arm around her shoulders and walked her to a TV monitor on the wall. There were twelve different scenes represented on one plasma screen. James and I stood under the heads.

"Jody," Em stepped to the right, removing his arm, "how does this work?"

"Right here." He pointed to one of the scenes.

"Oh, my God." She spun around and starred at me. "You and James are in the shot, perfectly clear."

Good gadget.

"Skip, you should see this."

If I walked to the monitor, I wouldn't be in the picture.

"There are twelve cameras in this showroom." Jody spread his arms. "You are being viewed from every angle."

I walked to the screen. It was unbelievable. James stood in the center of the room, viewed from every camera. "Dude, I can see you from twelve different positions."

"Doggie is my favorite, Skip."

We all ignored his comment.

"So, Jody, what are you suggesting?"

He patted Em on the back as she took three steps from him.

"Nothing yet. You get an idea of what this lady, the owner's daughter, needs and you call me, Skip. I mean, I could sell you a couple of portable cameras, voice recorders, and stuff like that, but until you have an idea of what this lady wants—well, you just stay in touch."

It was a plan.

"We're going to need some voice-detecting equipment." James was now walking around the room, touching the different items. "Like this." He pointed to a plastic power strip.

"Good choice, my man. You can plug in any appliance, lamp, whatever, and this baby will work just like it should. The microphone inside will pick up all the conversation in the room. Crystal clear. You can have your transmitter in the truck, at work, in your home, and attached to a recording device."

"And, of course, you've got the recording device as well." Em picked up the small power strip and shook her head in disbelief.

"And what's this?" James was pointing to one of the motion detectors mounted in the corner.

"Tell him, Skip."

"It's a," I knew I'd be wrong, "motion detector. We install them for security systems. It detects motion in the room. You can set the sensitivity level from low to high. That's what it is, right?"

"Meant to look like a motion detector, Skip." Jody smiled and walked to Em. "It's a camera, folks. See scene two on the monitor?" He laid his hand on her shoulder. She removed it.

"Jody." I should have explained the ground rules before we set foot in his store.

He spun around. "Skip."

"Um, the GPS. It's really that simple?"

"You've got to change the battery. Every couple of days,

you've got to go to the vehicle and change the unit. Or the battery."

"So, if you don't change the battery —" James had wandered back to the counter.

"You lose the signal, James."

"Middle of the day, night, early morning, you have to take the unit off the gas tank and replace it?"

"You've got it." Jody picked up the gray box and held it in his right hand. "You just slide under the vehicle and switch it out. Shouldn't take over thirty seconds."

"Hey, Jody."

"Yeah, Skip?"

"I really appreciate the fact that you're giving us this prep course on doing some investigation."

"Thanks, man."

"However —"

"However what?"

"Em and I are dating. We're a couple. I guess what I'm saying is, we have a really good relationship, and I need to tell you that."

He raised his arm in mock defense. "Jeez, I wish you'd said something. I mean—I wasn't coming on or anything. I'm not that kind of—well, I'm a friendly guy. What can I say?" A muscular, handsome, friendly guy who had the nickname of Macho Jody. And I needed to address that.

I'd taken a stand. Hopefully, she would realize that I loved her. Hopefully, she'd realize that the thing with Sarah was a job. A damned good-paying job, but nevertheless a job. I thought Sarah was hot, and I was intrigued with the hooker angle, but I really cared for Em. And I hoped this proved it. Maybe she'd thank me. Miracles do happen.

"Skip?

"Yeah."

He smiled at Em as she walked over to me. "It's just that, I don't know, that I never would have pictured the two of you. I mean, forgive me for saying this please, but —"

"But what?"

"Well, I only knew her when we were in school," he nodded to Em. She gave him a cold stare and nodded back. "But, man, she used to be so far out of your league."

CHAPTER FIFTEEN

"He's sleazy."

"Em, he's a guy." James and I stopped at the truck. Em's brand new BMW convertible was down the street.

"He probably uses those spy cameras to film *Girls Gone Wild* videos."

I'd checked Jody out on the Web. He was solid. Good reputation, fair and honest. "He didn't know we were dating, Em. Now he does."

Em smiled at me. "And you set him straight. My hero."

Her tight jeans and her black designer T-shirt hugged her cute little body, and I thought about what James and Jody had both said. About my league versus hers. Her blonde hair caught a slight breeze, and I felt a shiver.

"Let me just put the magnetic straps on the box." James climbed into the truck and pulled the GPS from the bag. "This is going to be so cool, Skip."

He was convinced we'd need it. To check on Carol Conroy, to track whoever her potential killer was, to follow whoever we thought needed following.

"Almost five hundred dollars of cool, James."

"Yeah, but it's on approval. If we don't need it, if we don't like it, he said we could return it." James snapped the bands together tightly around the box.

"Just don't make it too loose. It would be our luck to have the damned thing slip off and we'd have to pay him for nothing."

"Okay, let's go." We walked down to Em's car and she gave me a questioning look. I shrugged my shoulders. As usual, it was James's call. He tugged at the bands, seemed confident that they were tight, and he lay down on the ground, easing himself under the BMW. "Ah, this is easy."

"Yeah, but this is Em's car and there's nobody around to kick your ass for messing with his vehicle. If it was someone else's car, and you got caught —"

James pushed himself back out. "Those magnets are tight. It's gonna stay right where I put it."

"And you just want me to drive wherever I usually go?" Em wasn't 100 percent on board. Hell, it was my job and I wasn't 100 percent on board.

"Yep. We'll install the software on our computer at home, and we should be able to track you anywhere."

"I don't go to too many exciting places, boys."

James brushed himself off. "You should get out more, Em. Pretty girl like you. Show yourself off a little more."

"Screw you, James." She got in the car, started it up, and pulled out onto the street.

"Can't wait to get home and try this."

"James, if you had your way, you'd spend the entire profit on this kind of stuff."

"Only what we need, Skip." We walked back to the truck.

"I keep telling you, we don't know what we need. If anything."

"GPS, a little portable video cam with sound, that laser beam that picks up sounds through windows, and one of those power strips to pick up conversations in offices. That would be a sweet start, you've got to admit." James started the engine, and it coughed. It caught the second time.

"The problem is, you've got to have a receiver for the power strip, a recording device, and a laptop for the GPS, and something to capture the voice from the laser beam."

"Now you're getting the picture."

"James. Those cost money, man."

"They're going to make us money, amigo. Lots of money."

"Yeah, I've heard you say that before."

"And chicks dig dudes with money."

"*Office Space*, 1999. Actually a very funny movie." It was about working in cubicles for some big, impersonal company. After viewing the film, and laughing our asses off, James and I had sworn to never, ever work for a company like that.

"Good guess, pard. We okay back there?"

James had never learned to drive the box truck using the big side mirrors. Every time he tried to maneuver the Chevy one-ton box truck with the mirrors, we ended up having an accident or getting stuck. I leaned out the window and looked back. Five cars back, parked by the curb was a gray Honda Accord. Could have been coincidence, but it was the third time I'd seen one in a very short period of time.

The car that picked up the Asian man in front of the Red Derby Bar. In our parking lot last night. And now a similar car was five cars away.

"You're clear, James."

He pulled out.

"Circle the block."

"Why?"

"There's a car back there. A gray Honda that looks like the same car that was parked in our lot last night. And the same one that picked up that guy who was checking out Carol Conroy's Lexus."

"Gotcha." James eased the truck out of the parking space, a stream of brown exhaust blowing from the tailpipe. With the noisy muffler, the brown exhaust, and the coughing engine we'd be hard pressed to ever sneak up on someone.

Down the street and to the left, down by the big tennis pavilion with its fourteen clay courts, seven hard courts, and big stadium that seats over eight thousand people. How do I know? Em plays there. I couldn't afford the place. I mean they've had the Fed Cup, the Davis Cup, and who knows what else there. Out of my league.

James turned left at the next street. We got an angry look from an old lady who was crossing the street. Not because James almost hit her, which he almost did, but because as we passed her I could see another blast of brown exhaust that shot right at her.

Now he drove two streets down, and then left on the street where we'd parked. As we slowed down and creeped slowly up the street I could see the spot was empty.

"How many gray Honda Accords do you figure are in Delray Beach? Or Miami for that matter?"

Knowing James, he already had the answer. "How would I have any clue?"

"Just wondered. I'm guessing thousands."

"You're probably right."

"So, let's not get too paranoid."

A horn honked and I checked my sideview mirror. A long line of cars and small trucks stretched out behind us.

"You might pick up the pace, James. There are quite a few people lined up back there."

James glanced in his side mirror. "Yeah. I see them."

He could use the mirror when he needed to.

"And, Skip, about six cars back there's another one of those bastards. It's a gray Honda Accord."

CHAPTER SIXTEEN

"Are you sure you've got it installed properly?"

"Hey, you want to try it?"

James already knew that was the worst suggestion in the world. While my roommate was no whiz at the technology of computers, he could at least use the machine once it was hooked up. I've already pointed out that he was a whiz at Google, and the boy could kill at about a dozen online games. Texas Hold 'Em wasn't one of them, however. He'd gotten into some real cash games, and I had to help bail him out once or twice.

"No. But if you followed all of the directions, we should be able to pick up Em's car."

"Don't call her yet."

James wanted to call Em and announce her location. I already knew her location. She was almost assuredly home. Probably working on Daddy's books, and listening to the *Flight of the Concords* album.

"I'll figure this out." He punched in some numbers, referring again to the directions. "Okay, I'll bet this does it."

"Anything?" I was on the couch, my feet up, watching a Jerry Springer rerun.

"No."

"You did something wrong." Two heavy blonde women were trying to tackle each other as the guards kept them apart.

"Or didn't do something right."

"Yeah." God forbid James would do something wrong.

"Where do you think she is?"

"Home."

"Mmmm."

"Nothing?"

"Nothing. Where does she park when she's home?"

"Condo has a garage."

"Well, damn it. Why the hell didn't you tell me?"

"What?"

"GPS works off a satellite. If the vehicle isn't outside, there's no way we can tell where it is."

"So, should I call her?"

"Ask her to move the car *outside*."

She was going to love this. I dialed her cell.

"Em. You parked in the garage, right?"

"Sure."

"And the GPS works off—"

"A satellite. Skip, I'm sorry. I wasn't thinking."

"Do you mind moving the—"

"Car outside? No. Tell James I'll do it in the next five minutes."

Em was full of surprises. We waited.

"James—"

"Yeah?"

"The people you are trying to follow—"

"What about them?"

"Are you going to call them and tell them to move their cars outside so you can find them?"

He sighed. I was apparently his burden to bear. James came over and gazed at Springer for a while. "Where do they get these strange people, Skip? It's tough enough dealing with problems in private or with two or three of your friends. But to take it to Springer or weird Doctor Phil or Oprah? For God's sake, what are they thinking?"

What had I been thinking, letting James take charge of this case?

The phone rang.

"Skip? The car is outside."

James was already at the computer. He hit keys, dragged on the mouse, and I don't know what all. Thirty seconds later he had a huge smile on his face. "Give me the phone, amigo."

I handed him the phone.

"Em, you are at 1717 North Bayshore Drive."

There was silence as she apparently said something to him, then he handed the phone back to me.

"Em?"

"Call me if you need me, Skip." And she was gone.

"Congratulations, James. You got it to work."

"I did. I proved your girlfriend was right where she was supposed to be. And, I proved that she thinks I'm extremely intelligent."

I knew Emily well enough to know that she would never accuse James of being smart. "So what exactly did she say?"

"She verified the address."

"And? How did you extrapolate the fact that she thought you had a brain?"

"It was the way she said it, pard. She came on the phone and said, congrats, *Einstein. That's* where I live. Where the hell did you think I would be?"

I was glad to hear that Em and James were still getting along. It's important that children play well together.

93

CHAPTER SEVENTEEN

I pulled in early, right around seven a.m., not sure what to expect. One of our installation trucks was already there, unloading heavy boxes. There would be wiring, lots of wiring. And contacts, and motion detectors—real motion detectors—not like the secret camera we'd seen yesterday. We included smoke detectors in our package even though they had some installed. There would be control pads with secret passwords and codes for all kinds of things.

I'm surprised that things go as well as they usually do after we install a system. There are panic codes, breaking-and-entering codes, remote phone codes, fire codes, and more, and I figure somebody is going to screw up and all the whistles, bells, and alarms will go crazy because someone forgot to punch in a number. It happens, but not as often as you might think.

"Hey, Skip. This your gig?"

Andy Wireman was one of the senior installers. Honest to God, that's his name. Wireman.

"It is."

"Who's doing the running?"

Runners. That's what the installers called them. Michael called them supervisors. It was easier to hire someone part-time if you gave them the title of supervisor. "One guy who says he's done it before. Name's Jim Jobs. The other guy is my roommate, James Lessor."

"You've got a lot of contacts going in. What is it, forty windows, every office door, seven outside doors?"

"Plus all the smoke detectors and the remote camera equipment."

"Four cameras that can be accessed from a remote computer. This is going to be some operation."

Select people could access the cameras and monitor every movement in the company from thousands of miles away. Why they would want to escaped me, but they could. "So, Andy, this is going to make all of us some good money."

"Good job, Skip. The boys were excited from the get-go. And you, you'll make a nice commission on this."

I agreed. A nice hefty commission operation. "They're running a pretty important project inside. I guess they just want to take the extra precaution."

Wireman nodded and picked up two of the boxes, one under each arm. "You tell the runners we're going to keep 'em running. Michael said he wanted us done and out in three days. I think that's a little optimistic, but we'll give it a go. Give me a hand."

"Michael is a bottom-line lackey, Andy. He'd squeeze anyone to get his profit." I picked up two more boxes, and we walked into the building. A lone secretary manned the reception desk, eyeing us with a furtive glance.

"Are you part of the security system people?"

"We are."

"Do you have identification?"

We both pulled out our wallets and gave her identification.

I'd met the woman two other times, but I'd been with Sarah both times and apparently *that* was a different story. Sarah had pull.

She eyed the photo IDs and looked up at us. I even knew her name. Amanda. However, she acted like we'd never met. "Well, I guess you can go on in, but you'll pass another checkpoint before you get to the main plant. I should send someone with you."

"I've been here before, Amanda. I can show Andy the way."

She frowned, but nodded for us to go ahead.

Down the hall, past another desk where we showed our IDs, then into what appeared to be an assembly room. It was too early for the workers to be there, and I was surprised they'd left us alone.

"So this is where the big project is being designed?"

"It is." I remembered the first time I'd been inside. With workers at all the benches, silently punching computer keys and making whatever it was they made. And office number five, with a very dead body inside. I shuddered.

"And we're free to wander?" Andy set the boxes down, and glanced around. He was seeing it just like I did, but this time empty of any employees. The room was a circle, with benches, computers at different stations, what looked like small welding machines, and other assorted machinery that was foreign to me.

"Can I help you?" The uniformed guard stepped from a doorway on the perimeter of the circle. There were the five doors. They all led to offices. He'd stepped out of door number two.

"I'm going to be the chief installer for your security system." Andy stuck out his hand. The short, Asian gentleman kept his thumbs tucked into his thick leather belt.

"When you come back here, you should be escorted at all times."

Andy kept his hand out. "Andy Wireman. We're going to be working together, friend."

"Mr. Wireman," thumbs still in his equipment-laden belt, "someone should have walked you back here. From now on, please don't enter this restricted area unless you come accompanied."

"Got it." Andy glanced at me and slightly rolled his eyes.

The guard glared at Andy and me as he rested one hand on a holstered pistol and the other on a small metal gray canister. "You will have someone from our staff with you at all times."

It was my project. "Look, we're going to have a team of people in here who will be all over this building for the next three or four days. You're going to need eight or nine people to keep up with us."

The small man with the closely shaved head glowered at us, then pulled a cell phone from his belt. Punching in two numbers, he waited. "You're not making my life any easier."

Andy smiled. Mr. Congenial. I'd worked with him before, and when I was ready to kill the client, Andy Wireman always kept his cool. Then, at the end of the day, we'd go out with some of his guys for a drink. And after about four or five shots Mr. Nice Guy would start throwing bar glasses, screaming about the assholes he'd had to put up with all day long, and he'd get thrown out of whatever bar we were in. But on the job he was strictly professional. Strictly.

The armed, uniformed man talked in a low voice, turning from us, then spun around and pointed at me. "You're Skip Moore?"

"I am."

"Sarah," he heavily emphasized her name as if he didn't approve of the girl, "Sarah will be back in a minute. And, Mr. Moore, just because you're a close friend of *Sarah*, doesn't mean you can break rules."

The little guy walked to door number two, opened it, and stepped inside. The door remained open, and I assumed he was

97

watching us. I closed my eyes for a moment, thinking about his face. There was something familiar about the guy.

She came bustling in, if you could actually bustle in the high, high heels she was wearing. A wraparound skirt and a sleeveless blouse with a low neckline completed the outfit, and I saw Andy's eyes do a double-take.

"Skip, Skip, I am so sorry. Feng is very loyal to the company, and I told you we're working for the Department of Defense. We've got to really be careful that we don't have any slipups."

"I understand. This is Andy. Andy, Sarah."

She'd let the hair fall down almost to her shoulders, and the short skirt and sleeveless blouse highlighted her golden tanned arms and legs. I saw Andy's mouth open a little further. I should have warned him.

He held his hand out and she grabbed it. "Hi, Andy."

"So, Sarah, how are we going to work if there has to be a Feng everywhere we are?"

"There are actually nine guards. Six men and three women. They'll be at different stations watching."

"Nine Fengs?" Andy shook his head.

"Nine."

"We'll make it work, Sarah."

As supervisor I should have just told them to stay the hell out of my way, but Andy was in charge of installation. And Andy was Mr. Nice.

"Skip," she took my arm and pulled me across the room. "Sandy wants to talk to you. He wants to meet the players on your team."

I hadn't even been introduced yet. "Sarah, I need to talk to you about the down payment. Michael has put aside the rule, but we need that check as soon as —"

Sarah smiled, stood on her tiptoes, and kissed me on the lips. Took me totally by surprise. I could smell the subtle perfume, a light sent of flowers, and I could taste her lipstick, a very faint flavor of citrus. I didn't know what to say.

"Hey," she whispered as she stroked my arm, "we're romantically involved, remember. Got to keep up appearances." I immediately thought about Feng, watching the proceedings from office number two. The money issue? We'd address that at a different time.

I heard James's voice before I saw him. He was laughing his loud, over-the-top guffaw with someone else and their jovial attitude seemed wrong for this early in the morning. Then I saw them.

"Skip, amigo. Have you met Sandy Conroy?" He pointed his index finger at the president of Synco Systems.

"No." But James had.

"Sandy, this is my good friend Skip Moore."

Conroy had that somber look on his face, but he stuck out his hand and we shook. "James has been telling me a little about your background, Skip." I shot a look at James, who gently shook his head.

"My friend tends to exaggerate."

"On the contrary, from what he told me you are the perfect person to run this job. He says you've got a keen eye for detail, and he's assured me you're the man I can trust to put this together. I guess we made a good choice."

Sarah beamed. Her two boyfriends seemed to be getting along nicely. Who says you can't have your cake and eat it too?

I introduced Andy to Sandy and James, and a minute later Jim Jobs shuffled in, a tablet and pen in hand. Essential tools for a supervisor. Maybe he had done this before. I introduced J.J., as James had started calling him, and motioned to James to follow me.

"What's up, pard?"

"So you and Sandy are good friends?"

"Met him in the hall, Skip. He introduced himself, and we talked for a couple of minutes. That's all."

I dismissed it. "Listen, I know this is strictly paranoia, but there's an Asian security guy named Feng who has a bit of an attitude. He looks very much like the guy I saw outside the Red Derby. I'd love to know what kind of a car he drives."

"Feng. He's head of Sandy's security."

I looked back at Sandy, Andy, Sarah, and J.J. They weren't paying any attention to us. Feng probably was. "You and *Sandy* are such good buddies that he told you about his security arrangements?" I was pissed. I'd gotten James the job, and he knew more about it than I did.

"Hey, settle down, pard. He just mentioned that he should probably walk me into the assembly room or his chief of security, Feng, would have a fit. That's it, pal."

"Well, he's right." I took a deep breath. Then another, letting it slowly escape. I could have used a cigarette, but I quit smoking. "Anyway, as a runner, you have —"

"A what?"

"Andy calls you a runner. As a *supervisor* you have free run of the place."

"Except there has to be a guard with any of us at any time."

"Exactly. So, my friend, I'd like to know if Feng drives a gray Honda Accord. If you can time your lunch break with Feng's, you could get him to walk you to the parking lot. Then, you could see what kind of car he drives. What do you say?"

"You think Feng is —"

"I recognize him from somewhere, James."

"It's a great plan, amigo."

I smiled. James didn't hand out compliments too often.

"But unnecessary."

"James, call me crazy, but I'd like to know if there's any

chance Feng is the Asian gentleman who was fooling around with Carol Conroy's Lexus."

James nodded, brushing back his unruly hair with his hand. "And the same guy who drove the gray Honda in Delray Beach. Skip, I haven't had a chance to talk to you. I got here about half an hour early. I sat out in the parking lot, waiting for you to show up."

"Yeah?"

"Yeah. You parked all the way across the lot. I yelled, but you didn't hear me. Then I got caught up with Sandy when I finally came in and —"

"Yeah, yeah, yeah. What's your point?"

"Very simply, I saw Feng pull in. Didn't know who he was at the time, but I saw him get out of the car."

"What kind of car, James. Don't play games with me."

"Foreign. Not one of ours."

I should have hit the son of a bitch. "What kind of car, James?"

"Honda, Skip. Gray Accord."

CHAPTER EIGHTEEN

"It's too easy." Nothing came together like that.

"Some things *are* easy, Skip."

"So this Feng guy has been following Carol Conroy and you and me?"

"No guarantee that it's the same guy. And if it is, maybe he's just checking up, pally. Could be a logical explanation."

"Maybe."

"But," he hesitated, "if you're up for it, we can turn the tables."

"What do you mean?"

"We can follow *him*."

"James, we have a job to do. Neither you nor I have the time to follow someone."

"Yeah. What is your job, exactly? I mean, the installers are installing, J.J. and I are, as you so effectively put it, we're running. What do you do?"

"I make sure everything gets handled." Actually, I had the easiest job of the bunch. But I'd sold the project. The hard part was done. Unless of course there was a problem. There was always that possibility.

"How?"

"How what?"

"How do you take care of your end? What exactly do you do?"

"Look. My title is —"

"You've got a title?"

Never should have mentioned it. "It's not important."

"Skip, pal, come on. What is it?"

"Michael said that I was Person in Charge of the Project."

James laughed out loud. "Did you major in that?"

"Shut up."

He did.

"Look, as to what I do? I'll have the laptop with me at all times and coordinate the —"

"The laptop? What laptop?"

"Jaystone Security has a —"

"We've got that slow piece of crap at the apartment, that piece of junk from another century, and now I find out *you've* got a laptop?"

"Settle down, James." I checked over my shoulder as he raised his voice. I was hoping for a quiet conversation. "It's a company laptop." We did have a couple laptops that the sales staff shared. "I can only use it when we're on a job."

"Hooked to the Internet?"

"Of course. We've got one of those plug-ins with an antenna. You just plug it in and you're online. From anywhere."

James put his index finger on my breastbone, pushing. "You never told me, Pancho. But, if you've got a laptop with mobile Internet, I've got it all figured out."

"Yeah?"

"I got the GPS back from Em last night. It's in the car. Battery should be good for two days."

"And what are you suggesting?"

"Simple, Skip. We put the GPS on Feng's car."

It was simple. Simple and brilliant. Simple but illegal. Of course I didn't expect James to recall that part of the deal. "Do you remember what Jody said before we left his office?"

"Refresh my memory." James's eyes shifted as he watched the other installers walking into the room.

I put my arm on his shoulder, and we walked farther from the group, across the clean white tiled ceramic floor. In a hushed tone I said, "Jody told us that unless the vehicle had the user's name on the registration, it was against the law." A wife could track her husband, as long as her name was on the vehicle he was driving. But if it was someone else's vehicle, she is out of luck.

"Jody said a lot of things that he *had* to say. And what I heard, Skip, was blah blah blah blah blah."

"Listen, man —"

"Skip, we're not hurting anyone. We're just trying to see what he's up to. This guy may have been following you, Mrs. Conroy, and now both of us."

"Maybe it's a coincidence."

"Maybe it's not."

"Man, it's illegal to attach one of those things."

"Dude, we'll need another unit."

"What?"

"I told you. They only last for a short time. Battery has to be changed out. We'll switch 'em back and forth."

"Are you listening to anything I'm saying?"

"I believe you started this conversation by asking me to do a little detective work. You wanted me to follow this guy into the parking lot and see what kind of car he drove."

"And?"

"I'm taking it to the next level."

The morning was taken up with organization. Andy and his crew met with J.J. and James, and we all met with Feng and his eight Gestapo agents.

"We work on very sensitive projects." He addressed our small group as he paced back and forth. "It is a priority that we have a very tight security system, but we cannot let you folks wander around the premises. Whatever station you're working on, you will need to have one of our security persons with you at all times. Is that completely understood?" He always seemed to finish by looking straight into my eyes.

No one said a word. Around us about fifty men and women in white lab coats were sitting at their tables, oblivious of our little conclave. Quietly they worked their computer magic. Most of them just stared at their screens as we stood in a huddled mass.

James leaned in and whispered in my ear. "I'd like to be paid to sit on my ass and watch TV." I nodded. A quote from the movie *Clerks*, 1994. People who saw the movie claimed James and I were much like the lead characters. As if that were a compliment. As if.

"We will ask anyone who breaks this rule to leave." The short, little guy squinted and eyed each one of us, again finishing with me. Then he turned sharply and walked back into the office at door number two.

"I think we'll get along with this group quite well," said Andy.

I rolled my eyes, more for my own benefit than his. James and I walked with Andy and an attractive uniformed female out to the lobby where we'd left hardware for the main door system.

"Door contacts, motion detector, window contacts, smoke

detector, and camera mount." Andy checked them all off on a sheet of paper. He turned to one of the installers and James. "We'll be working most of the morning on the entrance."

The young lady with soft auburn hair, a gray uniform, and the thick leather belt stared intently at the equipment. Her authoritative tone didn't fit with the look. "Everyone associated with *this* installation will stay inside *this* building until *this* specific project, the main entranceway, is complete. Is *this* understood?"

Andy had stationed the other installers around the building, and each one had his own security guard. We had installers for the office doors, for the outside windows, and for three other camera mounts.

Our security guard was about five two, young, with flashing eyes, that dark auburn hair, and a name tag that simply read Callahan. I couldn't keep my eyes off of her belt. She had a gun and a holster, what appeared to be a Taser, a tear-gas container, a cell phone, pager, and two-way radio. There were at least two tools I didn't recognize and about two inches of just belt. I'm sure they were going to find something to add to those two inches.

"Skip, need to talk." James grabbed my arm and pulled me aside.

"James, this is a piece of cake. Just do the job and—"

"That's the point." He spoke in a soft voice. "Feng and the Nazi storm troopers aren't going to let us out of here. Meals are being delivered for lunch."

I thought the security was a little much. We'd licensed and bonded our installers, but I guess if you work for the United States government— "So? You get the bonus of a free meal. And I doubt if it will be crab."

James gave me a wry smile. When he worked at Cap'n Crab, he got free food. He brought home crab from work. Lots of crab.

Sometimes crab every night. We ate more crab than anyone I know, and we both were sick of crab.

"Are we going to follow our Honda Accord, Skip?"

"I like the idea. It scares me, but I'd like to know if this guy is working against us."

"Now think about this, pard. So what if he is? Is it worth taking this chance?"

James was getting cold feet? This wasn't like him at all. "Is it worth the chance? If this guy is messing with us, he's messing with my income. Come on, James, I finally get the chance to make some serious money and I'm not going to let some two-bit tin-horn security geek try to mess up my good thing."

"Glad to hear you say that, amigo." James stared out the glass door and floor-to-ceiling windows in the lobby. The parking lot was about two hundred feet away, and we could see the employee cars spread out on the asphalt. "His car is about ten rows back that way." He pointed to the right.

"So when you put the —"

"Hold on." James put his finger to his lips, a sign of silence. "I'm not allowed to leave till after we're finished."

"And?"

In a whisper he answered. "You are not involved in the actual installation. You can leave anytime you want."

"We had to set it up that way." I was whispering too.

"So, you're the point man."

"The what?"

"I can't leave, amigo. You have to put the GPS on Feng's gas tank."

CHAPTER NINETEEN

Andy needed some clarification on a couple of technical points, mostly regarding the removal of the old system, and I was glad to get that clarification for him. The system that was in place had to be removed. Not a tough call. Sandy Conroy stopped me in the hall and expressed his desire for this project to be clean, simple, and effective, whatever that meant. Sarah asked me to stop by her office and when I did, she closed the door and told me that if Sandy Conroy hadn't promised her the moon and stars, she might have been interested in rekindling our relationship from high school. Seriously. She actually said that. I didn't have the heart to say that a relationship with a hooker was probably out of the question.

    I was looking for excuses. Excuses not to leave the building. But eventually the excuses ran out. I found myself with nothing to do as the team of professionals went about their tasks. Jim Jobs, aka J.J., knew the ropes better than anyone and made some great suggestions, surprising even Andy. He pointed out some locations we might have missed, and J.J. had an uncanny sense about the positioning of the smoke detectors. I was feeling pretty good about the group, but not so good about my next assignment.

Signing out, I walked into the parking lot about ten thirty and headed for the Chevy box truck. I unlocked the passenger door, and there on the floor was the gray box, wrapped in plastic bands with magnets attached. A simple metal box that connected to a satellite somewhere miles above the earth. A simple gray box that would let us know, every step of the way, where Feng's car was located.

"All you have to do, pard, is slide under the car and attach the box to the gas tank."

I could hear his words. However, I'd never been on the underside of a vehicle. My father had. My dad left home when I was twelve years old, and I have few strong memories of the man, but I do remember he used to change his own oil. I remember him taking a large piece of cardboard, lying down on it, and sliding himself under his car. Isn't it funny? You remember the strangest things. But Dad, for all his ability to deal with mechanical objects, couldn't deal with human beings. Especially when it came to dealing with his family. He walked out on us, and no one ever changed oil in our garage again.

There was no cardboard in the parking lot. I was going to have to slide under the Accord on my bare back. Well, with the shirt on my back. I walked down the rows, hoping maybe Feng had an early appointment somewhere else. Maybe he'd taken off and the parking space would be empty. No such luck. The gray Honda Accord was hard to miss.

I almost believed that James had orchestrated the reason that he couldn't do this deed himself. This had been his idea, and I'd assumed he would take care of it. Instead, here I was. I knew it was ridiculous, but I could picture him taking Feng aside and saying "Hey, Feng. Why don't you make all of us involved in installation stay inside for the whole day? You could buy our lunch, and —" But I knew he'd had nothing to do with it. Even though he and Sandy Conroy were now best buddies.

The parking lot appeared to be empty of people. Eerily empty and quiet. Something didn't feel right. Probably the fact that I was about to break the law. I crouched down and peered under the car. How hard could this be? Attach the box to the gas tank. Just reach up under the car, and—wasn't going to work. The box wasn't grabbing the tank. The magnets weren't attaching. I assumed it would be a quick mount, but it wasn't. I scooted a little, my upper body now under the vehicle. The blacktop was hot, the muffler hung low, and I had to move to the rear of the car. I reached up and pushed the box against the gas tank. Nothing. Sweat ran down my forehead and into my eyes, and the hot asphalt burned my back.

I jammed the unit, shoved it, slid it over the tank, finally putting my hand up and pressing on the gas tank. It was then I realized the problem. The gas tank was plastic. Plastic. And even though I'd done poorly in science classes, I knew that magnets don't attach to plastic.

There's an entire metal frame on a car, and I ran my hand over some of the undercarriage. Would the magnets be strong enough to hold the GPS to other metal parts on the car? I'd have to give it a try. I could picture the GPS unit falling off and Feng finding it. Or, even worse, the gray box dropping off, and I'd be out five hundred dollars.

I took a deep breath, and reaching up, I placed the unit against a strip of gray metal. It snapped into place, almost like it was fitted for the position. I looked up, admiring my handiwork. That's when I heard the voices. Someone, two people maybe more, were walking the lot. I pulled my legs under the car and held my breath. The voices were close, and I could make out some of the conversation. Something about security. Something about letting him think that this would solve all the problems. It made no sense, but I latched onto words and faint phrases.

The voices were closer, and I curled into a fetal position, praying that the Accord would give me the cover I needed.

"When's the project going to be done?" The voice was low, rumbling, and now it sounded like it came from five feet away.

"One month. They'll get this security system up and running, and within three weeks Synco will start installing the software."

"When do they release the codes?" The deep-voiced speaker asked the question. And I knew who was answering.

The voice was Feng's. I would have bet on it. "We can't install the program unless they give us the codes."

The rumbler came back. "It's that simple?"

"We're banking on it," Feng said. "Ralph was supposed to get them. He was the contact, but you know what happened to Ralph." It wasn't a question. It was a statement.

"Yeah. I know."

Sweat continued to run into my eyes, running down my chest, as I was crouched into a tight ball, saying a silent prayer that I would not be discovered. Something on the ground tickled my right arm. Wearing jeans and a T-shirt for the installation day left me somewhat exposed, and I could feel this particular tickling on my right elbow. I shuddered and the sensation stopped. For a couple of seconds. I gave my head a short shake, trying to get rid of the perspiration from my eyes. Squinting, I peered down at my right arm and saw the large black beetle with gray antennas, chewing on my skin. My eyes stinging, I shook my arm and the beetle moved. I didn't follow him, just closed my eyes and prayed that he wouldn't return.

"You don't see any hitch?"

"None." Feng responded.

"It can't be this easy."

"It can. It will be. It is."

"Jesus."

"Are you Christian?"

"No."

Silence. Finally Feng spoke.

"We'll get the codes. The plan is the same. We will be victorious."

I could see their legs, Feng's gray uniform pants and polished black shoes, and the other man's black pants and scuffed loafers. And even though they spoke in hushed tones, I could hear their voices as if they were under the Accord with me. They were so close I could see lint on the fabric of their pants. Certainly they would realize I was two feet from them. They'd hear me breathing or I'd sneeze. Then I felt a funny sensation in my nostril, and I really started to worry.

"It's in your hands."

"I understand that, and I don't take it lightly."

There was no more conversation. The shuffling of shoes and the separation of the two men was audibly and visually evident, and I drew a deep sigh of relief. They were leaving. I couldn't have been happier. I sniffed, trying to stop the sneeze sensation. Once, twice, and then I sneezed, muffling it by pressing my face into the rough surface of the asphalt. Everything was quiet and I strained to hear even the faintest sound. And there it was. I heard the faint click, the opening of a door and a second later, the slam of a door. The suspension shifted. Someone was inside the car. I was under the car. This was not the way it was supposed to go.

A moment of silence. Then a roar of the engine, and I shuddered. I shuddered, then shuddered again. Someone, my guess would have been Feng, had started the Honda and I was directly underneath. Would the wheels run over me? Could the car scrape me off the parking lot? I was in an extremely uncomfortable situation. For some reason I flashed back to one of the dozens of Hardy Boys novels I'd read as a kid. Frank Hardy was in a do-or-die situation. With all his might, he pushed, pulled, or did something and miraculously escaped from a life-threatening situation. The guy was like Houdini.

I stuck my head out from under the car and dug my fingers into the asphalt, pulling with all my might. Any second he'd throw the Honda into drive and crush me into the pavement. I threw my arms forward, pulled hard, and only gained inches. Then, maybe a foot, and another. Again, and again. The car jerked forward and I curled my legs with lightning speed as the car lurched from the parking spot and the driver squealed the tires as he left the row of cars. I pulled myself forward, under another car, now getting the hang of it, my raw fingers scratching at the pavement. Under another car, huddling for just a moment, then easing out, my head swiveling this way and that, trying to see if anyone had noticed. I heard and saw nothing.

I lay on the blistering asphalt for a moment, running my hands over my arms, my legs, my neck, and head. I ached, but everything seemed in one piece.

And there I was, stretched out on the black surface, thanking God that I'd escaped with my life. Thanking anyone who would listen that I'd escaped with my limbs intact. Thanking my lucky stars that no one had discovered me. Thanking the spirits that protected me that I was protected.

I wiped my eyes with my left hand and took several long, deep breaths.

"So. You have one small job to do, and you end up sleeping on the blacktop."

James was looking down at me, shaking his head in mock disappointment. I'm telling you, there are times when I'd like to strangle him.

CHAPTER TWENTY

"Pard, he let us out on a short break. If I'd known we were getting the break, I would have done the job myself."

We sat on the solid cement slab behind our apartment in cheap green and white Walgreens lounge chairs, drinking cheap Genny long-neck beers. I'd accepted the beer from him, even though I'd paid for it, but I hadn't said a word. I was still shook up over the GPS incident. The one that my roommate suggested. The one he was going to handle. Until he conveniently couldn't do the job.

James took a deep drag on his Marlboro, letting it drift into the air. I took a deep breath. Secondhand was better than starting up again. And besides the health issue, I couldn't afford to smoke.

"Skip, I will admit, I talked to Eden, and she sent me to Sandy's office. I asked him if he didn't think we should be allowed to leave the building for even half an hour."

"Eden?" I'd never heard the name.

"Eden Callahan, the cute security guard."

Leave it to James. The next thing would be he'd have a date with her.

"By the way, I asked her out for next Friday."

And I hadn't even considered that. Not *asking the guard out on a date*, but asking for a break. I'd gone along with Feng's program. The little soldier rode roughshod over everybody and I'd let him do it to me.

"Sandy said we could take a break and passed it down the line, and so we did." He stared at me, waiting for my response. I just took a long swallow of beer. "Anyway, Feng was furious. He was stomping around, just totally pissed off that someone had gone over his head. Of course, as short as he is, just about everything goes over his head."

I smiled.

"See, you can't stay mad too long."

I gazed down the row of apartments, the little cement porches like a board game, one after another. Cracked, pitted, stained concrete, littered with cheap grills, kids' broken toys, and worn out lawn furniture. Just beyond our pathetic living quarters there was a mud brown ditch, half filled with brackish water that flowed with the runoff from somewhere. I was mad. But only mad because I was settling for this miserable existence. I wanted success as much as James, maybe more. Maybe for different reasons. James wanted success that his father had never achieved. I wanted success to show Em that I could amount to something. James and I both had something to prove.

And even with this job, even with the nice paycheck at the end, I still felt like success was just beyond my reach. And that almost getting myself killed this day was probably not the way I was going to make a million dollars.

"Listen, you did a great job, amigo. You got the GPS under his car."

"At the risk of killing myself." I could feel a crick in my back and the soreness of my arms and legs.

"Yeah, but you're alive and we can track that little weasel."

"James, it was stupid. We did it on our own. Mrs. Conroy didn't even ask us to do it. We had no business—"

"Skip," he stood up, tugged his baggy shorts up high, and walked back into the apartment, returning moments later with two more cold beers, "we did have business. Somebody died in that building a couple of days ago. Could be suicide, could be murder." James twisted the top and tossed it over his shoulder. Nobody kept up the back of our apartments. Nobody kept up the front either. "And this little guy shows up every time we turn around."

"Still—"

"No *still*. Carol Conroy comes to you and says there's some kind of mystery going on there, and I maintain that we have a right to check it out."

"Well, what's done is done. The GPS is on his car. If it hasn't fallen off yet."

"I called Jody. He said that it should stay on. The magnets are strong."

I looked back the other way, more apartments stretched out to the road. I saw J.J.'s. rear screen door, hanging from only one hinge. What kind of a handyman lets his own door go unrepaired? What kind of a security guy can't even put a GPS on a car without nearly sabotaging the entire effort?

"So, you're going out with this—what's her name?"

"Eden. Eden Callahan. Like, garden of Eden. All the fruits—the delights."

"Yeah. James, I don't know my Bible that well, but I think there was a snake in the garden as well."

He thought about that for a moment, leaning back in his webbed chair and sipping on his beer. "That's fitting, isn't it?"

116

It was.

"And if you'd just bring the laptop home with you, we can follow this guy. From home and from any mobile location. Pretty cool, eh?"

I had the laptop in my car.

"I've got his car spotted on the computer inside. He's at a residential address. I assume it's his home."

Five hundred dollars down the tubes. It was on approval, but if we bought it, we'd have spent that much to prove, without a doubt, that, when not out and about, Em was parked at home. We'd now proved that Feng, after work, was at *home*.

"Come on, Skip. You're still upset that you got stuck putting the GPS under the car. It wasn't my fault. You know me, pally. I would have done the dirty deed. Relished it."

"Did you know that the Honda had a plastic gas tank?"

"I did. Looked it up on the Internet."

It figured. "Did you know that Feng stopped three places yesterday afternoon?" I wanted the element of surprise. I got it.

"I didn't install the program until I got home. How could I know that?"

"I loaded it last night on the laptop. I've been following the little guy all day. On the laptop's screen."

"You son of a gun. And you never told me. Leave me out to hang, eh? You're getting into this aren't you?"

"A little."

"So where's he been?"

"Addresses. That's what I have. I have no idea if these are businesses, maybe a restaurant."

"So we could drive the same route and see where he's been."

I nodded. "We could do the same thing. Take our lunch hour and follow his path. Except that gas costs money and nobody is paying us for these little jaunts."

"True."

"All right. I'm making enough on this job, let's do it. Tomorrow for lunch we'll follow his path, just to see if anything sticks out. Happy?"

"I am, my man. We're officially spies."

CHAPTER TWENTY-ONE

The work was going slower than we expected.

"The old system is harder to get out than I thought it would be," Andy said.

"We're under a pretty tight deadline." I didn't need any more problems than I already had.

"Skip, when you're dealing with a building of this size, there are bound to be surprises."

One of the surprises was that we still didn't have our 50 percent down. Michael had called on my cell phone, eating up my minutes, and told me to check into it.

"Skip, we've put you in charge of this project. I'm taking some serious heat from Jaystone. Now, don't let me down. You just walk into that office and tell them that we can't work like this. We're covering all the hardware, software, the labor, and blah blah blah blah blah." That's what I heard.

One crisis after another. As the Person in Charge of the Project, I guess that's what I was paid for. Putting out fires and finding solutions. So far, I hadn't done a very good job.

Sarah was in her office, door number three, right next door to Feng's door number two. There used to be some show on television where people had to choose a door to see what their prize was. I was starting to believe there weren't a lot of prizes behind any of these doors.

"Skip, what can I do for you? More problems with Feng?"

Damn she looked good. A sleeveless shell top of gauzy white, and a cranberry-colored skirt that hit above the knees. Either she had money, or she knew how to bargain shop. And she wore it very well. Em was a sharp dresser when she needed to be, but this girl was just plain hot.

"No. No Feng confrontations. Not yet. Michael called today and asked about the down payment on the security system."

"Do you mean we haven't sent that yet?"

"He says no."

"Skip, I apologize. I'll call bookkeeping, and I'll let Sandy know. He won't be happy about this. Don't you worry about it anymore. Do you understand? I'll take care of this right away."

"Sarah, I've got one more money question."

She gave me a quizzical look. "Yes?"

"The bonus."

"Bonus?"

"Yeah, you know, for pretending that you and I —"

"What about it?"

"When, you know, when do —"

She frowned, sitting behind her glass-topped desk, and reached down, tugging her skirt just a little farther down. People who live with glass desks— "I told you that Sandy was getting a big payoff."

"You did."

"You'll get paid for your . . ." she hesitated, "extra services, when *he* gets paid. Is that a problem, Skip?"

"No, no, no. I just wondered. We hadn't really talked much about it, and —"

"If that isn't a problem, is there anything else?"

There wasn't. I'd gotten nothing. But, I'd been promised everything, so it was all good, right? Sarah motioned with her hand that I should leave, and I had the impression her message was "don't let the door hit your ass on the way out." The room was about twenty degrees colder than when I'd gone in.

I walked up to the entranceway and Andy and another installer were pulling cable from the ceiling.

"Skip, this is what I'm talking about. I think there was another system that someone used a long time ago, before the newer system was installed. So this means two old systems that were up there. We need to clean this out. I'm thinking we're going to have to tack on a day or two extra."

I didn't like the sound of that. Michael would be upset, Michael's bosses would be upset, and somehow I knew this was going to affect my commission.

Jim Jobs was on a ladder halfway down the entrance hall. "Hey neighbor." He smiled at me, taking ceiling tile out and stacking it on top of his ladder. "Andy tell you that there might be two systems up here?"

"He did."

"Not that I'm takin' credit or anything —"

"Credit?"

"Yeah. I found 'em yesterday. Told Andy, we can't be puttin' new lines in when we've got all these old lines. Not just the last installation, but one from a long time ago." He gave me a big smile and if those two front teeth weren't missing, I might have considered punching them out. J.J. reached up and pulled another tile from the ceiling. Damn.

This guy was supposed to be a runner. Now he was a technical consultant? And he was cutting into my paycheck. The worst part was, I'd hired him. Was there a sign on my back that said "Dumb Ass"?

"Hey, pard." James came walking through, carrying a cardboard box under each arm. "I guess we've got Feng backed down from that 'do not leave the building' crap. Sandy and Sarah say as long as we are checked when we leave, we're free to go to lunch. Good deal, eh?"

"*You* got the permission?"

"I just asked Sandy, Skip. Hey, no need to get upset. You're in charge. You're the man. I just wanted clarification."

What happened to Person in Charge of the Project? I think the entire title evaporated that morning. Almost everyone on the project knew more than I did, and had taken more responsibility than I had. I looked at my cheap Timex watch. It was nine thirty in the morning. Nine thirty. The day had just started, and I was ready to go home. For good.

By noon I'd run into two more problems. The manufacturer had sent the wrong smoke alarms and we were short by twenty motion detectors. Unless we could pull them from another job site, it would be another two or three days from the time they were shipped. My head throbbed and I wanted a beer. Two, no make that three beers, back to back.

"Ready to rumble, amigo?"

"What?"

"Lunch? A little trip to see where the Fengmiester went yesterday?" He stood in the entranceway, pointing to the glass door.

"I shouldn't leave, James. There are about a million problems with this project, and —"

"You need to get away. Come on." Throwing his arm over

my shoulder, James walked me out the door. "We'll follow up on those addresses, stop at a little bar I know and have a sandwich and a beer. You'll feel better. Trust me."

I get into so much trouble when I trust James Lessor.

CHAPTER TWENTY-TWO

We walked to the truck in a drizzle. The only problem with the drizzle was that the truck's wiper had one speed. Very, very slow. About a month ago, during a heavy cloudburst, James had to stick his head out the driver's-side window to see where we were going.

"We can take my Chevy."

"No. Let's use the truck. I mean, it's a new business venture, this spy thing, and I think we should use it." The idea seemed to make sense to him.

James climbed in and started the engine, black smoke from the tailpipe swirling in the wind and rain.

"I was thinking about a sign. We could stencil it on the side."

"What? Spymobile? I tend to think that would give it away, James."

He rolled his eyes. "Settle down, pard. Now, tell me what kind of a business everybody needs from a service truck."

I thought for a moment. Everybody had to eat, but they bought their food from a grocery store. Or a Schwan's truck. That didn't work. Locksmith, auto repair, carpenter—

"It's easy, Skip. A couple of years ago they even sent one to the space station to fix the toilet. A plumber."

"I remember that."

"Well, I'm thinking we open a plumbing business."

"That's your cover?"

"Lessor and Moore Plumbing. Or maybe Buddy's Plumbing. Or —"

"I get it, I get it." From deep in the back of my brain I remembered a quote from Albert Einstein. Somebody in college shared it with me. "If I had my life to live over again, I'd be a plumber." I'm sure it was taken out of context. Or, maybe not.

"We're good to go anywhere. Nobody's going to question a plumber. Some poor schlob's crapper is backed up or the pipes have burst in his kitchen or his drains need to be cleaned out. Everybody needs a plumber sometime in their life. Am I right?" We hit a bump and I thought the bottom of the truck was going to fall out.

"Do we want the truck permanently decorated with a sign that advertises a business we really don't have?"

James lit a cigarette with one hand, clutching the wheel with the other. The steering on this vehicle was tough enough with two hands, and when he hit the next bump in the road the truck veered, almost nicking a car in the other lane.

"Okay, let's get a magnetic sign. Take it off when we're home."

"Sure. I guess that works."

The rain had become a downpour, beating against the glass, and the windshield was streaked with dirty water, some running off the top of our truck, some splashing up from puddles in the potholes.

"Pard, check your addresses. I think we're coming up on one right now." I was surprised he could see anything.

I'd written down the three addresses where Feng had gone after work. They were all within a fifteen-square-mile area surrounding Carol City. I pointed out the crossroad, and James took a right onto Palm Breeze Way. Where they came up with these names I have no clue. The romantic name of the street was quickly disproved by the run-down shacks and shanties that lined the street. Pothole after pothole caused splash after splash and bump after bump and two blocks in I thought we were going to blow the entire suspension. What was left of it. And then, like magic, the rain stopped. The sun peeked through the clouds and steam rose from the pavement.

"Right there. Stop." A two-story cement-block building, about the size of a convenience store, sat on a solitary lot. Weeds grew up around it, and red and black gang graffiti covered the otherwise colorless structure.

"This was one of his stops?" A gentle rain had started up, filling the temporary reprieve.

"Appears to be. According to the computer."

James pulled over to the curb into what used to be a small parking lot. He jumped from the truck and ran up to the building, never succeeding in dodging the raindrops. He yanked on the heavy metal door, which refused to open.

Getting back into the truck, he shook the water from his face and hair. Like a dog. "Padlocked. Rusty old padlock. I don't think the place has been open for years."

"Well, he was here."

"Let's hit the next place."

"Probably about three miles."

"We can do this." He started the truck, and we drove down Palm Breeze Way. The shabby dwellings just got shabbier.

A left on Bianca Drive, another curving left onto Bonita Boulevard, and I saw a small laundry on the right. Chinese letters in the window, and under them the name CHEN'S LAUNDRY.

"So he had to drop off clothes."

"Disappointing so far, eh, pard?"

He pulled back out on the road, and I glanced in my side mirror. "James, check out your mirror."

He glanced out. "Is that gray car an Accord?"

"I believe it is."

"There's a lot of gray Hondas in Carol City, Skip."

"Or, maybe Feng is hitting his stops again."

The car hung back a couple of blocks, then turned off the road, and I lost it. "Must have been someone else."

"You've got his license number."

I thought for a moment. I'd been intimate with his car. We'd been physical, and I didn't even have the number. "You must have taken it down, James."

"Jeez. Great spies we are." James banged his fist on the steering wheel. "What's our last stop?"

"This is stupid. Let's go to the bar you talked about and have a—" I stared hard into the side mirror, making sure of what I saw.

"What is it?"

"Gray Honda. Maybe two blocks back." There were a couple of cars and another box truck between us. I viewed the Honda as it maneuvered behind the other vehicles.

"How would he know where we were?"

"It's probably all a coincidence."

"Where do I turn, pard?"

"Next street. Forty-seventh."

He turned and picked up speed. Not much, but a little. The engine chugged along. The Little Engine That Could. There were some commercial buildings, then a rundown strip mall with three of the five businesses boarded up.

"Any sign of the graymobile?"

There were none.

127

"On your right, James. Right there."

He stepped on the brakes and there was a metal on metal sound. Another problem with the truck. We needed new brakes.

"It's a day care center."

"So Feng's got a kid. He had to pick him up." James shrugged his shoulders.

I noticed the name. Recognized the name. Tiny Tots Academy. Somewhere Carol Conroy had picked up one of their pencils. I was sure she didn't have any kids. "Keep driving."

He did. Swerving to avoid the caverns in the road and trying to maintain a speed at about forty miles per hour. Quick for Forty-seventh avenue. I glanced in the mirror and there it was. No mistake. A gray Honda. It never slowed down at the day care center, but hung back, blending in with the light traffic.

"He's back, James."

"Son of a bitch. He knows exactly where we are."

"I should have brought the laptop. Why didn't I?"

James took a sharp right, then a left. Then back out to Forty-seventh. "You never thought about him following us."

"If I had it, we could tell if the Honda was Feng. It would be so easy. We'd just check out his car, and we'd know immediately if it was him."

"Don't beat yourself up, pard." James braked hard, the grinding and squealing painful to my ears. He took a hard right into a parking lot of a small restaurant. ANITA'S PLACE. The sign in the window said *closed for family emergency*. It was a Mexican restaurant. Just as well. I'm not a big fan of Mexican food.

James opened the door and got out of the truck.

"Hey, man, it's closed." I yelled out the window after him.

He didn't respond, but ducked down, and I lost sight of him. I jumped out of the truck and looked around. No sign of James, no sign of the gray Honda. Nothing. "James?"

Everything was quiet. A couple of cars passed, kicking up a

spray, and the gentle raindrops spattered around me. Nothing. "James?"

"Skip, here. Check it out."

He was nowhere.

"Skip?"

From under the truck.

For the second time in two days I scooted under a vehicle. "What?"

James pointed to the gas tank. "Check it out, pally."

Feeling the wet pavement through my soaked shirt, I gazed up. Fastened to the metal tank was a gray box, very much resembling a GPS unit.

CHAPTER TWENTY-THREE

My cell phone rang on the way back. The ring was Springsteen, the musical opening to "Born in the U.S.A."

"Mr. Moore?"

I didn't recognize the voice.

"This is Carol Conroy."

I reached over and nudged James. He glanced at me and took his eyes off the road as we hit a crater that went halfway to China. The truck shook like we'd encountered an earthquake. We had to do something about the shocks. "Yes, Mrs. Conroy. What can I do for you?"

"For what I'm going to pay you, I hope you can do a lot." There was venom in her voice.

"What do you have in mind?"

"I need to know what's going on in one of the offices at Synco."

"What's going on?" Maybe someone was having sex on a desktop. Maybe someone was doing a second set of books or taking drugs.

"Is there any way that you can record conversations? Without being obvious?"

"Mrs. Conroy, can you hold on for just a moment?"

"Of course."

We were pulling into the Synco Systems parking lot, and I scanned the blacktop looking for Feng's gray Honda. It didn't seem to be on the property. "James," I put my hand over the phone and spoke in a loud whisper, "she wants us to bug somebody's office." It hit me that no matter how much this lady was willing to pay, I could be in a lot of trouble. But I also remembered that this lady thought her life was in danger. If I could save a life—

"We can do that."

"Yeah? What if we get caught?"

"She's calling the shots, amigo. She's the owner's daughter. Not only that, she's the president's wife. She's a double threat, amigo. If she tells us to do something, it's part of the job."

For the right amount of money, you can justify just about anything. Sarah Crumbly had already reached that conclusion. James seemed to have always been there. And, for a split second, I thought about James's rationalization and figured he was right. This was going to be a really nice paycheck.

"Mrs. Conroy?" James drove through the puddles and parked the truck in the identical spot he'd parked it this morning. He turned off the ignition and we sat there listening to the engine sputter and crackle. "We can probably handle that." Feng's office. It had to be. And, it would serve two purposes. We could find out what the little man's agenda was. Find out why he was following us, and, at the same time, we could report to Carol Conroy on his conversations.

"Good. How soon can you report to me?" Maybe she was trying to get evidence on the little guy so she could go to her father. Maybe she needed to worm her way back into papa's good graces. This was my imagination at work, but it all made sense. She'd told me that she and her dad were not on the best of terms. Finding a mole in the company might help cement that relationship and at the same time help her insure her inheritance. Of course, this was all a guess.

"How soon can I report to you? Um, tomorrow. Will that be soon enough?" I couldn't wait to give her the news that Feng was the guy who was messing with her Lexus.

"No. That's not soon enough. However, it's probably the best you can do."

The lady was a stone-cold bitch. Getting a shot in as often as she could. "We'll find a way to do it."

She was quiet for a moment. I could hear her breathing on the other end of the line. "Mrs. Conroy?"

"Yes. Just do it, okay?" I wasn't *sure* that she was *sure*. The tone of her voice led me to believe that maybe she was hesitant. But here was someone who thought her life may be in danger, and she was taking steps to find out.

"Okay. You can call me late tomorrow afternoon, and I'll give you a report. We'll have some sort of recording, or notes." James and I would figure out how to do it later. Right now, I just wanted to cement the project. And my bonus. I wanted to nail Feng myself. And we could get this done.

"Okay."

I hung up the phone.

"We're going to bug somebody's office?"

"We are."

"Feng?"

"Yes." And then it hit me. Just as the phone rang again.

"Hello."

"Mr. Moore, I seriously wonder if I hired the right person for this job. Are you a complete idiot?"

"I can assure you, Mrs. Conroy, this *will* be taken care of."

"You don't even know whose office I want you to monitor. I am seriously reconsidering my decision here."

I realized she'd never told me whose office needed bugged. But I'd figured it out on my own. I just didn't want her to realize that James and I had already started looking into Feng.

"Mr. Moore, I want you to gather conversations from office number one."

"One?" One? That couldn't be right. And yet I realized Feng was number one in my thoughts.

"Office number one. Sandy's office. My husband."

CHAPTER TWENTY-FOUR

"It's impossible, Skip. You can't fall into this much crap. Nobody can get themselves into this much of a mess." Em sat wedged between James and me as our truck chugged down the highway toward Delray Beach.

I'd attached the GPS unit from our truck to the UPS truck that stopped twice a day at Synco Systems. Learning from my mistakes, it took me about two minutes this time. Let Feng follow "Big Brown" for a while. So I didn't think the complaint was entirely warranted. I mean, I was adjusting.

"Em," James shot her a glance, "it's not like we've been exposed to this kind of thing before. You can be as critical as you want to be, but we're in virgin territory here."

I heard her growl. "James, I blame you for ninety percent of this."

"Your boyfriend is innocent. I take all the credit."

I wanted to strangle both of them. "Why don't the two of you grow up and quit throwing blame around?" I used the popular phrase that seemed to be the dumbest one of the decade. "It is what it is."

"And that's exactly what it is." James jerked the wheel, avoiding a Porsche that cut us off, and kept his eyes straight ahead.

"Look, we're going to be at Jody's store in about ten minutes. We have a mission, and I'm—*we're* being paid well for it." This had started out being *my* project. Obviously I wasn't comfortable in my own ability. I'd asked these two people to participate. A bad decision.

No one else spoke for the next seven or eight minutes. We listened to the tinny radio. There was an electrical short somewhere in the system and it cut in and out. The sound quality was second only to the crappy rap music selection James had chosen. Finally, we pulled up next to Jody's spy store.

"You know," James said, "we don't really need three people to buy a simple bugging devise."

"No." I agreed. "I volunteered to do this myself. But you two decided it couldn't be done without your expertise."

The three of us walked into the store, and Jody greeted us from behind the counter.

"Hey, Skip, James."

"You remember Emily. My—" I remembered how he'd almost made a play for her the last time.

"Girlfriend." Emily finished the sentence. "He has a hard time with that."

"No." I corrected her. "It's just that I still can't believe I'm dating someone as hot as she is, and I stumble every once in a while." I wasn't going to let this sleazy guy move in again on Em.

James rolled his eyes. Em grabbed my arm and squeezed it.

"As we said on the phone, we need a listening device." James was scanning the walls, checking out the inventory.

"Well, there are several things I would suggest. First of all, there's the power strip." He pulled a three-outlet power strip from behind his counter and handed it to me. "I showed you this the last time." Jody beamed a smile at Em. "You turn on the red switch, just like you always do. Then, you plug it in. No one has a clue, and you hear every voice in the room."

"That's what we need, pard." James was nodding his head up and down.

"Hold on, friend. Then there's the light switch, the body microphone, and the motion detector."

James nodded as if he understood. Trust me. He didn't.

"If you need to move it around to different locations, the power strip is good. I've also got a ball."

"Ball?" I looked around. Didn't see a ball.

"Right here." He opened the palm of his hand. "Barely the size of a Ping-Pong ball. Now this is a camera and a microphone."

Jody set the ball on the counter as we hovered over it. He pointed to a flat-screen moniter on the wall, and we could all see ourselves.

"You guys are setting up a security system, right?"

"We are."

"Then these two items here would be perfect. Remember these?" He pointed to the wall behind him. "You thought it was a motion detector. Pretty good imitation, huh?" The small, curved plastic apparatus was mounted on the wall, facing us.

The thing was dead on. To the eye there was no way to tell it was a camera. I dealt with motion detectors on every installation. "It looks exactly like a motion detector. If it was a real detector, anytime something moved in front of it, it would trigger an alarm. The alarm is usually programmed to call the security company and they send out the cops." But it wasn't real.

Jody walked back to the monitor, flipped a switch, and we were all treated to another live shot of ourselves. "It's a really good camera and a microphone. So you'd be getting quality video as well."

"Wow." James stared at me. "If it can fool an expert, it should fool a layman. Pretty good."

Em watched the monitor and brushed her hair back from her face. "So Skip could have that installed and it would appear perfectly normal for the security system?"

"Exactly."

"Wow."

"But I'm thinking the item up there might be the best of all." He pointed above our heads. A smoke detector was mounted to the ceiling, and again we all appeared on the flat-screen monitor. "That baby covers the room, and the sound is great."

James looked at me, a big grin on his face. "I told you that Jody would come through. These are pretty cool, eh, amigo?"

I had to admit. There were companies making a living inventing these spy things, so there must be a lot of sneaky people in the world. "You must sell a lot of these to industries for espionage. Or maybe checking up on employees?"

"Some. Most of them, they're used by spouses."

"Woman checking up on cheating husbands?" James smirked.

Jody shook his head. "No. Men checking up on cheating wives. Mostly."

It was Em's turn to ask a question. "What?"

"I know, you think of straying husbands, not wandering wives. If I was in business, let's say north of Atlanta, I'd be dealing with philandering husbands. But south of Atlanta, it's where the rich sugar daddies retire. The old men bring their money and end up marrying girls half their age or younger."

"Ah," James seemed to get it. "And the old geezers need to keep an eye on the little fillies because they know that most of them married for the money."

"Something like that." Jody pointed at the monitor with all

the locations clearly marked. "Twelve out of fifteen clients are men tracking wives."

"A clear case against marriage." James laughed.

"So, my choice would be the smoke detector."

I let out a deep breath. "How much?"

"This one I can sell you for about a hundred seventy-five dollars. All you need is a computer, and when you remove the secure digital card, what the industry calls an SC card, you can plug it into your computer and see and listen to everything that happened in the room."

"That's a steal, Skip."

I gave James a sharp look. He hadn't put up one cent yet. Oh yeah, the truck. That was always his investment. As long as it continued to run.

"The card inside?" I was thinking about taking it out, putting it back in, taking it out—

"Well, if you want to do this fast and easy, you just mount the detector. The card inside is motion and sound sensitive and should last about six hours. As I said, you just take off the cover, take out the card, and play it on your computer."

"Just?"

"Well, you could hardwire the thing, but there's cable and drilling and running it into ceilings and walls and—"

"No, no." That's what we were doing for the legitimate part of our business. This had to be quick and easy. "Never mind." I looked up, studying the white piece of plastic. What had I gotten us into? So someone, probably me, has to go into the office, climb up on a chair or ladder, remove the card, replace the cover, and get out of the office alive.

James was looking up too, and I noticed Jody was looking at Em. "And, amigo, someone has to go back in and replace the card."

"There's that too."

138

"You can buy an extra card." Jody looked anxious.

"I'm not sure I can afford the one I'm buying now. Any chance we can lease this smoke detector? Rent it?"

"Can't do it. You have to do a permanent mount. But I can let you have it for half down and half once you get it up and running."

I had one hundred dollars on me. Not much more until the bonuses and commission came in. I reached in my pocket and pulled out three twenties. "Can this be the down payment?" I was netting a minimum of $10,000 from Carol Conroy. Another $5,000 if this camera picked up any evidence that she was interested in. James was right. I had to make this investment.

"Sure. I can take that. And I can expect the rest in what? A week?"

"Maybe two?"

"Because we go back, Skip." He winked at Em. I never did like the guy too much, but he had good taste in women.

Jody dropped the detector in a plastic bag, wrote a receipt longhand, and we concluded the transaction.

"There's one other thing you should be aware of."

"What's that?"

"There's a camera detector that's pretty hot right now."

James leaned in. "A camera detector? To detect the camera that is used to detect something else?"

Jody gave him a funny look. "Let me show you." He walked to one of the shelves and pulled off a small chrome mechanism with an eyepiece. "Here. Look through this at any of the cameras I've mentioned."

James aimed at the smoke detector. "There's a red light."

"Yep. Try the motion detector."

"Wow. There's a red light."

"And on it goes. If you ever want to see if someone has infiltrated *your* place with a camera, all you have to do is —"

"The Teddy Bear has a red light."

"All you have to do is —"

"And the calendar. Wow. This is so cool."

Jody cleared his throat. "All you have to do is aim this at everything in your home or office and you'll know immediately if there's a camera, secretly recording what goes on. If you want, I can add that to the sale."

Em was faintly smiling. "Ah, the tangled webs we weave."

"No." I was emphatic.

"Skip, it may come in handy, pard, I mean —"

"James. No." I turned to Jody. "So, we're all set." I was anxious to leave.

"Um, Skip. We'd talked about another GPS to switch out while the other was charging."

Jody smiled. "Can't let you try two of them out, but I can make you a great deal. Why don't I wrap up the second one and —"

"No. No thanks. We'll recharge the other one and take our chances." I glared at James. I knew very well he'd demand an equal split of the money, but he had yet to pay a cent. "A fake smoke alarm and we're in business. That's all we need for now."

"Fake?" Jody looked very disappointed. "Skip, not so fast." He pulled a pack of matches from his pants pocket and tore one off. He struck it on the pad, let the flame burn down and held it up to the ceiling. The piercing siren started immediately.

"What the heck?" I plugged my ears.

"It actually works." He was shouting against the loud noise. He waved his hands, apparently stirring up an air current, and the noise abruptly ceased. "Nothing fake about it."

"Son of a gun." James had that toothy grin on his face. "That's even better."

Jody walked back into the rear of the store, and James put

his arm around my shoulders. "Wise decision, my man. Wise decision."

Em rolled those eyes. "I doubt if you've ever made one yourself, James."

"Teaming up with your boyfriend, miss. That's always been a good decision."

And what was she going to say about that?

CHAPTER TWENTY-FIVE

On the way back I pulled out the laptop, stuck in the card, pulled out the short antenna, and logged on. With the stroke of a key I had Feng's car. "James, you won't believe this. He's back at the laundry."

"Guy has issues with clean clothes. Maybe it's the place all the guards have their uniforms cleaned. You've got nine guards over there, pally."

"And," Em pointed out, "you can't be sure he didn't figure out you had installed a GPS on his car. He might have planted it somewhere else and we're following someone else."

That would mean he was as smart as I was, and I doubted that. "We'll know in a minute." I pointed at the screen. "He's leaving, and—" I waited, watching the little blip on the map, "it appears he's headed back to Synco Systems."

"We should arrive about the same time he does, pard. We'll just see."

Everyone was quiet as we drove back. The truck ran rough, and James managed to hit most of the potholes in the narrow streets, but other than that the ride was uneventful. We were probably going to arrive about twenty minutes late, but no one from my company was watching the clock. Wireman would probably notice, but he'd never say anything. He never seemed to sweat the small stuff. Until after work when he was loaded.

I was thinking how I could get the smoke detector installed. It was similar to the ones my company used, but ours were connected by phone line. I would have to concoct some story about how we had to install a separate detector in office one.

"James," I broke the silence, "Jody seemed to be pretty sure that no one installing this thing would know it contained a camera."

"Pretty sure."

"So there's only the one drawback."

"Getting that chip in and out. Yep. There's that."

We didn't say anything else until we got back to Synco Systems.

When we pulled into the parking lot, Feng's car was there and our UPS truck was parked in front of Synco Systems. I wondered if the little guy had figured it out yet. Or was he tracking a large brown truck and a guy with brown shorts and shirt? And the scary part was, if he knew we'd switched the GPS unit, then he'd figured out that we knew he was a suspicious character.

Em left in her brand new powder blue 335i BMW, heading back to her luxurious condo, and James and I went back to work. Eden gave James a big smile when he walked in, and I had a hunch that their date on Friday would go very well. She was a good-looking girl, even in her uniform, and if I didn't have two girlfriends at the moment, I would have been interested.

J.J. came up and patted me on the back. "Hey, Skip, we got all the old cabling out of the ceiling and the walls. It was easier than we thought. So, we're ready to start installation this afternoon. Thought you'd be happy about that."

I nodded, looking around for Andy Wireman.

"You looking for Andy?"

"Um, yeah, sort of."

"Got pulled off the job this afternoon. I guess you guys needed him at another location. He asked me to kind of run the show till tomorrow when he gets back."

I couldn't believe it. Andy Wireman had turned over this job to Jim Jobs? I was as surprised as I was pissed off. This was my project, and I trusted Andy. And furthermore, I needed to get someone to do my dirty work. I studied him for a moment, then figured he'd have to get it done. "Listen, Jim, did you know that we are short a bunch of smoke detectors?"

"We're short twenty some *motion* detectors. We have enough *smoke* detectors, but they're the wrong style."

Where did this guy come from? I was in charge of the project and I couldn't even remember that.

"Regardless, the president, Sandy Conroy, needs a smoke detector in office number one."

"You want me to install a smoke detector that's the wrong style? Why would we do that?"

Andy would have just done it. This guy was taking his temporary power way too far.

"I've got one I'd like you to install."

"If we put it in, we'll just have to take it back out when the actual ones arrive."

"Jim, I don't care." I held out the plastic bag with the detector/camera/microphone inside. Can you have one of the installers put this detector in office one?"

J.J. glared at me. His face was red and the spiky hair on his head made him look like a short devil.

"Please."

"Am I in charge or not?"

"Why?"

"Because I don't think it's a good idea to switch things all around like that. That's why."

"Then no. You're not in charge. I am. And if you have any questions about that, call my office."

"Okay, okay. No need to get all upset." He was scratching himself between his legs. I handed him the plastic bag, and he looked inside. Reaching in he pulled out a piece of paper.

"No." I panicked and grabbed it from his hand, tearing the receipt in the process. I glanced down and saw I'd managed to snag the part that said SPY STORE and the price.

"This is highly irregular."

"Irregular?" If he'd seen that receipt, he would really have thought it was irregular. "You've never worked for us before in your life. You've already pushed us back by two or three days because of your little 'discovery' that a third system was in the walls. And now you're telling me how to run my operation?" I surprised myself as I got worked up. Pushing my index finger against the guy's breastbone I continued. "You have no idea who we are or how we operate. All I'm asking is that you have some-one install this smoke detector in office one. Is that clear?"

J.J. stared right through me.

I continued. "Because if it's not clear, I can arrange to have you back at your apartment by the end of the day. Maybe you could spend the afternoon fixing your rear screen door."

My neighbor gave me a frown, brow all wrinkled. "Jeez, Skip. I'm just trying to do my job."

"So am I." I was breathing fast and my heart rate was up. Just getting my cardio exercise. "Then I guess it's clear."

He nodded.

"Great." I started to walk away, aware that Eden Callahan had observed the entire interaction. I was hoping she wouldn't mention it to Feng. Or worse yet, mention it to Sandy Conroy.

"But I will mention this to Andy." His back was to me. "This isn't the way I'd run an installation if this was my account." He shrugged and turned back to his ladder.

"Thank God it's not your installation, J.J." I caught myself. "Jim. Albert. Whatever your name is."

"You'll have it in that office before five. Is that soon enough?" He kept his back turned toward me, but his message was strong.

Eden was watching us, her eyes shifting back and forth.

"We thought it would be a good idea to make sure the president was protected against a fire." I smiled at her and she just gave me a puzzled look, shrugging her shoulders.

"Okay."

"Good idea, huh?"

She nodded and turned away. Maybe not the brightest girl. James liked them just slightly dense. Pretty, but dense.

"Thanks, Jim."

He grumbled and worked his way up the ladder.

What the heck was Andy thinking putting this bozo in charge?

"I'll talk to Andy tomorrow morning."

"You do that, Jim. If you're still working here." I walked away, hoping I didn't have to deal with the guy the rest of the afternoon.

CHAPTER TWENTY-SIX

I caught up with James in the hallway and told him that Jim Jobs's temporary assignment had gone to his head.

"So J.J. is showing some attitude, pard. I wouldn't worry. It's still your show." He just shrugged. "Might want to take it easy on him. After all, we do have to live next to him."

James was taking charge again. Jim Jobs was taking charge. I needed to step up and deal with this. There should be only one person in charge. Me. And there was a lot of money riding on this project. Forget James, J.J., Wireman, Feng. This was *my* project and I was in charge of getting it done. I couldn't, I wouldn't, let anybody screw it up.

"So, what about the smoke detector?" James whispered the question.

"He promised to install it. Before five o'clock. Of course I had to threaten him. And he also promised to talk to Andy tomorrow about the proper way to supervise an installation."

"Don't let him get to you. Andy Wireman will do it your way, amigo. You told me you've worked with him before. I feel certain he'll let you call the shots."

James saluted me, as if that confirmed *I* was in charge, and walked away, carrying a box of connectors.

I needed a cigarette, but I'd given up smoking. I needed a beer, but couldn't indulge myself for three more hours. I took about five deep breaths, felt dizzy for a moment, then decided to see how *my* project was progressing.

I walked into the room where all the offices were located. Number two was open, and Feng stood in the doorway, surveying the activity in the main room. He had his hand to his mouth and it appeared he was picking his teeth with something. When he observed me, he gave me a wry smile from across the way. I felt like waving, but I didn't.

Three installers were on ladders, working up in the substructure of the ceiling. James walked over, handing them tools from below. It reminded me of a acene from *Grey's Anatomy* where the nurse hands Dr. McDreamy his tools.

"Scalpel."

"Yes doctor."

"Clamp. Retractor."

And all around them sat the silent men and woman at their computers, all wearing white lab coats like they were in an old James Bond movie where Ernst Blofeld had his minions in uniforms, working on a diabolical plot to capture the world. They pecked like chickens at their keyboards, never even looking up. James and I would have been playing games, poker and blackjack, and checking on possible porn sites. I wasn't sure that these people weren't. It was just that they were supposed to be inventing something for the Department of Defense, and watching porn and playing blackjack were never really that productive. At least in my experience.

An installer walked by me with a ladder and headed for office one. The door was shut. He knocked, then opened it. A moment later Sandler Conroy walked out, frowning. I could

guess why. His workday was being interrupted so that our camera could be installed. I had a hollow feeling in the pit of my
stomach and my heart jumped. I said a silent prayer that no one
would ever find out what was inside that smoke detector.

Conroy spoke to Feng for a few seconds then turned and
pointed at me. He walked over and looked me straight in the
eyes. I froze. How he'd figured it out in this brief amount of time
I had no idea.

"Mr. Conroy—"

Conroy's rage was obvious. The red from his face broke
through the tan, and I was afraid I was not only to be arrested,
but possibly to be taken behind the building and beaten to death.
He'd figured it all out.

"How much longer?"

I didn't say anything, but the fear in my eyes had to give
me away.

"I said how much longer?"

"How much longer what?"

He pointed to the installers.

"Do you mean how much longer will we be here? How
much longer will it take to finish the installation?"

Conroy nodded.

I felt weak. Like you do after the first shot of whiskey at the
end of a long day. You feel that sense of release.

"Well, sir, we had a shipment problem. I would expect the
motion detectors and the alarms to be here tomorrow, and I—"

"How much longer?"

"As I said, it all depends on—"

"Young man, I asked you a question."

"Two more days?" I'd learned in school that you can't answer
a question with a question, but I tried.

"Get it done." He spun on his heel and walked out of the
room.

149

CHAPTER TWENTY-SEVEN

"Does he always lock the office?"

I'd been watching. Sometimes he did, sometimes he didn't. But regardless, Feng the oppressor was hanging out almost all the time. So just waltzing in to retrieve the card would be under Feng's watchful eye. Well, so was the UPS truck. Under Feng's watchful eye.

"You know, pal, we can't ask one of J.J.'s henchmen to go in and retrieve that chip."

"We knew that going in. It was part of the problem. You thought the smoke alarm was a good idea, James." We knew it would be a problem. And I didn't like the installation crew referred to as *J.J.'s* henchmen.

I studied the door to office one. Conroy had gone in and the door had been closed for probably over two hours. If he was on the phone, we might have something. But one of us had to retrieve it.

James and I were standing at the entrance to the hallway that led outside. Maybe seventy feet from the entrance to all of the offices.

"Have you kept an eye on his office?"

"Well, not for the full two hours. But I figure if he talked on the phone we'd get some good audio."

"No one else with him?" James was watching the closed door.

"I didn't watch the whole time." There could have been someone who walked in. I'd only seen maybe half the action.

"Yeah. We're going to have to keep an eye on that office."

"We're going to have to do more than that. James, we're going to have to retrieve the card. This is such a bad idea." It really was.

James put his elbow in my ribs. I jerked my head in his direction and he nodded to the office one door. Sarah, lovely Sarah, was walking out.

"Whoa!"

James watched as she walked back to her office. "I'll get that card, Skip. I will. I just thought of a way."

My selfless roommate. My best friend. Looking out for me. And I knew the real reason.

"Man, can you imagine the video tonight if something was going on between those two?"

My childhood compadre, looking out for me. It was ten minutes till five and if I was going to report to Carol Conroy the next day, I had to get that card.

"I'm going in, sarge." James nodded to me. I'd half expected the salute.

"What are you going to tell him?"

"We have a problem."

"What kind of a problem, Mr. Lessor?"

"There's a technical glitch with the smoke detector."

"And?"

"This will only take a minute."

"Okay." I'd bought into it.

"Wish me luck." James picked up a ladder that had been carelessly left leaning against a wall. He lifted it over his shoulder and slowly walked toward Conroy's office.

Feng watched. His eyes were glued to James's stride. When my roommate arrived at the door, he set the ladder down and leaned into the office. Within twenty seconds Conroy stormed out. He stood outside and scanned the computer room. Once again his eyes rested on me, and with a swagger he started his walk.

I could have walked away. I could have run for cover. But my best friend was putting himself on the line. For the possibility of seeing a steamy sex scene, yes, but it was what we were hired to do. I stood my ground. I had to stall this guy. Had to give James enough time to pick up the last three hours of conversation and action. I was dripping with sweat, but I stood my ground.

"Moore."

"Yes, sir."

"I told you this was to be taken care of. In short order."

"You told me that three hours ago, sir."

He frowned, and shot me a sideways glance. "This is the second time someone —" he waved his hand toward his office, "someone has interrupted my work. Do you understand this?"

"I do."

"When I'm in my office, work around me."

"Sir?"

"Do something else. When I'm out of the office, get Feng. I'll give you and your partner permission to work in the office. You're the only ones. Got it? And Feng will be there the entire time. Understood?"

We had access to the office any time he was out of it? Feng had no idea what we were doing. Of course, he didn't trust us. He'd proven that by putting the GPS under our car. But all we had to do was work on that smoke detector once or twice, take the card out, put it back, and take it out, and my job was finished. Sandy Conroy was giving us carte blanche?

"Understood."

"Then that's that." He brushed his slightly unruly black hair off his forehead, straightened his tie, and took another look around the room. "This will work out much better. Just make sure that Feng is in the office."

"No problem."

"I have a lot of important papers in that office. Not to mention documents and files on the computer."

"I can imagine."

He looked at me through squinted eyes. "No, I doubt that you can. Anyway, thank you for getting me the smoke detector. We'd be up a creek if that office burned down."

The guy was thanking me for setting him up. This spy business was just getting stranger and stranger.

"And tonight, can you park your car at Sarah's?"

James would probably be upset that we didn't have a smoke detector at Sarah's condo too. "No problem."

"Okay then." He turned and walked toward the reception area and I watched James walk out of the office, ladder under his arm. I hadn't noticed his T-shirt before.

> *Live every day like it was your last*
> *Someday you'll be right.*

CHAPTER TWENTY-EIGHT

James pulled out of Sarah's parking lot, and I watched my cheap car fade in the distance as he gunned the engine. We inched ahead. What a poor excuse for a vehicle. "You got Feng's GPS on the screen?"

I did. He was parked back at Chen's laundry. "He's safe and sound."

"Then let's watch a little of this." James pulled the card out of his T-shirt pocket and handed it to me.

Sliding it into my laptop, I punched a couple of keys and a grainy screen opened. The first word I made out was *Warning*. They'd listed a number of rules and regulations regarding the recording device. I was pretty sure that we'd broken most of them. After you break one rule, like planting the GPS unit under Feng's car, then they get easier to break. Actually, I prefer to think we just *ignored* them. It sounds a little better than breaking the rules. Not much, but a little.

"What do you see?"

"James, if there is anything between Sarah and Conroy it

won't happen till the end of the card's play time. Probably a couple, three hours from now."

"Can you fast forward it?"

"No."

Again the screen went fuzzy and I could hear the door open. As it closed, a head came into view. Dark hair breezed by and the picture cleared up. Sandy Conroy sat down at his desk and pulled out the keyboard mounted underneath. He punched at six or seven keys and stared at his computer screen.

"What's he watching?"

"I can't see. But I watched him turn on the computer. Honest to God. I just watched him turn on his computer."

"There's some excitement you don't get everyday. Settle down, pard."

"James, do you realize what just happened?"

"You're losing it, Skip."

"Did I tell you what I heard Feng and the guy with scuffed shoes talking about in the parking lot when I was under his Honda installing the GPS?"

He thought for a moment. "Codes. Getting codes. Installing using codes. Something like, 'you can't install a program without a code.'"

I was surprised. He'd paid some attention.

"You said it didn't make any sense."

"Didn't. Still doesn't. But I just cracked a code."

"You what?"

"How do you get into a computer?"

James yelled out the window and flipped his middle finger at a bright yellow Mustang that cut him off. I felt certain he'd chase it if he thought the truck could get anywhere near up to speed. After glaring through the windshield for several seconds he glanced at me.

"You turn it on, Skip. Don't play mind games with me."

As if he didn't with me

"What are you getting at?"

"Then what do you do, James? After you turn it on."

"Punch in some lame password like Beerville." James had come up with it. I wouldn't take credit for that.

"Won't open unless you punch in that password?" He didn't understand what I'd just seen.

"You know it won't."

"I just watched Sandy Conroy punch in his password."

"So?"

"From above the computer. From the smoke detector camera, James. The one we had installed."

"Yeah? So what?" He was irritated.

"James, I can zoom in and steal his password — his code."

"Oooh. Are you sure?"

"I'm positive."

"You saw the code?" He was silent for a moment. "That's pretty impressive. But do we need to do that?"

"I don't know, but that's how easy it is."

"You just watched him, dude. You actually saw every key?"

"I did. If I replay it a couple of times, I could walk in and open everything in his files."

"So we know his code. And there's got to be some heavy stuff on that computer."

"You'd think."

"Mmmm. So what are you thinking?" No longer irritated. A little bit of intrigue and James was engaged.

I hadn't been thinking much of anything, but it just kind of spilled out. It made sense in a perverse way. "So I'm thinking that Feng was talking about installing programs using a code and this other guy told him that it was up to Feng to get it done. They were counting on him. I mean, maybe he's setting up a spy thing at work."

James shook his head. "Come on, pally, what are the chances that he'd be doing the same thing we're doing?"

"James," I shot him my pity look, "you're the one who found the GPS unit under the truck. We're pretty sure that Feng attached it that night in our parking lot. And at the same time we were bugging Feng's wheels. What *are* the chances?"

"There's that."

"Could this have anything to do with Ralph Walters being killed?" I don't know why I said it, but it just seemed to fit.

He was silent for a moment. "You saw Feng messing around with Carol Conroy's Lexus."

"I'd swear it was him."

"When he left in a gray Honda, someone else was driving. Could have been the guy in the scuffed shoes."

"Could have been."

"Then Feng starts following us in a gray Honda. By now he knows that you're dating Sarah. He knows you had drinks with Conroy's wife, and he knows you're setting up a security system for Synco Systems. He also knows we're on to him. By now he's figured we took the GPS off our truck and put it on the UPS truck."

That's what we knew. And all combined, it meant nothing. Absolutely nothing. I just wanted the money. Damn, I wanted the money. And I didn't want anything to come between me and the money.

"And you think this all leads back to Ralph Walters's murder?"

My brain was screaming. "James, it doesn't really matter."

"What do you mean it doesn't matter?"

"I'm — we're getting paid for three things. Installation of the

157

system. Me pretending to date Sarah. And bugging offices for Mrs. Conroy. I guess I'm saying who cares if Feng is a counter-spy?"

"You know you just said something, amigo. Something that triggered a brainwave."

"What?"

James wheeled the truck into our parking lot, bumping the sidewalk with his front tires. "We're installing a system."

"We are."

"So are they."

"They?"

"Synco Systems. We're installing a system, with codes, pass-words, and who knows what, so Synco Systems will be safe — *while* Synco Systems is building a security system for the Department of Defense, so they'll be safe, which will have codes, passwords, and who knows what."

"Yeah? So what?"

"I wish I knew. Maybe Ralph Walters knew what it meant. Codes, passwords, programs. Maybe Carol Conroy is afraid she knows too much. She thinks someone is out to kill her, Skip. That's why we've got the side job."

The loud, cackling laugh startled us both, and I stared at the screen. Sandy Conroy was staring intently at *his* computer screen, laughing at the top of his voice. I wish I could have seen what he was looking at. I needed a good laugh.

"Man, I hate to say this."

"What?"

"I feel really dumb mentioning this."

"James, what are you talking about?"

He hesitated, cranking the windows of the box truck, letting air into the vehicle. "Skip, promise me you won't tell anyone I said this."

I could do this. Most of the things James said, I would have been embarrassed to mention.

"I think we should talk to Em about this."

"What? You want to talk to Em?"

"She's usually pretty levelheaded about these things."

"I can't believe you're saying this."

"Come on, you know most of our attitude toward each other is just for show. I mean, she knows what's going on, including your pretend tryst with Sarah. I'm sure she'll have some good ideas. Just don't tell her this was my idea."

I seriously don't think Em likes James. But it didn't make a lot of difference. "James, I don't want to go any further with this. I've got three paychecks coming, and if I screw around with any of them —"

"Yeah." Sandy Conroy picked up his phone. It took us both by surprise. There he was, down below, barking into his phone. It looked like he was doodling on a pad of paper as he talked, and it felt like we were watching one of those really bad movies that come on at three in the morning. The lighting was harsh, the sound was scratchy, and the acting was cheesy.

"You come down to the office in about an hour. We'll talk."

Silence for thirty seconds. This thing needed fast forward.

"Look, you little bitch, there's a lot going on you don't understand. When the time is right, it's right. You don't say a word about my wife or what's been going on between the two of us. Do you understand? Sarah, I swear I will destroy you if you mention one word of this relationship to anyone. Man up, little girl. It will be over soon enough. I want to see you in one hour, do you understand? In my office. In the meantime, stay in your office, and pull yourself together. I told you things would be fine once we finish this project."

James was staring at the screen. I was staring at James. He

still hadn't shut the engine off, and with the cost of gas it was getting rather expensive.

"Show a little maturity. I'll come over tonight."

I felt sleazy. This was a private matter and here we were like Peeping Toms. On top of that, I was being paid.

"It's like a bad movie, Skip."

Everything was quiet for a moment. I assumed Sarah was talking on the other end. Probably from her office.

"And the worst thing is, I don't know any of the quotes."

Conroy was rubbing his forehead, and I actually felt sorry for the guy. He was juggling his girlfriend, the former escort; his wife; his business; and dealing with the death of his vice president.

"I'll tell your friend, Skip, to park his car at your place tonight. Just in case." A pause. "One hour. You see me. In my office."

He'd mentioned my name. I shouldn't have been surprised, but I was.

James turned off the engine, and nodded toward the computer. "We should probably leave it on and see what else transpires."

"Probably should." I was hoping I wasn't the topic of conversation again.

"So, why don't you just turn that card over to Mrs. Conroy tomorrow, pardner? That would be the thing to do."

"Well now, I can't very well do that, can I?" She'd know my situation and cut me off. Damn. James knew it and I knew it. We were screwed.

"Amigo, we're in a world of shit."

I had to agree with him. Greed can get you into a whole lot of trouble.

"Skip, let's talk to your girlfriend. As negative as she can be, she may have some very positive suggestions."

All I could think about was how she'd roll her eyes, sigh, and let me know that she was tired of my immature attitude, tired of the situations I managed to get myself into, and tired of my best friend James. Oh well.

CHAPTER TWENTY-NINE

I called her when I walked in the door. The laptop continued to run on the kitchen table. Every once in a while I heard Sandy Conroy grunt, chuckle, laugh, or cough. I couldn't wait to see what the conference between Sandy and Sarah was about.

"Skip?"

"Em. Can we meet at Ester's?" Quick and formal.

"Ummm, yeah. You're making this sound like a business meeting rather than a date."

"Ummm. Yeah. It sort of is."

"Doesn't sound good."

"No. No. No. It's all good. I just need to run this idea by you." I glanced at James and he nodded in affirmative.

"Okay. I'll be there. What time?"

The movie probably had another twenty minutes to run. "Half an hour."

"You're not in more trouble, are you?"

"Me?"

She didn't laugh.

I went back to our small kitchen table and stared at the

computer screen. Nothing was happening, but Sandy Conroy's clacking at his computer and occasional noisy outbursts kept the camera and microphone activated. The phone rang, and I looked around for a second. We don't have a phone, just our cells.

"Yeah."

Conroy waited a minute for the person on the other end.

"All right, you tell Jason Riley that we go into production in three weeks. Three weeks. And we need the codes by then. Hell, you tell him we need them before that. Some story about how we have to program in some stuff to the security system. We weren't aware we needed them this soon, but since Tony Quatman isn't around any more yada yada yada."

More silence.

"Look, I don't care what you tell him. You're good at making things up. Just get the codes." He shook his head back and forth and then slapped his desk with an open hand. The loud slap bounced off the cheap sound system in the computer. "I wish Ralph was handling it too, damn it. It worked a lot better that way. But he's not with us anymore if you remember." The person on the other end must have tried to abdicate some responsibility. I could almost see Conroy roll his eyes in disgust. "You're in charge of it now. Do you understand? It's in your hands." The deliberation was taking entirely too much time and we didn't have a lot of time.

Watching someone on the phone when they don't know you're watching, gives you a whole new understanding of how they react to situations. Conroy doodled on a pad, tapped his foot, kept looking around the room like he thought someone was hiding somewhere. The man was obviously very uncomfortable with the conversation. I checked my watch. Whoever was on the other end was taking a long time to make his case. Minutes went by and I checked my watch again. Finally Conroy spoke.

"Look, the thing with Ralph is taking care of itself. There's nothing else they can prove. It's going to be ruled a suicide." He stretched his neck and rolled his shoulders. "No, I don't care what his wife thinks. And we know that Tony, Julia, and her husband won't be back anytime soon to discuss the matter with anyone. Understand this. It's up to you. You've got to get it done. I told you. Everyone agrees that it's in your hands."

I'd heard the man with the scuffed shoes say that to Feng. *It's in your hands.* What did it mean?

"I'll take care of Carol." Again with the doodling, the stretching, "It doesn't matter what that means. I said I'll take care of Carol, okay?"

This was taking far too long. Finally James and I watched Conroy hang up the phone, put his head back, and close his eyes. It was almost as if we were afraid to speak because he'd hear us and realize we were eavesdropping.

Quietly James said, "Did you get any of that?"

"Understand it? No."

"Who was he talking to?" It could have been anyone.

"Where did Tony and Julia go? They won't be back any time soon? What does that mean?"

"And, dude, all that stuff about the codes. Who is Jason Riley?"

Just then we heard the knock on the door. This time James was the one who cast a furtive glance at our apartment entrance before he realized the sound came from the video. Our original spy movie.

I checked my watch. We had ten minutes to get to Ester's.

"James we can pick this up when we get back."

"Amigo, no."

"Sarah, is that you?" Conroy looked up from his computer.

"Dude, Em's going to be pissed off enough as it is. No reason to start her off by being late. Okay?"

He gave me a mournful look. "Been waiting all day for this, pally. Would it hurt you to —"

"James, a couple more hours won't kill you."

"Hold on. It's locked." Conroy punched several keys and pushed himself back from the desk.

"Skip? Amigo —"

"Really, dude, we've got to take off."

"Pick it up where we left off?"

"Promise." Conroy was walking to the door and as he unlocked it I shut the computer down.

CHAPTER THIRTY

Ester's has Southern cooking down pat. Grits and gravy to corn-bread and hash, these folks have it. But this wasn't a grits and gravy meeting. Coffee and a clear head were all that we needed. And you fill your own coffee cup at Ester's. We did.

Em stared at me with her blue eyes, and I glanced out of the window, noticing how much her new blue BMW matched those eyes. Was it intentional?

"You boys are in trouble. Up to your eyeballs. I can see it, and I can smell it."

James frowned. "I wouldn't say we were in trouble. It's just that your boyfriend may have overextended our abilities."

I nodded. There was a lot of truth in that statement.

"And you called me because?"

I'd promised James I wouldn't tell her that he'd made the suggestion. "I think you bring a clear head to the table."

Em smiled, self-consciously pulling her hair back behind her ears. "A clear head?"

"Yeah." I took a long swallow of coffee, trying to clear *my* head.

She shifted her gaze to my roommate. "And you, James? Do

you think I have a clear head?"

I swear, I know that they have a real problem with each other, but there are times when it's almost like they're flirting.

"It's clear enough, Emily."

"So explain the problems."

I did. As embarrassing as it was, I told her how I'd finally got myself trapped. I wanted to leave out major parts of the story, but I told her everything. Except the story about Sarah being a hooker. I know, I know, it's an important part of the story, but it just didn't seem important at the time. And I'm sure that Em would have really had a problem with that issue.

She sat back and closed her eyes.

"Em." Sitting next to her, I put my hand on her arm. "Are you okay?"

"I'm fine." She breathed deeply. "Look, I knew most of this, but it seems to have escalated quite a bit. I mean, there's a lot to digest here."

She had at least grasped that.

"I mean, first of all, going to Carol Conroy tomorrow with that card—I mean she'll know right away that *you're* not having an affair with Sarah. Her husband is."

That's one reason I love her. She gets to the point.

"But there's so much more to this. Carol Conroy thinks she's marked for murder. She thinks that Ralph Walters, Tony Quatman, and his secretary may have been killed, and you're being followed by this gray Honda. I mean, guys—"

"So you're just as confused as we are." James had half a smile on his face.

"Maybe."

"Maybe?" I wanted her to elaborate.

"This company, Synco Systems, has one big project. Right?"

I stared out the window, seeing the empty parking lot. "It's all we know about."

"It's a federal government project, right?" She took a sip of her coffee. Two creams and a packet of Splenda.

"It is." James sounded cynical. He was wondering about his decision to include Em.

"Let's back it up to that project, okay?"

I wasn't on the same page. I must have looked like I didn't understand.

"Tell me again about the government project."

I figured if I was in charge of the security installation, I should be the one to tell her about the Department of Defense project. "Synco Systems is banking on a project for the Department of Defense. This system is supposed to protect the Department of Defense from any outside intrusion."

"There was this big retail chain that had all their customers' credit information on their computers." James had jumped in, leaning over the table. "Two guys in an old Pontiac used a laptop in one of this company's parking lots, and they stole all this personal information. All from a wireless laptop. It's crazy. The FBI got lucky and found them before they could sell the information."

"So this system is supposed to stop that from happening?"

I chimed in. "It is."

"Guaranteed to stop anyone from stealing information from the Department of Defense."

"That's the general idea, Em." I'd gone over it twice now.

"That's where it starts, guys. *If* Ralph Walters was killed, it goes back to this project."

"You think?" James looked puzzled.

"If you're being followed, it goes back to this project. The GPS unit on your truck? Same thing. The disappearance of Tony Quatman, his secretary, and her husband? Department of Defense project."

"You know this?" James appeared to be amazed.

168

She tilted her head and stared at him. "Of course not. What do you think I am, a psychic?"

"But you just said—"

"Problem solving one-o-one, James. When faced with a problem, you have to go back and start at a certain point. As far back as you can go. In this case, that starts when Skip sold the job. The reason for the sale? A contract with the Department of Defense. So we'll start there."

"You sound so confident."

"I have no clue. But you two—you don't even have a starting point. Now I've given it to you."

"So your theory could be all wrong."

"Could be."

The gray Honda drove slowly past the restaurant. It took me by surprise, but I could swear that the driver slowed down, and even though I couldn't see him, or her, it appeared they were checking out the parking lot. Probably looking for our truck or my car. It was time to check for another GPS unit. This spy versus spy thing was getting old.

"James—" I motioned to the window and he looked.

"I checked the truck before we left Synco, amigo. No GPS."

"So what are you going to do about the card and Carol Conroy?" Em went right back to the problem at hand.

"If I give it to her, she'll know I'm a phony. She'll be totally aware that Sarah is not dating me. And, she'll have evidence that her husband is having an affair."

"That's what she's paying you for, Skip." Now she sounded like a mother.

"Yeah, but when I give it to her I've effectively lost that part of the job. She may fire me from the security job for leading her on, and she may cancel the contract we've got with Synco Systems."

Across the table, James looked glum. I wasn't feeling so good about it myself. We needed the job.

"I lose the bonus from Sarah, my commission on the sale, the bonus from Carol Conroy, and I'll probably be fired from my job. Other than that —"

"So don't give it to her." Em sipped at her sweet, creamy beverage. "That's the answer, right?"

"Like you said, I'm being paid to —"

"You're being paid to listen and report. Smart move, Skip. *Tell* her about the conversation on the phone. The one about codes, about Ralph Walters and Tony Quatman. Give her a written report. If you have to, transcribe the conversation. Tell her that you can't release the recording due to technical reasons. The machine had a short in it and you can't get it to play back again. But you have the basic information."

I was formally put in my place. I couldn't believe my girlfriend had figured it out over coffee.

"You know President Richard Nixon used to tape conversations in the Oval Office at the White House. And when he was called on by Congress to produce the tape of a conversation he had that was somewhat incriminating, they found that seventeen crucial minutes had *accidentally* been erased. We read about it in history class. Remember? But I'm sure you guys already figured that out. You've got a way to get rid of the phone call from Sarah. It's the only solution, right?"

"Yeah." James nodded his head up and down, up and down, up and down. There was such a thing as overdoing it.

"Sure. We just wanted to know what you thought."

"Same thing you guys thought." Em sipped her coffee and stared out the window. "Find a way to spoon-feed her everything else, but don't play the Sarah card. Not yet at least."

"Sure." It all sounded so easy.

"There's that gray Honda again." Sarah pointed out the window as an Accord slowly cruised by.

"Are you sure it's the same one?"

"The license plate matches, and the dent in the passenger's door appears to be identical. I'd guess it's the same car."

James had been the one who wanted her opinion. It could have been the best idea he'd ever had. Em had already identified the problem, identified the starting point, solved the immediate problem, and recognized the enemy. Was it any wonder I loved this girl?

She went home in the BMW, and James and I drove home in the truck. There was no GPS under the truck. I slid under and checked the undercarriage myself. James was strangely silent as he drove, and I kept thinking about Em's insight.

We'd driven for about five minutes, the brakes grinding and the engine sounding rough when he said, "I'd thought of that, you know. Just tell Carol Conroy what she needs to know. Nothing more. It was pretty much where I was going with it."

"Yeah. I'd thought of it too. But it's always nice to hear someone confirm your thoughts, right?"

"My thoughts exactly, compadre. Just because we've got a high-tech surveillance system in place, doesn't mean we have to share everything with her. We can control what she knows."

"True." But then I was taking Carol Conroy's money under false pretenses. And it was a lot of money. But if I leveled with her, then I'd probably lose the entire gig. And was it legal to bug Sandy Conroy's office in the first place? I wanted to go somewhere and just scream for about five minutes.

When we walked in the door, James pointed at the computer. "Turn it on, amigo. We need to see how the day ended."

I hit the power key, awakening the computer from hibernation mode, and the warm glow on the screen showed me the password box. James and I used *Beercity* on our ancient PC. The company code on the laptop was *Password*. It was my boss Michael's brilliant idea. I always figured that *Beercity* was a lot harder to crack than *Password*, but Michael was the boss. I punched in *Password*, and in a moment the screen glowed.

Conroy pulled the door open and Sarah walked in. She stood still for a moment and he stalked back to his desk, sitting down and staring at her. Slowly she walked to the sole chair in front of his massive wooden desk. She sat down, pulling her dress down to her knees.

"What?"

"You scare me."

"Sandy, I scare *you*?"

"You start with your insecurities, your 'do you love me, I love you' little whines, then it moves on to demands. 'When is this going to be over? When are you leaving her?' I can't have this, Sarah. It's got to stop."

"And all I'd like is some reassurance." She sounded shaky.

"You've got it. I tell you that every time. You've got all the assurance you need. Every minute. But it's all I can say at this moment. There are things going on you're not aware of, and if you'll just let me work through them, it will be all right in the end. Do you understand?"

She stood, walked to the desk, and put both hands on the oak, gripping it tightly. "Obviously no. I don't understand. You just told me that I wasn't aware of certain things. If you can't share with me, then —"

Conroy jumped up, almost knocking his chair over. "Stop it. Stop. You're driving me crazy. Maybe this was a bad idea."

She was close to tears, I could hear it in her voice. Wavering, higher pitched, choked, she said, "I have turned everything over and —"

"What? What did you turn over? The fact that you were a call girl, and you've put that on hold for a while? You've quit turning tricks because of me? Is that what you *turned over?*"

She screamed, picked up a ceramic coffee cup, and threw it at the wall behind him. The cup smashed to pieces.

Conroy was out from behind the desk in a second, holding her by the shoulders. "I'm sorry. Sarah, I'm truly sorry. I know, I know how tough this has been on you. Ralph's suicide, Carol, and everything else. Please, baby, be patient. Understand I'm going through a lot right now."

She sobbed softly, pressing her body against him.

Conroy brushed at her hair with his hand. He stroked her back, pulling her closer and I felt like a shit. How could I watch this?

"Tonight. You and me baby —" The screen went blank.

"What?" James's eyes were as wide as saucers. "Power go out? What?"

"The card ran out of time."

"Damn!"

"James. She doesn't have a clue what's going on. I was hoping we could get some information from her, but —"

"Wasn't quite what I was hoping for either, but one heck of a show, eh, Kemo Sabe? One heck of a show."

I had to agree with him. The movie ended with a bang.

CHAPTER THIRTY-ONE

The package arrived at Synco Systems at seven a.m. the next morning. Addressed to Skip Moore and stamped **CONFIDENTIAL**. I could only hope that it was a box of smoke detectors or motion detectors, but that wasn't meant to be.

"Skip." Andy Wireman walked up and put his hand on my shoulder. "Your runner seems to be a little bit upset with how things went yesterday."

I hated confrontation, but "Andy, where did you get the authority to put him in charge?"

"Skip, Michael called the shot. I had nothing to do with it."

Michael. What an idiot. Putting someone like J.J. in charge. And I knew the only reason it got under my skin was that I almost wasn't able to get my smoke detector installed. That, and the fact that I was supposed to be in charge. Not some handyman.

"So Jim tells me that you put a smoke detector in the president's office?"

"He wanted temporary protection, Andy. Conroy even

thanked me last night. He said if that office burned up, this company would be in a lot of trouble. This is my project. Title being — well, person in charge, and I've got the authority to —"

"Hey, man, I'm with you. We're on the same exact page, okay? It was a very smart move. And if it makes you feel any better, this morning your neighbor, Mr. Jobs, is back at being a runner and there's no problem. Just wanted you to know."

"Thanks, Andy."

I carried my confidential package to a quiet corner of the computer room, and I used a packing knife to cut through the tape and paper on the large box. Feng was busy instructing two of our installers, and the doors to Sarah's and Sandy Conroy's offices were closed. My guess was that they had not come in yet. Still making amends for the lover's spat they had yesterday.

"Dude," James walked up, "the office isn't open. I can't get the card in place if the office is locked. We need to get this thing back up there."

I'd forgotten to tell him. And it was a great moment, the kind a supervisor likes to spring on his employee. "No problem, James. You go up to Feng, tell him that you want to work some more on the smoke detector, and he'll let you in. He'll watch you reinstall the card and won't say a word. He also won't have a clue as to what you're doing."

James studied me for a moment. "I'm serious, Skip. I'd like to get this put back in, but I can't get into Sandy's office."

"I'm serious too, James. See Feng."

"You're messing with me, amigo. I don't appreciate it."

I rolled my eyes, picked up the package, and approached Feng. "Excuse me. James needs to get into Mr. Conroy's office to do more work on the smoke detector. Can you please let him in?"

Feng frowned. He looked back and forth at the two of us, and I saw James giving me the 'I told you so' look.

"How long will this take?"

"Not more than five minutes. This time." I knew we'd have to take it back out in three or four hours.

"Okay. Follow me." He headed down to Conroy's office as James closed his wide-open mouth.

"You've got to know how to handle these people, James."

James grabbed a ladder from an installation team and double-timed it down to office number one.

My large package was half open and I couldn't wait to see what was in it. There was no return address and no clues on the outside. I went back to my corner and glanced up at the entrance as Sarah came waltzing in. Conroy's mistress was wearing a gray suit, a simple white blouse, and sensible black shoes. Her dress told me she was in no mood for frivolity. She gave me a grim smile and walked directly to her office, unlocking the door, opening it, and slamming it shut. Apparently the night had not gone well.

"Excuse me." The soft voice surprised me and I spun around, almost cutting my index finger with the box cutter.

"Yes, Eden. What can I do for you?"

"Mr. Wireman would like to see you up front."

I sighed. Just a couple more minutes and I'd solve the mystery of the big brown box.

"And, have you seen James today?"

"Um, yeah. He's working on a smoke detector." I nodded toward Conroy's office.

"Great. If you happen to run into him, please tell him I'd like to speak with him."

Her brown eyes sparkled. I tried to picture her in something other than the stiff officer's uniform with the heavy, heavy belt, the gun, the tear gas, and all the other paraphernalia. There was a cute figure under there.

"I'll tell him. Can I give him a message?"

She blushed. I could see the color rise in her cheeks. "We're supposed to go out tomorrow night. Sort of a date."

"Yeah. He told me."

"Well, of course. I mean, you're his roommate and all."

"Is there a message? A problem with the time? The date?"

She shuffled her shiny shoes. "No, no. Nothing like that. I just wanted to tell him—"

"Yes?"

"That I'm looking forward to it. The date, I mean."

"So is he."

"Oh, good. Because he hadn't mentioned it again, and I thought maybe he, well, you know."

God deliver us from insecure women. And thank God for men who are always very secure in their relationships.

I clutched the brown box under my arm and walked up to the entrance. Wireman looked down from a ladder, giving me a broad smile.

"Skip. Over there." He pointed to the reception desk. There were two large packages on the counter, not unlike the one I had under my arm. "The new smoke detectors."

Not good. "How soon will they be installed?"

"I'm thinking tomorrow, Friday."

We'd have one more day to use the one in Conroy's office.

"The sooner the better." I just wanted this project to be over.

"Well, I was thinking. We could start with the president's office. You know, get him taken care of first—wire it in and—"

"No. No. We've got the temporary detector already installed. That can be the last one you install."

"It's up to you."

"Yes. It is." Person in charge of the project or whatever. I started out to the parking lot, the brown package under my arm. This was a far better idea. Open this in private.

"Mr. Moore?"

"Yes, Eden?"

"You're not allowed to take anything from the building."

"This is personal, Eden. See?" I held up the remaining paper that was clearly stamped **CONFIDENTIAL**. Skip Moore.

"Makes no difference. Once it is received here at S.S., it remains here. Sorry."

I couldn't believe it. I didn't even know what was in the package, and she was telling me I couldn't take it outside. I felt like telling her that James was going to stand her up, but he probably wouldn't agree to that. I think he wanted to see what was under that gray guard uniform too.

I walked back to a corner in the computer room, sat on the floor, and stared at my package. Then, with a single determination, I attacked the box with my box knife.

"Skip —"

"Go away, James."

"But —"

"I'm busy." I sliced tape, ripped paper, and finally cut through the box itself. I sensed James still standing over me.

"What the heck is that?"

I ignored him. It was the worst part of my birthday. The worst part of Christmas. Ripping open the packages. Bending back fingernails, paper cuts, trying to untie ribbons that weren't meant to be untied. Finally I could see inside the box. Another box. Damn.

James had lowered himself, sitting on the floor across from me. "Dude."

I ripped the cardboard from the first box, finally making a tear wide enough to pull out the second box. This was the one with the printing on the side. But the envelope inside was what caught my eye first. I yanked it out of the box and shoved it in my shirt pocket. By now I was ready to put a match to all the paper and cardboard and tape.

I looked up and James was staring at me. "Where did you get the package, Skip?"

"Special D, James. No problem. Confidential to Skip Moore."

His eyes were wide, and he froze as I took the box knife to the tape that sealed the box.

"Skip."

"What? Can't you just leave it alone?"

He leaned down, grabbing the box from my hand as my box knife went flying. James started down the hall, package under his arm, running as fast as I've ever seen him run. I struggled to my feet, charging after him, hitting my pace and in seconds feeling winded and weak.

"James. Where are you—" Eden Callahan yelled as she jumped back from her post, and Andy Wireman staggered on his ladder as James ran by. Wireman held on as James hit the glass door with his shoulder and plowed on through, racing into the parking lot.

I got to the door as he heaved the box twenty feet in front of him, fell to the ground, and buried his head under his arms.

I stood in the doorway trying to catch my breath. The burning in my lungs wasn't going away anytime soon. My roommate lay there for at least sixty seconds and I just kept gasping for air, thinking I was probably going to throw up.

I watched him pull himself to his feet, staggering as he walked back to the building. As he got closer I could see him sucking in oxygen. We were a real pair.

Finally he reached the door, and I pushed it open for him, barely able to move the heavy metal and glass. James walked in, leaning against the inside wall, eyes closed and his hand over his heart. I knew exactly how he felt. Finally he slid to the floor, slumping over, and breathing heavily.

Eden stood on the far side of the entrance area, hands on her belt, not saying a word. Wireman had come down from his ladder and was just standing there, staring at James.

Then my best friend opened his eyes, and saw the three of us. He also saw the two installers who were standing out in the hall, and J.J. who had walked in, looking very confused by the scene.

"Well," James paused, surveying the growing crowd. "If it *had* been a bomb, you'd all be safe."

People were nodding their heads in agreement, and I had no idea why.

We sat in the van, James just staring out the window. Andy Wireman had suggested a short break and I couldn't argue with that. James reached into his pocket and pulled out a cigarette. I reached into my shirt pocket and pulled out the envelope that had been in the package.

"Well, read it." He held the cigarette without lighting it.

I tore it open, unfolded the paper, and read out loud.

Dear Skip and James,

I'm always running across new "stuff" that people can use to spy on other people. I don't always have a personal use for the equipment, but I think you may find a use for this particular item. We've talked about it before, but I'm offering it to you for a demonstration if you're interested.

I stared at the dented, broken box James held in his lap. *The Sound Max.* It was an infrared microphone recording device. The letter continued.

This baby will pick up and record sound from 200 yards away, and all you have to do is aim it at a window. Is it legal? Probably not. So be careful. I'm offering it to you as a demo. If you get into trouble with it, you can't come back on me. I'd like it back in two weeks with your thoughts and comments. Oh, and my regards to Emily.

Thanks, guys.

Jody

Regards to Emily? It was a shot. But, he had sent us The Sound Max. I didn't know why, but he had.

Finally James lit his cigarette and looked hard at the match before he tossed it into the parking lot. Taking a deep lungful of smoke, he slowly exhaled and frowned.

"Damn."

"The Sound Max, James. The Sound Max."

"Yeah. You know, if it wasn't a bomb, that was going to be my next guess."

CHAPTER THIRTY-TWO

"I understand there was an incident at Synco today." The cold, harsh voice of Carol Conroy added to the day's wonderful turn of events.

"Yes, there was."

"Care to comment on it?"

She wouldn't take no for an answer. "We've been a little on edge. With the suicide and your fear of being killed, I think my friend was taking some precautions."

"Mr. Moore. You and your friend acted like idiots today."

"Maybe. But I have a transcript of your husband's phone conversation from yesterday. And that is what you're paying me for." The lady was paying me big bucks to be an idiot. Her idiot. I swallowed whatever pride I had.

"Because of your actions today, there are a number of people in that company who are asking questions. I wanted to run this inquiry or," she paused, apparently not sure what to call it, "this, this mini-investigation, quietly. Very simply, I asked you to record conversations from office one. Now everyone is talking about a bomb threat. It certainly adds to the confusion, doesn't it?" The lady was obviously irritated.

I drank my second Yeungling of the afternoon and listened to James rattling around in his bedroom. He should be the one dealing with this. If he hadn't freaked out. "Mrs. Conroy, I have a transcript of the conversation. It's what you asked for."

"An actual recording of the conversation would be infinitely preferable. I believe that's what I asked for."

I thought back to our original conversations. "And I think I promised you notes."

"So I'm to take your word for what was said?"

I'd spent three hours last night with the word processor trying to get it all down. And I had no idea how to erase the conversations with Sarah. So a transcript was going to have to suffice. I couldn't possibly give her the video card without giving everything away.

"We had a little trouble with the recording device. I mean, you only gave us a day to install the unit and —"

"Audio? Or audio and video?"

"Mrs. Conroy, I have the transcript if you'd like to see it. Printed out. It's the best I can do under these conditions." The conditions being that I didn't want to play the original recording for her. Plain and simple.

She was silent, but I could hear her breathing. Sarah had been right. The lady was a bitch. "I'll meet you."

I thought about the money again. It's all I could think about. I wasn't born with an aggressive personality, but I was salivating thinking about the payoff at the end of this assignment. "Mrs. Conroy, I realize there may be more to do, but if I could just get an advance on what we've done so far —"

"Mr. Moore. You've already done considerable damage on what you've tried to accomplish so far. The phony bomb scare, no actual recording of Sandler's voice, just your transcript. I'm really unhappy with how things are going. Are you clear on that?"

"Mrs. Conroy," James was banging on something in his

room, making it hard to hear on my cheap cell phone, "I will do everything possible to quiet things down and get you the information you want."

"And when your job is finished, then I'll pay you. Not until then. Do you understand? I don't want any misunderstanding."

Damn. And there were expenses I needed to cover. There was a moment when I thought she was going to refuse to pay. Now she sounded like I'd get my money, but who knew when? "And where would you like to meet?" Not the Red Derby again.

"I know where you live. I'll be there tonight at seven p.m."

"Fine." She knew where I lived. That scared me.

"And, Mr. Moore, there isn't any chance that Sarah Crumbly will be at your apartment is there?"

"Sarah?" Why would Sarah come to our dump? We couldn't afford her. I quickly remembered why. "No. Nope. No chance. No way. We're not seeing each other. I mean tonight. So, there's no chance tonight. No chance at all. Nope." I could have gone on, but it was time to shut up.

"And your friend?"

"James will be here." Damn straight James would be here. I didn't want to deal with this lady alone.

"Ah, good. But I was referring to Emily."

I felt a chill go down my spine. I had no idea what she knew. How she knew. But I had the presence of mind to keep on going as if her question was perfectly normal. "No. Just James and me. A quiet night at home."

Again, she was silent.

"Mrs. Conroy?"

"I would think that after the ruckus you caused this afternoon, a quiet night would be just what you need." She hung up the phone.

CHAPTER THIRTY-THREE

"Dude." James walked out of his room. "I've got something to show you."

"James, I just talked to the ice queen."

"Ah, the lovely Mrs. Conroy."

"Yeah. She wants to come over tonight at seven to pick up the transcript."

"I'll be sure to disappear."

"No. I don't think so. She's upset with you — and with me, and we both need to be here to take some wind out of her sails. Got to calm her down, James."

"Then I'll have about five beers just before she shows."

"It might not be a good idea."

James walked to the refrigerator and opened one. Something smelled spoiled, and I couldn't imagine what it was. We use it primarily for beer. Maybe that leftover crab James brought home last week. Sometimes it doesn't stay as fresh as it should.

"I can hear her now, Skip. 'Mr. Lessor, I smell alcohol on your breath.'"

I knew the Will Smith comeback from the movie *Hancock*. "That's 'cause I've been drinkin', bitch."

Neither of us cracked a smile. It had been that kind of a day.

"Let me show you. Just stay there."

James walked back into his room, then reappeared with a tripod and what appeared to be a short telescope. It was wired to a box he held in his hand.

"Ta-da."

I shook my head. "So not only will it pick up sound at two hundred yards, but it will withstand a throw of twenty or thirty feet."

"You got it, pard."

"Jody would be proud."

"It still works, Skip. Must be the Lord's will." He gave me that charming smile. "And by the way, amigo, can you check on Feng's car? Track that little sucker and see where he is right now?"

I flipped on the laptop and watched as the Miami map came into view. I scanned the screen, looking for Feng's little blip. It was still surprising to me that he hadn't figured out we were tracking his car.

I found the Honda. "It's sitting still at the moment. It's right near that day care center."

"Maybe the guy's a pervert, hanging around a school yard."

"We've got nothing on this guy, James. Nothing. I say we drop it."

"Humor me."

"I think I do that every day."

James ignored my sarcasm. "What time is it?"

I checked the computer. Five thirty.

"The dry cleaners is what, ten minutes from here?"

"The dry cleaners?"

"The one Feng stopped at when we first started tracking him."

186

"About ten, yeah."

"Let's jump in the truck. Take the laptop, and let's see if he goes there next."

"And what's that going to prove?"

"Probably nothing. But we're taking along The Sound Max. Maybe give it a test run."

"What?"

"I asked you to humor me."

"You've already got us in trouble once today."

"I can do better than that. You know I can. What's my record?" He folded up the tripod and started out the door. "Grab the laptop, pard." He walked out the door. Over his shoulder he yelled. "Five times in one day."

"When?"

"When we were fifteen. I'll fill you in on the way."

Feng moved while we were en route.

"Following his ritual?"

"He's headed toward the dry cleaners. It may be a quick stop. Honestly, James, he's probably just dropping off laundry."

"We'll soon find out, amigo."

"When we were fifteen? You set a record for getting into trouble? Why don't I remember this?"

"You probably weren't paying attention. Yeah. That must be it, because for just one day I set a personal record for doing things I shouldn't have done. Mind you, Skip, I'm not saying I'm proud of all the things I did, but . . ." He hesitated. "Ah, what the heck, I am proud of them. If I remember right, I started that day in Miss Naab's class, glued her grade book to the desk and she blamed you. I think you almost got a couple days off on account of that one."

"Damn. I knew that was you, but you never admitted it."

"So gluing the book was number one. I got you in trouble, which was number two, and for number three I skipped track

187

practice. Number four on the list, I 'borrowed' Mom's car and picked up Janice Richards. Being fifteen years old, I obviously didn't have a license. We parked in back of the old mental hospital, you remember that old decrepit place, and number five and last on my infamous list, I got to second base with Janice. All in all, a pretty good day."

"You're a nutcase. Do you know that?"

He just beamed and kept on driving.

"Feng stopped."

"Was I right? He stopped at the cleaners?"

"It would appear."

"We'll be there in three minutes. There was a parking lot for a deserted gas station across the street. We can pull in there. Think he'll recognize the truck?"

"I still have no idea what you have in mind."

"Just be patient. All will be explained, Grasshopper."

I watched the screen and Feng's Honda didn't move. James hit a pothole on Bianca Drive and I thought we were going to lose the muffler. He turned onto Bonita Boulevard and there it was. Chen's Laundry. He pulled up beside the cleaners. A gray Honda Accord was parked directly in front of the establishment.

"There's an office in the back, and those big plate-glass windows in the front. Where do you think he is?"

"If he's just dropping off laundry, he'll be out in the front by the counter. My guess is that's it."

"My guess is that he's in the office."

"Why does it matter, James?"

"You thought he was suspicious. You were sure he was following us using a Global Positioning System. Now, I buy into that and try to find out more, and you want to walk away from it."

"All right, are we going to sit here and debate where he is?"

188

"I thought we'd *prove* where he is." James pulled across the street to the abandoned cement-block building. They were plentiful in Carol City. If you wanted an abandoned building, complete with pitted cracked asphalt parking lot and weeds about ten feet high, you could find one in every other block. Some had been converted into churches, but most of those had reverted back to abandoned concrete-block buildings.

James backed up the truck so the rear was facing the plate-glass windows across the street. He got out of the truck and motioned for me to do the same.

I gazed at the laundry, a dirty white stucco building with a faded sign propped up in the front window that said OPEN.

James rolled up the back of the truck and climbed in. I followed.

"Okay, Kemo Sabe, we're going to see what the gossip is." He set the tripod about halfway back in the box of his truck and aimed the wand at the front window of Chen's.

Putting on his headphones, he pulled the trigger.

I watched the small metal box that was wired to the wand. A meter was flashing. "The meter, James. It's flashing."

He nodded. "We've got contact."

We were buried far enough back that it was dark, and although I doubted that anyone was watching, I was sure they couldn't see us.

"Extra starch in the shirts, Skip."

"You can hear that?"

"Here." He pulled off the headphones and handed them to me. I put them on, leaned over, and pulled the trigger.

"Yes, Mrs. Crider. We'll have them for you Tuesday. Oh, it's no trouble at all. I'll ask Su Ning if she will sew two new buttons on the shirt." The sound was clear, although I picked up street noise that was pretty loud.

In a minute, a woman emerged, turned right, and walked down the sidewalk. I could hear what sounded like an industrial strength fan running in the background, but there were no voices.

"Nothing else, James. You might be right."

"Let's head up the street. We can get a straight shot into the office window if we park back in the next block."

I was getting into the spirit of the whole thing. We left the sliding door open, and I stayed in back with The Sound Max. James drove out of the small parking area and past Chen's, stopping about a block away. Through the rear of the truck I could see the back window of the dry cleaner. James came around and climbed back in.

"How do you know that's the office?"

"I don't. But aren't offices always in the back?"

I shrugged my shoulders. We had nothing to lose.

James put on the headset and pulled the trigger and I saw the meter flashing red and green. He was shaking his head and I wished we had two sets of headphones.

"He's in there." James was talking at about twice his normal volume.

"James. You don't have to yell."

"Oh, yeah." He was quiet for a moment. "They're talking about Mr. Chen's business."

"Oh, well that's got to be exciting. How Su Ning sews her buttons or what?"

"No, shhh."

I was quiet for a moment.

"How Mr. Chen will be able to retire after this next project. How he is looking forward to closing the shop and—" He got quiet for a moment, then pulled off the phones and handed them to me, motioning that I should put them on.

"The codes. It's imperative Feng. We should have them by now."

"Obviously we had a slight problem. There was a death in the immediate family."

"You must put some pressure on to get them. Now. How much more emphasis can I put on this?"

"This is a sensitive area. It's not possible to just walk in and demand—"

"Feng. This group forgets where they leave laptop computers with worldwide secrets on them. They allow workers to walk off with nuclear material, personnel information, and all types of secure matter. Feng, our own Chi Mak stole thousands of pages of information on weapons, nuclear reactors, and propulsion systems for U.S. submarines. For twenty years this organization was blind to his theft. They are the most inept establishment in the world. All we are asking for are the combinations. They should fall all over themselves to give them to you. You ultimately need them so you can install your security software. All we are asking is that you get them early. Early, Feng. We need them — *now*."

"You are right." Feng sounded remorseful.

"We've stressed this to Mr. Conroy."

"Once there was a breach in our own security we did take care of it. That took some time, and we didn't want to raise any red flags. You must understand that."

Chen or whoever the other party was laughed. "Red flag?"

"The parties who had the information are no longer with us. There were four actual incidents." I knew that voice. It wasn't Feng. Who was it? I'd heard it before, recently, and I listened intently.

"And you would like me to compliment you on your ability to deal with problems in your own business? I'm sorry, Feng. I

191

cannot do that. You have been retained, at a very high price, to take care of those situations. It was your job."

Feng once again jumped in. "They learned about the project, and we removed them. There is a level of trust that I have to gain now."

"And there's a time frame that has been moved up. Remove the obstacles, and give me the codes. Do you understand?"

"Yes. I understand." I could tell by his voice that he didn't.

"Feng, to you this is a job where you will be paid. Very well, I might add. But you don't really understand. Maybe Conroy does. But you don't. You don't understand what we can do with these codes. What Chi Mak accomplished is nothing to what we can do. But that's for another day and another time. Let me put it very clearly. If you don't produce the codes in the next forty-eight hours, I'll find someone who can."

"Yes."

"If you let anyone interfere with the project—anyone, I'll find someone else. And your involvement with our plan will be permanently erased. I have pressure, Feng. You couldn't believe the pressure that I have."

Codes and combinations. James was looking at me with a frown on his face. I could sense he was worried about what I was hearing. I handed him back the headset. I didn't need to hear any more. It was all being recorded on a card, so we could play it back later that night. It sounded to me like Feng's life was being threatened.

James listened intently, nodding as if in agreement with the Asian men. Finally he pulled the earphones off and turned off The Sound Max. "What is going on?"

"James, you tell me. Does it even have anything to do with Synco Systems?"

"Oh, come on. Every word. I think this thing is very shady. Very shady."

My phone blared "Born in the U.S.A." and I glanced at the caller's number. I didn't recognize it. "Hello."

"Skip? This is Andy Wireman."

"Yeah, Andy." I glanced at the clock on my cell phone. 6:40. We had to hustle to get back. Mrs. Conroy would be there in twenty minutes.

"We've got a serious problem."

That's exactly what we needed. Every project needs a very serious problem. "Andy, can it wait until morning?"

"No."

I sighed. James picked up on the urgency and moved in closer. I tilted the speaker toward him. He may as well know whatever Wireman knew. James and I, as usual, were up to our asses in this thing. "Tell me what the problem is."

"You know that smoke detector that James installed in Conroy's office?"

We both looked at each other. My hand started shaking and I seriously thought I would drop the phone. James shook his head back and forth like he didn't want to be reminded of that smoke detector.

"Yes, Andy."

"It went off."

"It went off? There was a fire?" Jody told us that it really worked. I just hadn't considered there would be a real fire.

"It went off and there was no fire. A false alarm."

Whew. "Well, what could be the problem. It's defective and we'll switch it out for one of ours tomorrow." Problem solved. No wonder I was Person in Charge of the Project, or whatever I was.

"No, Skip. We went up and opened it, trying to quiet it. And Skip, this smoke detector is unlike any I've ever seen. I think you need to come over here immediately."

"Immediately?"

"Immediately."

Mrs. Conroy was coming over, and I had to be there for her. Wireman was concerned about the detector and I couldn't leave him with that. "Andy, can this wait maybe one hour?"

I could hear conversation in the background. "I don't think so, Skip. Sandy Conroy is here and he wants some answers right now."

CHAPTER THIRTY-FOUR

"Skip. I can handle this. You need to get to Synco, pronto."

"Damn it, James. She's not a happy camper. If it was just handing over the transcript, but I know she wants more information."

"Even better. I can't give it to her. We can put her off, because I know nothing. Nothing."

"But you do."

"She doesn't know that. I'll play dumb."

I let the comment slide. "What am I going to tell Conroy? Wow. I can't imagine what I'm going to say to him. I am in so much trouble." I couldn't even fathom how much trouble. It was like, when we were doing it, it was an adventure. Now, there was a likelihood that I'd broken the law and could be arrested.

James took a sharp curve, braking as he rounded the corner, and the shrill sound of metal scraping metal gave me chills.

"James, I could lose my job over this."

"You could probably go to jail over this." He was thinking the same thing.

"*You* installed the detector."

"Hey, boss. Didn't *you* tell me to?"

"James—"

He swerved to avoid a parked car, straightened out, and gave the old truck some gas. "Amigo, we've talked about this. Carol Conroy gave you permission—no, she actually *asked* you to install a listening device in her husband's office. She didn't say why. She just told you to do it. Just like you told *me* to perform the actual task." James pulled into our parking lot. He rammed the sidewalk with the bald tires, and we both took a deep breath.

Carol Conroy's Lexus was nowhere to be seen. Grabbing my laptop, I stepped out of the truck, and walked down to the Cavalier. I'd be in the office in ten minutes.

"I'm going to hand her the envelope, and tell her something came up at Synco. You couldn't make it, but asked me to give it to her."

"Exactly."

"If she wants to check on that, she can drive by Synco and she'll see your car in the parking lot."

"James, please. If she asks about Sarah, if she mentions Emily—"

Doing his best Sgt. Schultz from *Hogan's Heroes* imitation. "I know nothing. Nothing, Colonel Hogan."

"Wish me luck, James. I just hope they don't have the cops there. If I need bail money—"

"I haven't got it, pal."

I didn't hold out too often on my good friend. But once in a while— "James, seriously, if I need money—"

"You won't. This is going to work out. Just have faith, pard."

"Listen to me. If I need help, money—"

"I'll find some."

"No. In my room, on the second shelf in the closet, there's a Shel Silverstein book. *Where the Sidewalk Ends.*"

"Okay."

"Page sixty-three, there's three hundred dollars."

"Got it." He didn't even look surprised.

I got into my car and on the third turn of the key the Cavalier coughed to life. I'd planned on putting some of my new wealth toward a new car. It didn't appear I was going to see any of that wealth any time soon.

There was a poem on page sixty-three that I still remembered. When you're a kid it's easier to memorize things, and I'd memorized a poem called "Who." And I thought about the second verse of that children's fantasy. The exact wording wouldn't come back to me, but it was something to do with having X-ray eyes. Who can fly and who has X-ray eyes? And who will be the man no bullet can kill? I will.

X-ray eyes. That's what we'd had last night when we watched Sandy Conroy's office from the ceiling. It was all amazing. I'd actually had X-ray eyes. I'd witnessed conversations and confrontations. I'd seen and heard things that were meant to be private. And earlier this evening I'd listened in on strangers' intimate conversations that were foreign to my ears. It had been exciting, exhilarating, and now I was going to pay the price.

Flying, with X-ray eyes, and being the man no bullet can kill. Who can do all that? I will.

CHAPTER THIRTY-FIVE

On my way over, I concentrated on what could have happened. Somehow the detector was set off. Maybe Conroy smoked cigarettes or cigars, and even though Florida had passed a no-smoking ban, he *was* Sandy Conroy. The laws weren't made for some people. People like me for instance. I didn't seem to have too much trouble breaking the law. Putting GPS units under cars, cameras in office ceilings, taping private conversations.

What would they do to me? A police car came up behind me and I froze, slowing down to a crawl. He pulled to my left and zipped on down the road, paying no attention to the criminal that was almost in his grasp.

James was right. I'd have to give up Carol Conroy. It was all I could do. Tell them that she offered us money to tape conversations. But that meant that I'd be fired from Jaystone Security Systems. That meant that Sarah and her boyfriend wouldn't pay me what they'd promised, and that meant that Carol Conroy certainly wouldn't give me a cent. And if I was convicted of a felony, I couldn't imagine Em sticking it out with me. And how many years could they give me for that crime? And how much of a fine?

How did criminals who did long time in prison ever make enough money to pay the fines? And when you came out of prison as a convicted felon, who would ever hire you? You could sweep floors, maybe work at a fast-food restaurant, work on one of the fishing charter boats, helping some rich guy bait his hook and clean his fish. But what kind of a life could you possibly have?

I pulled into the nearly empty parking lot, glancing around at the seven or eight cars that were still there. Wireman's truck was up front. There was a yellow foreign sports car. I didn't recognize the body style. Head of security was not there. But I knew where he'd been about twenty-five minutes ago, and I knew what he'd said. I had a recording of what he'd said. Just another crime of mine.

I dreaded this confrontation, more than any meeting I'd ever had, but at least there were no cops. No Feng. I walked by the yellow car. A Lotus Exige. Man, that car was hot. Something like 260 horsepower under the hood. I didn't have to wonder whose machine it was.

I pulled on the front door and it opened. I was half hoping it was locked. No one was at reception, and I thought about James' remarkable exit today from these same doors as he threw the package into the parking lot. Was that just four or five hours ago?

Down the hall, past the rows of computers and worktables where technicians performed their software magic during the day. I stared at the offices, all in a row. The door to number one was open and I could hear soft conversation.

Play dumb? Admit to the crime? Blame James? Confess that Carol Conroy had offered me money? Take the heat myself and throw myself at their mercy? Whatever made me think I could be a spy? I didn't have the guts for it. Especially when I got caught.

If somebody captured me and threatened me with anything,

I'd spill it all. I'd tell them whatever they wanted to know. I have no idea what made me think I could be a spy. I had to think more clearly the next time I started to make these irrational decisions.

Slowly I walked to the door. "Sorry it took so long."

"Get in here." Conroy pointed his finger from behind the desk. Wireman sat in the only chair in the room. I'd seen Sarah in that chair.

"Look, Mr. Conroy, I—"

He picked up the smoke detector from his desk. The top half and bottom half were separated, and I glanced at the ceiling where it had been earlier today. A new detector was installed. Apparently someone had come in after hours and wired it in.

"We hired your company based on the quality and the speed you could bring to this project."

"Yes, sir."

"So can you explain this?"

I didn't know what to say. So, I just stood there like a dumbass. Andy Wireman sat in his chair, his hands folded, watching the two of us with a grim look on his face.

"Can you?"

"No. Well, yes." Sweat ran down my neck. I wanted to scratch an irritating itch on my rib cage, but I was frozen in place.

"Which is it? No or yes?"

"It's not what it seems." It just came out. I had no idea where to go with that. It was *exactly* what it seemed. A card with a small camera lens.

"It's not what it seems? What is that supposed to mean? Look at this." He was almost shouting now, as he leaned into the desk and rested his elbows on the surface.

I did. I stared at the smoke detector. It was preferable to staring at his face, which was covered with a deep scowl. His eyes were wide open, and I was glad the man was behind his desk and not in front of it. His hands were clenched tightly around the white detector.

"According to Mr. Wireman, your friend installed a —" he paused, looking into the section that housed the camera lens and card. I closed my eyes and held my hands at my side, fingernails digging into my palms. "Installed a piece of crap. A smoke detector that is barely functional, and you chose this one to install in my office. He tells me that it's a very unorthodox piece of equipment. That no company should ever use something this bizarre and you chose this to install in my office?"

"Sir —"

"Moore, as I pointed out, we hired you for the quality and speed you could bring to this project. Right now I'd fire your ass. If you weren't already into the project, I'd have you out on the street." His eyes had narrowed and he was breathing heavily.

I should have been petrified, but all that was running through my head was the fact that he didn't know it was a camera. Obviously he didn't have a clue. Not the first hint that he held a camera and microphone in his hand. I wanted to jump up and down. I wanted to shake his hand and hug Andy Wireman. I kept my emotions under control.

"I've got a very important project that needs major security. I've got a timetable that is tighter than a rat's ass. And I'm dealing with crap like this? It went off today, Moore. Screaming that intolerable shrill scream, and there wasn't a fire. *There was nothing.* Do you hear me? Nothing."

With that he threw the detector against the far wall. It hit with a thud and fell to the floor. Just like the coffee mug Sarah threw against the other wall.

"Mr. Moore, Mr. Wireman. Get this project under control. Get it done, and get the hell out of here. Do I make myself clear? Perfectly clear?"

"You do." I shouted it. "I'll see to it. Andy and I will get it done in record time, and there will be no more screw-ups."

"Take that piece of crap with you."

I looked up again. Not so much at the ceiling, but just up, thanking God. Silently thanking God, over and over and over. I picked up the two halves of the detector, nonetheless for the wear, and exited the room. I was dizzy with excitement and could feel the blood pounding in my head. He'd asked me to take it with me. The evidence. I was convinced I would be walking out in handcuffs. Instead, I had the evidence in my hand. I wasn't sure things could get any better.

Wireman walked out and closed the door behind him. He gave me a sheepish look. "I'm sorry, Skip. When it went off, he blew up. I told him the truth, that it was an inferior piece of equipment, and he asked that we wire him a new one even though it was after hours. Of course, we did it. It was his idea to call you in tonight. I didn't mean to get you in trouble. Honestly."

"Andy, no problem." I was elated. There were no problems in the world. "It was my mistake. Totally mine. I never, ever, should have put that detector in."

"Just out of curiosity—"

"Yes?"

"Where did you get that? It's got some things in it I have never seen. Some card, and a tiny glass—"

I interrupted. "The main thing is, Andy, I'm not going to install anything like that again without your approval. Got it?"

He looked at the detector in my hand. "The insides of that thing are strange, Skip. Do you mind if I take it home and study it?"

That didn't sound like the plan I had in mind. "Andy, no more problems. Let's just get this thing done, take our money, and go home. Is that okay with you?"

He smiled. "Got it."

I walked through the building, out the door, into the parking lot, wanting to jump up high and kick my heels. Looking down at the smoke detector in my hand I saw the card, clipped tightly to the case. We could actually play it on the computer tonight and see and hear what happened today. We could listen to the recording from The Sound Max and analyze what Feng and Chen were talking about. I could get out the calculator and once again add up all the money that was mine once this project was completed. I could even dream about what I was going to spend that money on. I figured I'd better stop at Gas and Grocery and get a case of beer to celebrate.

It was going to be a glorious night. We were back in the spy business.

CHAPTER THIRTY-SIX

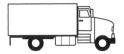

I called Em on the way home. I didn't want to alarm her, but I thought she should know a little of what had transpired. After all, Carol Conroy seemed familiar with her and I was hoping to find out why.

"The smoke detector went off?"

"But no problem, Em. No one suspected a thing. It was amazing."

"Skip, you could have been discovered. I mean, that's a felony isn't it?"

"I'm not a prosecutor, Em. Don't know that much about the law. Anyway, it's out of the office."

"I'm glad you're safe."

I told her that James was passing along the transcript of the conversations Sandy Conroy had in his office. And I did mention that Carol Conroy asked if she was going to be at the apartment tonight.

"Carol Conroy knows about me?"

"Seemed to."

"How?"

"It probably wouldn't take much checking to see that you and I are seeing each other."

"So, does she know that the Sarah relationship is a sham?"

"I don't know. I was a little afraid to ask her."

Em was quiet. I could hear her thinking. Really. When she thinks, you can hear those wheels spinning. "See what James has to say and call me back tonight. I want to get his take on it."

"James?"

"That's what I said."

I about drove off the road. James and Em were starting to scare me. They both were seeking each other's opinion. If I was a suspicious person, I'd almost wonder if they had something going on between them.

Pulling into the apartment complex, I parked next to James's truck. The Chevy continued to cough and sputter even after I'd turned off the key and I wondered how much a tune-up would cost.

I opened the door and stepped inside. He was sitting on the sofa. "James. It's all okay. Conroy had no idea that the smoke detector was a camera." I laid the two halves of the malfunctioning smoke detector on the kitchen counter.

"Skip—"

"Hey, it went very well." Turning to my roommate, I gave him thumbs up. "I mean, even Wireman had no idea. We skated on—" I heard the toilet flush in the bathroom and seconds later Carol Conroy walked out.

"You had a camera in his office?"

James looked at me and rolled his eyes.

"Hey, Mrs. Conroy. I didn't realize you'd still be here."

"Obviously." She'd dressed down in jeans, jeweled sandals, and a frilly cotton top, but her attitude was still haughty and one of total control.

"So you got the transcript?"

"So you have pictures?" She shot back at me.

"Um, Mrs. Conroy asked if she could stick around till you got back. I didn't see any problem, so I agreed." James shrugged his shoulders.

"There was something you wanted to ask me?" I wanted to get off the camera conversation. My high had been brought back to earth in a hurry.

"A smoke detector that doubles as a camera? You've been holding out on me, Mr. Moore." She looked right at me, standing there by the evidence.

"It . . . it malfunctioned. Doesn't work properly. No film, just scratchy sound. That's why I did the transcript." The frown on her face told me she wasn't buying it. Not 100 percent.

"Mr. Moore, can we talk outside?"

"We can. I have to tell you that James knows a lot about what's been going on. He's my partner and he's helped with your project."

Carol Conroy ran her hand over her forehead as if in desperation, and slumped onto the couch next to James. I sat in the remaining chair.

"My life is in danger."

James leaned toward her, touching her hand. She allowed it. I was surprised, but she left his hand on hers. "Mrs. Conroy, Skip already told me that you think someone's after you. That's a pretty heavy statement to make. What makes you think that someone would be out to kill you?"

She shifted, still leaving his hand on hers. "I told Mr. Moore. The vice president of my father's business was murdered. I'm certain of it. Ralph Walters was killed. I believe the man who developed the software that we are currently manufacturing, Tony Quatman, was killed. And I believe it's possible that his secretary and her husband are either involved or dead as well."

"Can you tell us why you believe this?"

She was softening up. "No."

I stood up and went to the refrigerator. "Anyone want a beer?" I had a case in the car, but I wanted it cold. For some reason our refrigerator almost freezes the beer.

"Mrs. Conroy," James had removed the hand, "you've got to tell us why."

"I can't. I don't know why. It's something to do with the project."

No one had said that they wanted a beer, so I pulled one out and popped the top. "Can you tell us what the project is?" Sarah had told me it had to do with the Department of Defense, but I wasn't supposed to know that.

"It's a government contract. We've had them before. But this project, this one seems to be a little more special."

"If you don't know exactly what it is, then why would someone want to kill you? I mean, if you don't know anything?"

"Because *I* know that Sandy is being very secretive about this specific job. Because *I* know that Ralph Walters found out something he wasn't supposed to know, and the next day he was dead. Because my husband doesn't trust me, just like I don't trust him. And *I* believe that Tony Quatman found out that Synco Systems was going to do something illegal or unscrupulous with the software program, and he was eliminated."

"Mrs. Conroy, even if all those things are true, it's tough to believe that someone is going to kill *you*."

"Oh, it's not just someone."

"Who is it going to be?"

"I know, you're laughing at me."

I shook my head. "No. I promise you that we're not laughing. I think we're both a little concerned that you're going out on a limb here." I took a deep swallow of beer.

"No limb. It's going to be my husband or Feng."

"Really?" James sat back and cocked his head.

"Really, James." James? I was still Mr. Moore. James was now on a first name basis.

"Because of the aforementioned reasons."

"Those. And the fact that he's going to leave the company when this project is finished."

I knew that. And I'd told James. But I didn't get the impression it was common news.

"I think Ralph may have found out about that as well," she said.

"Carol," James was trying out the familiar style, "even if he's leaving—"

"Boys, he *is* leaving. Let's drop the charade, okay? I need your help. I've told you what I know. If you have any more information that you're not sharing with me, please, give it to me. I understand that my case is weak, but I know what's going to happen. And I want to stop it. I think that Sandler is planning on destroying my father's company, I think that he's going to find a way to kill me in the process, and I know that he's going to take off with his little girlfriend, Sarah Crumbly." She shot me a cold, hard glance. "Yes, Mr. Moore. I know that he's seeing her. No more games. Either you're with me or against me."

It had been a day of ups and downs. I didn't know what to say. But leave it to my roommate.

"Carol, we're with you. No more games. We'll give you everything we can get. Give us until tomorrow and we'll lay out all that we've found."

She stood, obviously a little shaken, and walked out of the apartment. A moment later I heard her Lexus start.

"It's been a long day, pard."

"It's going to be a long night, James. We've got three hours of video to watch from the smoke detector, and the audio from Chen's laundry to listen to."

"Part of the job, Skip. We're spies."

CHAPTER THIRTY-SEVEN

We listened to the audio again. I knew that second voice, the voice of Chen, and I couldn't figure out how that was possible. The voice just jumped out at me.

"So you took dry cleaning in there one time?"

"James, you know better. I've never taken dry cleaning anywhere. Other than a couple of sport coats, I haven't got anything worth dry cleaning."

"Those jackets, amigo, maybe you should visit Chen's."

I was working it over in my mind when I heard the knock at the door. I figured out who it was before I'd even answered it.

"Guys, you got me involved in this, so I'd better know everything." Em went to the refrigerator and grabbed a beer. No glass. She drank her Yuengling from the bottle.

I told her what Carol Conroy knew. We shared the audiotape with her, and she listened intently.

"You've Googled this Chi Mak?"

"It was on my list," James said sheepishly. We weren't exactly coming up with all the answers that Em was. He walked to our computer sitting on the wobbly stand next to the stool in the kitchen.

"Where is Feng? Right now?" Em looked at her watch.

I punched in the code on my laptop for his GPS. "Looks like he's back at Synco Systems. Working late."

"And I'll bet that Sandy Conroy is telling him about the smoke alarm incident." She pressed her fingers together, staring into space.

"You're right." I knew Mr. Conroy would tell his head of security about the smoke alarm. But I had the evidence. No one could prove a thing. The smoke detector was on our kitchen counter, the two pieces lying face down. I wondered if Sandy Conroy had rendered it inoperable when he threw it against the wall. "This would be the time to have a listening device in there. I'll bet he and Conroy are talking right now."

James looked up from his screen. "This Mak guy was found guilty of espionage. The story is right here." He read from the screen.

Chi Mak was convicted of taking computer disks from Anaheim defense contractor Power Paragon, where he was lead engineer on a sensitive research project involving QED, a propulsion system for Navy warships, according to an FBI affidavit. He also e-mailed photos and reports about the QED system to his home computer. Authorities say Mak and his wife copied the information onto CDs and then delivered them to a relative, Tai Wang Mak, who encrypted the disks and then was scheduled to fly to Hong Kong. From there, Mak allegedly planned to travel to Guangzhou in China to meet a contact.

"And during their conversation at the laundry, Chen is bragging on this guy."

"Em," James kept scanning his screen, "this guy was stealing stuff for maybe twenty years before anyone figured him out."

"Great story." I was watching Feng's car, a blip on the computer screen. It was on the road, moving at a pretty good clip. "But what does it have to do with Synco Systems?"

Em took a long pull on her bottle of beer. "This Chi Mak was *stealing* Defense Department secrets."

"Yeah. Big time." James nodded emphatically.

"Synco Systems is *working* on a huge project for the Defense Department."

I thought about it for a moment. "Em, this Chi Mak was an engineer. He had access to *all* the information. We're pretty sure that Synco Systems is making a system that will *protect* the Department of Defense from having anyone like Chi Mak hacking into their computers. They're trying to stop people like Chi Mak." The two stories were diametrically opposed. There was nothing that brought them together. "And Synco Systems has no information. They have no plans — no idea what the Defense Department is planning. Feng doesn't have access to any information within the Defense Department. To my knowledge anyway. Chi Mak had the plans in his hands. He was even designing some of them. If you're designing a propulsion system, it's one thing. Then you have all the plans, and you have the capability of stealing those plans. If you are designing a security system to stop that theft, it's an entirely different story."

James sipped on his beer. "We're in Miami. Defense is, where? In Washington, D.C., right? They may as well be in different countries. Synco Systems has nothing. Just the software they're designing, and that's not going to be ready to go for another two or three weeks."

"I just think there's something lying right on the table, and we're missing it." Em sat on the couch and pressed her fingers into the fabric.

"Maybe not." I stood and was pacing. As much as you could pace in the tiny abode we called home.

"Oh, so maybe there's been a suicide or murder and the disappearance of two employees for *no* reason. Maybe Carol Conroy is just paranoid. Maybe this Feng is following you guys and Carol Conroy as just some sort of exercise. I suppose that could be." Em smiled and slugged down another swallow. "Hey, boyfriend, bring me another beer."

I did. And one for James and myself. We were now officially out of Yeungling, and I went outside to get the case from my car. The moon was coming up, and I realized the late hour. We hadn't even looked at the video card yet. I hefted the case up on my shoulder, not needing any lower back strain at an early age, and turned to go in. I heard a car enter the lot, and turned briefly. The headlights were off, but I could make out the shape on the far side of the parking lot.

I walked into the apartment, case on my shoulder, and Skip and Em looked up from their conversation and applauded. Whenever someone is bringing the drinks they get the accolades.

Carrying the case to the refrigerator and setting it down, I turned to Em. "Well, do you have it all figured out by now?"

She gave me a smirk. "No. But one more of these, and I'll have to crash here tonight."

That wouldn't have been all bad. We always spent the nights at her place, but if she really wanted to, well— That's when the front window shattered and I heard the sharp crack from the parking lot. Like a whip, a firecracker. Like a gun. I froze.

The glass shattered in our second front window and I heard another sharp crack. You always wonder what you'll do in a tense situation like this. I lunged at Em, tackling her around the hips and knocking her to the ground. Later, she said I'd actually bruised her, but I couldn't have cared less. Climbing on top of her I screamed. "James, get on the ground. Now."

He was sitting there, his mouth half open, watching me covering Em. Then, like a tottering bowling pin he fell from his chair and for just a moment I thought he'd been hit by a bullet. James stretched out flat, his eyes riveted to mine. A second later I heard the sound of more broken glass and something rattling. I glanced up at the computer stand and saw our old P.C. explode into dozens of pieces.

"Damn." James had crawled under the kitchen table and couldn't see the stand, but he knew what had happened.

I pulled my cell phone from my belt and punched in 911.

"Nine-one-one. Do you have an emergency?"

"Someone is shooting at us." I was screaming.

"What is your address?"

I gave it to her, trying not to shout.

"Sir, is anyone injured?"

"Ma'am, if you don't get someone out here immediately, we'll all be dead. Damn the injured part."

"Sir, I've already alerted the authorities. Now please, you have to tell me if anyone is injured."

Something whizzed overhead and crashed into a lamp. "Not yet."

"Can you take cover?"

"I'm lying on the ground, lady. Three of us are hugging the floor. It's the best we can do." Em squirmed under me, but didn't say a word.

"Is there a bathtub? Or someplace safe you can go to?"

The bullets had come right through the windows. Even if we wanted to change our location, it would have been a bad decision. The minute we would rise up, someone could get hit, and none of us wanted that to happen. "Ma'am, I just want to know someone is coming."

"Miami Gardens Police are on their way. Would you like me to stay on the line until they arrive?"

I could hear a siren in the distance. No more gunshots. "No. Thank you."

"You're certain?"

The sound of the siren was louder. "I think we'll be fine. Thank you for being there." I felt like we were doing a commercial for General Motors' OnStar. "Em, are you all right?"

"You're a little heavy, Skip. Other than that, I think I'm okay." I stayed on top. There was no guarantee the gunplay was over.

I'd expected a run-in with the police tonight. It's just that I expected to be arrested for bugging Sandy Conroy's office. Instead, local cops were in rescue mode. Our rescue.

"James?"

"I'm here, pard." His voice was quaking.

From underneath me I heard, "Skip, thank you for covering me, but seriously, I think you can move off of me now."

So I slid off of Em, still hugging the floor. The siren was closer now, screaming with a mournful wail. Still no shots.

We were silent. The three of us realizing how lucky we were to be alive. I reached out and grabbed Em's hand, secretly wishing I could grab James's hand as well. She squeezed, and I felt a chill go through my body. I shivered and squeezed back, looking into her eyes. She had tears running down her cheeks.

"Hey, Skip?"

"Yeah, James."

"Is it safe?"

"I don't know, man. I wouldn't go putting my head out the window. But I do know one thing."

"What?" Em asked quietly from the floor.

"It's gonna be a mess. Windows, the computer, the lamp."

"Holes in the wall. God, I hope they didn't hit the beer or the refrigerator. Why us?"

I didn't have an answer. A couple of guesses maybe.

"You guys know more than you think you do." Em was still

hugging the floor, her face buried in the cheap carpeting, stained with beer and cigarette burns.

"But Skip —" James sounded more upbeat. The fact that no bullets had flown by in the last ninety seconds may have had something to do with that.

"What?"

"Is it safe?"

"Safe?"

"Is it safe?"

It had been a long time, but I remembered the answer. Amid all the craziness, the gunfire and near death experience, James was still playing. It was dangerous because someone was still out there, trying to kill us. But I answered. "Yes, it's safe, it's very safe, it's so safe you wouldn't believe it."

Em raised her head, looking at the two of us, still lying flat on the floor. "Are you two crazy? Wait. Don't answer. I know."

"You already know we're crazy, Em," James chuckled softly.

"Yes. There's no question about that. Crazy enough to almost get us killed. But I know the movie."

"Movie? What movie?"

"Guys, I know the name of the movie."

James strung her along. "How do you know there's a movie involved? Em, don't give me that. No. No, you don't know what movie that's from."

The siren shrieked as it pulled into the parking lot. I could see purple light, combination of red and blue, as it streamed through the window, or what was left of the window. There was a slight commotion as voices outside got louder, and still we lay on the floor, afraid to sit up.

The siren drifted off, and there was a pounding at the door. "Police, open up."

Slowly I pushed myself from the floor, and as Em stood up she brushed at her clothes, shaking shards of glass from her hair.

I turned to my two best friends. "We cannot say anything about who might have done this. We've got no proof. Agreed?" The two of them nodded their heads. "Officer, I'm going to open the door. Nobody in here has any weapons." The cops hadn't asked, but I didn't want any accidents. We'd already been shot at from a distance. Didn't need to have it happen at close range.

I pulled the door open, and two young officers with pistols drawn stood on either side of the doorway. A small group of neighbors was gathered outside, and I thought I saw Jim Jobs at the head of the group. I remembered his scolding voice when I first had James install the fire alarm in Sandy Conroy's office, and I wondered if my comments to him were strong enough to give him reason to shoot out our windows and blow our computer to kingdom come.

"Thank God you're here." James crawled up off the floor and offered his hand. Neither officer took it.

"Who called about the gunfire?"

"I did."

"It came from —"

"The parking lot."

"We have another officer checking that out." He glanced around the apartment. "Do you have any drugs in this apartment?"

I couldn't believe he was even allowed to ask the question. "A case of beer is about the strongest thing we carry."

He nodded. "I'll need to take a report." The younger uniformed officer walked in and started making notes as he moved around the living room. The guy was probably about our age, maybe younger. This was the officer of the law who was going to save us from a sniper? A guy younger than I was?

"*Marathon Man*, James." Em gave my roommate a grim look.

"Pardon?"

"When Laurence Olivier is torturing Dustin Hoffman he says 'is it safe?' and Hoffman, trying to get away from the pain says, 'Yes, it's safe, it's very safe, it's so safe you wouldn't believe it.'"

James shook his head. "You're good. You're very good. I can't believe you came up with that."

"Sir, would you step outside for a moment?" The older officer motioned to James and the night got a lot longer.

CHAPTER THIRTY-EIGHT

The cops left a little after midnight. They'd questioned us individually, then together. Did we owe anyone any money? Did we use drugs, did we buy drugs, did we sell drugs? After the exhaustive interviews, they worked the apartment over, digging out three slugs from the walls. They combed the parking lot, looking for I don't know what. All I know is that we were glad when it ended.

We'd called a 24-hour home improvement company, Twenty-Four Seven, that the police recommended and they boarded up our windows. Em stuck around and helped clean up the broken glass and computer pieces. The computer hadn't been worth much, but it's all we owned. The company laptop was untouched. My jackass boss Michael would be so happy. I promised myself when I got paid from everyone, I would buy the apartment its own computer. Something new and state-of-the-art. Something cheap. I had a lot of plans for that money. Travel with Em, a new car, computer, maybe upgrade our lodging—the list was endless. Maybe put back a couple of bucks just in case Em and I decided to take this relationship to the next level. Not that either of us was ready for that.

"We should have told them about Feng. About Jim Jobs." James was having second thoughts. "Skip, we should have told them the whole story. Carol Conroy and Sandy and Sarah."

"Hey, James. You did a great job in giving them just the basic facts. We were sitting here and somebody started shooting. That's all we know for sure. Don't even think about blowing it now."

"Blowing it?" He buried his head in his hands. "Skip, I wanted to tell the cops everything and ask them to solve the problem. It's been a game up until now. It's no longer a game, pard. We came this close to being killed."

"The cops made it clear they thought it was a drug thing." Em sat on the couch, scowling. "Our age, this location," she flung her arms out. "You guys need to get out of this place."

"It's what we can afford, Em." James shot her a dirty look. "It is what it is."

"James, maybe it *was* a drug thing." For the last hour I'd had this thought in the back of my head.

"What?"

"Maybe somebody picked the wrong apartment. It's not that we haven't seen deals going down here before." We'd seen drugs being sold in the parking lot, and the cops had conducted at least three raids in the two years we'd lived here.

"Yeah. Maybe. But what are those chances?"

"James, Skip is right. If we told the police about Feng and the rest of that crew, the cops would think we were smoking something. What were you going to say? That Skip is *pretending* to be Sarah's boyfriend, so maybe her *real* boyfriend shot the place up? Or maybe her boyfriend's wife shot the place up? Or would you tell the story about you guys bugging Feng's car and maybe Feng shot the windows out to get even or to scare you? Or would you use the story about bugging Sandy Conroy's office and maybe he found out and decided to kill you?"

Em brought it home. Each one of those scenarios was entirely possible. We were in some deep, deep shit.

We sat on the couch, the three of us, drinking strong, black coffee at twelve thirty a.m. We should have all collapsed by now, but the fear and the energy fueled by the caffeine kept us on the edge of our seats.

"Who ordered your security system?" Em stared ahead, watching some spot on the far wall.

"Synco Systems." What was she thinking?

"Why?"

"Because they wanted to upgrade. Wanted a better—" and then I remembered. In my first conversation with Sarah, she'd mentioned that a new client had demanded that Synco Systems put in a new system. "It was one of their clients."

"Any idea who?"

I thought about it for a minute. A new client had told them they wanted Synco to install a better security. Presumably to make sure no one broke into the plant and stole that client's software secrets. "I do remember. I think she said it was the government."

"Our government?"

"Yeah. I'm sure of it. She said someone associated with the United States government made the request."

"The government wanted a new security system installed at S.S. to protect the security system that was being designed for them."

"Sounds convoluted, but yes. That's what she said."

James spoke up. "The security software package that Synco is working on right now is for the Department of Defense, right?"

"It is. Sarah said it's a secret, but she's under the impression that the Department of Defense is the client."

"So, we can assume that the Department of Defense is responsible for your big sale, Skip." Em smiled at me, stood up, and walked to the window. "Did you guys have renters' insurance?" She tapped on the plywood.

"No."

"Just wondered." She paced with a nervous energy. "Do you remember what we talked about yesterday at lunch?"

Could that have been just yesterday? A lot had happened since then.

"Going back to a starting point? Well, we started when Skip sold the job. But now we know that it goes back a little further. It starts when the Department of Defense asked for a new security system to be installed at Synco Systems."

"Why does it start there?" James had a cynical tone to his voice.

"Because they were afraid someone would break in and steal the plans for this sophisticated software program that is being installed on their computers."

"Makes sense." I nodded.

"The Department of Defense is making sure that their new security system is secure."

"And? You're just going around in circles." James was frustrated. Late hours, caffeine, and a headache usually do that to him.

"It's all right there. The murder of the vice president, Carol Conroy's paranoia, even Sarah's relationship with Sandy Conroy. I can feel it."

"But you can't tell us what it is?"

"Feng's part of it. That conversation you recorded this afternoon. We need a couple more pieces of the puzzle. That's all."

"Where are we going to get them?" I had no idea where she was going with this.

"Anybody ready for bed?" James jumped to his feet.

"I couldn't sleep if I tried." Em kept pacing in the small room.

"Then let's go back to Synco."

"Right now?" I couldn't imagine what he planned on doing.

"Right now. Skip, you've got the temporary code, and at this moment the motion detectors and security devices aren't hooked up. We'll never have a better chance to walk in and check out Conroy's and Feng's offices."

"For God's sake, James, we've already broken some sort of law. I almost got myself arrested tonight and —"

"That's the point, amigo. You didn't. What you almost got tonight was killed. We can walk into those offices and go through files, paperwork, and whatever else we want to look into. Let's find out why someone tried to kill us. There are no detectors to stop us. After tomorrow, all those security devices will be hooked up and nobody will be able to get in. Am I right?"

"You're right."

"And Skip, there's something else."

"What's that?"

"We can get into Sandy Conroy's computer."

"We can?"

"Don't you remember, compadre? We've got the code from our little smoke detector spy on the ceiling."

He was right again.

"Em?"

"What are you going to do if you get caught?"

"I tell them that we couldn't sleep." Caught up in the spirit of the caper, I continued. "I came in to make sure that everything was ready for tomorrow's hookup." I figured it might have a chance.

"You know that will never stand up." Em set her empty coffee cup on the kitchen counter.

"You keep a lookout at the entrance and it won't have to." There were two ways in. The main entrance was the only one

222

that was ever used. The rear entrance would only be used for an emergency.

"I know this is one of the worst ideas you guys have ever had." She brushed her blonde hair off her face. "And you've had some really bad ideas."

"But?" I watched her walking from one end of the room to the other. About nine medium steps.

"Em?" James drained his coffee.

"*But* I'm going to go along with you."

"Because you want to help us? Because you and I have a relationship, and you're sticking by me?"

"Because somebody took a shot at me, Skip, and I am pissed."

CHAPTER THIRTY-NINE

James reached behind the driver's seat and pulled out a rolled mat. "My friends, I will magically transform this vehicle."

"We could use a little magic tonight." I watched as he waved the rolled vinyl above his head.

"Watch as the old box truck, magically becomes—" James turned his back to us, unrolled the vinyl, and placed it against the driver's door, "The Water Connection Plumbers."

"The Water Connection?" We could barely read the sign in the dim light of the parking lot.

"What is a plumber responsible for? Water in. Water out. Therefore, The Water Connection. The Water Connection Plumbers." I had to admit, the name worked. I just hoped he'd checked the Yellow Pages to make sure there wasn't another Water Connection.

"Guy I know from Cap'n Crab printed them up for us. Pretty cool, eh."

"Problem is, James, you don't know one end of a wrench from the other."

I could see him smile. Someone had then taken the letters and intertwined a silver *W*, *C*, and *P*. It actually did look pretty cool. What bothered me the most was the phone number, displayed in a putrid yellow.

"Skip, that's your number." Em looked puzzled.

"If someone calls to check up on us, it can't be a fake number." James had thought it all out. "They've got to believe we're a real plumbing company. If we're out on a surveillance call, all you've got to do is answer your cell with 'Water Connection.'"

That didn't bother me too much. The people who called my phone were Em, James, and one or two other friends. My mother and I hadn't spoken in years, so she wouldn't call. And with the others, I could always explain. I'd just tell them I was moonlighting as an answering service. What bothered me was the minutes. Every time someone called to check on the phony business it would cost me time on my plan. Hopefully the bonuses would more than make up for the extra cost.

"And I didn't want you to feel left out, Skip." He walked to the passenger side and unrolled a second sign.

"James," I opened the door and let Em in, "I just hope nobody recognizes the truck."

"Perfect disguise, Skip. Perfect. Once the signs are in place, nobody realizes it's the old truck." Of course, he was right. Superman could put on a business suit and glasses and everyone thought he was Clark Kent. Thin disguises worked everywhere. Grow a mustache, shave your head, and no one would recognize you. People would focus on the sign now, not on the truck.

We stared at the apartment as James backed out, gazing at the large plywood squares that covered our windows. It was another reminder that someone had tried to kill us. I saw someone walking slowly up the sidewalk and they waved. I thought it might be Jim Jobs, but I couldn't be sure. It was after one o'clock in the morning, and there was still life at the complex. I flashed back to the night I'd seen someone in the parking lot under the box truck. No matter what hour of the night, there was life at the complex. There was soon to be life at Synco Systems.

I kept my laptop on my lap, feeling that it was a lot safer with me than sitting in the apartment. And if Feng was moving around this early in the morning, I could check up on him. It still amazed me that the man hadn't stumbled on the GPS unit under his Honda.

"Got three of these." James reached over and handed each of us a cheap plastic flashlight.

"Three?"

"They were cheap. Four for five bucks. And they don't last very long. I already tried one, but I've got three of them left. Just take them in case, okay?"

Green, blue, and red.

"I think we're in business. If anyone wants to back out, say so now. We're on a nonstop mission, boys and girls."

"You're sure this is a good idea?"

"It's the Lord's will, my man. Must be. It feels right."

"In other words, James, we're on a mission from God."

He didn't miss a beat. "*Blues Brothers*, Aykroyd and Belushi, 1980. We're on a mission from God."

"Do we have any idea what we're going to find?"

"Pieces to the puzzle, Skip." Em sounded full of determination. Determination and caffeine.

I much preferred an exact definition of a mission. But I had to admit, this mission had no definition. We were almost as clueless as we had been from the beginning. But this time we had the code to the big guy's computer. And that might make a world of difference.

James drove out of the lot, and I could see the shadow of a figure standing in front of our apartment. I'd bet on that figure being Jim Jobs, and I thought again that maybe he'd been the shooter tonight. If he was, maybe he was disappointed he hadn't killed one of us. And if it was Jobs, and he planned on breaking into our home after we were gone, I wished him a lot of luck. The only thing of value in that apartment had been the case of beer and the PC, and the PC had been blown to hell.

CHAPTER FORTY

The parking lot was eerily empty. Dark and empty. And the stark brick building was outlined against the sky. James wheeled into the asphalt acre, circled the lot once, then drove back out.

"Changed your mind?" I had no idea what he was thinking.

"Would a plumber make a call to *this* business at *this* hour of the morning?"

Em turned to James. "If there was an emergency call, yes."

He turned right and drove for another block, finally pulling up in front of a small concrete-block house. "If we park here, we could be calling on any one of ten houses. A much more logical location."

"Plumbers at this hour of the morning?"

"Broken pipes, backed up toilets, they don't know the difference between night and day, Skip. A business like Synco Systems is closed, but homeowners are there around the clock—you never know. When a resident of this affluent neighborhood needs the Water Connection, we're as close as their phone."

As close as *my* phone.

"As plumbers, we've got to be vigilant twenty-four hours a day."

I said nothing more as we opened the doors and stepped out of the truck, flashlights in hand. Often there's nothing left to say when James is done. We remained quiet as we walked a block and a half to the headquarters of Synco Systems.

"Skip, you've got the temporary entry card and the code?"

I stepped up and inserted the card. A green light flashed on the small electronic pad, and I turned the handle. The door swung quietly inward. The numbered pad was mounted on the right. With another light flashing red, I punched in 45693 and waited until I heard the shrill whine of the signal. Punching in 45789, the whining stopped and everything went still. For a brief time, I had total access to the facility. With the code to the building and the code to Conroy's computer, the place was mine.

A security light from high on the wall cast shadows on the lobby, now showing our silhouettes on the far wall.

"Before we go any farther," Em looked around, scouting out the location for the first time, "this is breaking and entering. We're on very dangerous ground, guys."

I held up my entry card. "It's certainly not breaking. I've got the card right here. Remember, we're just doing some preliminary work for the hookup tomorrow." We all knew that excuse wouldn't last ten minutes.

"Em, why don't you be the lookout." James was looking around the area like he'd never seen it before. I chalked it up to being nervous.

"If anyone finds me here, they'll wonder why a stranger is in the lobby. It makes more sense if they find one of you. You have a reason to be here."

I spoke up. "You're right. However, I know the computer code and James is familiar with the office. He's been in there a couple of times installing the smoke detector and taking out the card."

She sighed. "Fine. I think it's a dumb idea, but I'll do look-out. What kind of signal do you want?"

"If you have time, a 'Hey guys, someone is coming' would be nice."

"Screw you, James."

I was somewhat relieved. The two of them were back to their normal relationship.

Things had been going almost too smoothly.

"But if you get caught by surprise, if someone shows up and you didn't catch it, then get back to the office as quickly as possible."

She said nothing.

I took Em's arm and walked her back to the work area. "Number one. Right there. That's Sandy's office. If you need to see us, that's where we'll be. Okay?"

It wasn't okay for any of us. But we needed some information, and we needed it now.

I left Em sitting in the lobby behind the reception desk. James and I walked down to Conroy's office, and when I punched in a temporary code the door opened. I thought for a moment about the three Synco Systems offices I'd been in. Ralph Walters's office, where we'd discovered the dead body, Sarah's office where I'd gone in to ask her to please pay the deposit on our security system. I remembered the glass-topped desk and those fabulous legs and short skirt visible through the glass. And then there'd been Sandy Conroy's office, where I'd been dressed down several hours ago. And here we were, back at the scene of the crime.

"If someone hadn't shot at us, James—"

He raised his hand and shook his finger in my face. "But they did, amigo. Someone took three shots at us."

"Could have been a mistake, James."

"You know better."

The dim security lights cast a pallor over the office as James and I stood there, not sure where to start. Three oak veneer file cabinets lined the far wall, and other than the papers on Conroy's desk, his computer was the only item that might hold secrets.

"Tell me again what we're looking for."

"We'll know when we find it, pard." He pulled open the top file drawer in cabinet number one. "Not locked. Probably nothing valuable in here."

Placing my laptop on Conroy's desk, I sat behind the large wooden structure, realizing it would probably be a long time before I was ever in a position like this in my professional career. I pictured myself as Sandler Conroy, CEO of a big, successful company, married to the owner's daughter.

"Skip, you look like you belong."

In jeans, sandals, and a Green Day T-shirt, I doubted that.

"Just think. You marry Em, take over her daddy's company, and you become the next Sandy Conroy."

Could happen. "Never happen, James. Remember, she's way out of my league." I pulled out the piece of paper where I'd written down the code. A series of numbers and letters that were probably some word or combination that meant something to Conroy. I knew for a fact that people still used birthdays, phone numbers, anniversaries, and other common threads in their life so that they could remember their codes and passwords. The problem was that other people knew those birthdays, phone numbers, and anniversaries too. And with that information, identity theft was rampant.

Pulling out Conroy's keyboard I punched in 305-805-500-1AC. The screen on his desk blinked and a box appeared.

Failure to complete password.

Checking the paper in front of me, I punched in the code again. 305-805-500-1AC.

Once again the box appeared.

Failure to complete password

"How you comin'?"

"I know I copied it down right, James. I watched Conroy punch it in. It was on my computer screen." I'd watched the action ten times. I was sure I was right. "Maybe he changes it daily."

"Do people do that?"

"If they do, we're screwed." I wouldn't put it past him. Conroy seemed like the kind of guy who would guard his privacy with his life.

"Mmmm. Let me see that."

I handed him the paper, thinking about how much trouble we could be in and hoping that Em was all right.

"Seven numbers in a phone number, right?"

Standing up, I nodded. I opened the office door and gazed at the dimly lit work area, down to the entrance hall where I hoped Em was still sitting.

"And the area code is three numbers. Well, if you got the numbers wrong, just one digit, we're screwed. We'd be punching in numbers all night."

"Let's assume the numbers are right."

"So let's say it's a phone number. Okay. Does it ring a bell?"

"If you dial it, maybe."

He thought about that for a moment, never cracking a smile. "Skip, let's go with the number. If you got that right, then that leaves two letters. *AC*."

"What do those stand for?"

"Could be as simple as the first and third letter of the alphabet. A and C. That could be it."

"But it's not the first and third letter." He wasn't thinking. "Because it doesn't work. It's got to be something else. People use initials, James. Even when they install our security systems. We

232

always suggest a random number because it's much safer. But they end up putting in the kid's birthday or their wedding date or—"

"Their initials?"

"Yeah. Like, Sandy Conroy. S.C."

James glanced again at the keyboard. "One letter off. If you thought Conroy was punching in an *A*, it could have been an *S*. *SC*. The *A* is right next to the *S*. Could be his initials."

"Could be." I'd studied Sandy Conroy at his computer for ten minutes. Watched the video over and over. I was certain it was *AC*.

"You were trying to see his code from up there. That's quite a ways." He pointed toward the new smoke detector.

I sat back down behind the desk. "Some systems only let you try the code twice before they shut down. If I punch another code in that's not right, this thing could freeze up."

James leaned over, putting both his hands on the desk. "This isn't one of those systems. I can feel it, amigo. Punch the code back in and substitute an *S* for the *A*.

I punched the code slowly, as if each number and the final two letters were precious cargo and I was scared of breaking them.

305-805-500-1SC

Nothing happened. I stared at the screen, concentrating with all my might. I thought that if I focused all my energy on that code it would complete the cycle, and we'd be inside Conroy's information bank.

Then, as if hit by a sudden bolt of lightning, the screen went black. Dark, dark black, and I felt my heart drop into my stomach. I could almost hear the power system drop away to nothing. "We're screwed, James." For a second I couldn't breathe. "Really screwed. Honest to God. It's gone. The entire computer just shut down."

"No." James took three big steps and came to the back of the desk, peering over my shoulder. "Oh, shit. This can't be good."

"It could get worse. Tomorrow morning he'll know someone tried to hack the system."

"Damn. What if it alerts him at home? I mean right now. Could this system alert the cops? Jeez, Skip, would that be possible?" His eyes were wide open and I could see his fear.

"We are so screwed." I wanted to bolt from the office, run screaming down the hall, grab Em, and get out of the front door before anyone had a chance to react. The screen had shut down, gone black, and everything was deathly quiet. There was no hum of the computer, not even the sound of James breathing. I was shaking and my palms were moist as I watched a gradual gentle light spread across the computer's flat screen, and a soft green background frame the emerging words.

Welcome Sandler. What program would you like to open?

CHAPTER FORTY-ONE

"I hope that when the world comes to an end, I can breathe a sigh of relief, because there will be so much to look forward to." James was taking deep breaths of relief as he spoke. I knew exactly how he felt.

"*Donnie Darko*, right?"

"Pard, I don't even know what movie it's from right now, but I am extremely excited to see that screen light back up."

"Brings up another point, James. He still may have something on here that tells him a program was compromised."

"We're inside. That's all that matters right now."

I studied the screen. A list of prompts was lined up on the left side, and I read each one carefully.

"Codes." James was ahead of me.

I hit *Codes* and watched the screen open up. There was a series of numbers, each one highlighted with a name. Number seven on the list was 305-805-500-1SC (computer code).

"And look at that. There's the safe combination. Where the hell does he have a safe?"

"James, we could break into just about anything this guy has. How can someone just leave this stuff on his computer?"

We read through the list. There were codes for ATMs, savings accounts, checking accounts, market accounts, insurance accounts, and several coded accounts that I didn't understand.

"You know, we don't get it, because we're not there yet." James tapped his fingers on the desk, still over my shoulder and breathing down my neck.

"We're not where?"

"If we had the kind of money this guy has, maybe we'd understand."

"No. If I had the kind of money this guy has, I'd be protecting my codes. That's what I'd be doing."

"Dude, he is."

"Is what?"

"Protecting his accounts, his codes, man."

"James, we're reading his private information. How is that protecting his accounts? I can see every one of them. If I can break in, then —"

"Skip, think about it. If we hadn't had a camera on the ceiling, this stuff would be totally private."

You can't plan on everything. And you never planned on a ceiling camera. James had a point. "So you're saying no matter how secure you are, you can never be as secure as you need to be?"

"I'm just saying, pardner."

"You're probably right."

"Try DOD."

It seemed as good as any other. I moved the arrow to DOD and pushed enter. A small box flashed in the lower left-hand corner.

Blocked

"Won't open."

"Two minutes ago you said the same thing about his computer."

236

"James," he was frustrating at times. Most of the time. "I don't have a clue how to unblock this."

I could feel his hot breath as he leaned in closer, scanning the computer screen. "There's an open box in the upper right-hand corner. See it? It says 'information.'"

"So?"

"Type in DOD."

"What the hell *is* DOD?"

"We'll never know if you don't get busy and type that in."

I did.

"Push enter."

I did. The screen went black, and I'll admit that my stomach knotted up and my chest was tight, but I had faith this time. The screen opened back up.

"There it is, pally."

The words on the screen explained a lot. Department of Defense. DOD.

I dragged the arrow to enter. The next page opened like an orchid blossom, and I watched as the words spread into outline form on the screen.

"Can we print this?"

"James, if we try to print this —"

"We don't have time to read it all here."

"Why should we read it at all?" I was getting cold feet. Hadn't heard from Em in seven minutes, and every tick of the clock was pushing us to the opening hour.

"Read it, but do it fast."

We both stared at the screen, reading the first page.

Ralph Walters: Original contact person with DOD
           (too many questions)

Jason Riley: DOD contact

Tony Quatman: Developer (wants a larger cut)
Feng: Contact between project and Chen's group
Chen: Contact to China group

Riley says DOD has made a decision to change computer codes once security system is installed. Necessitates stepping up date to receive current codes.

Feng must impress importance on Riley. Convince Riley that we need to go into system early, preparing system for security software.

I turned and looked at James. "There's a Chinese group involved."

"And what does that have to do with stepping up the time-table on codes?"

"Damned if I know."

James stayed over my shoulder, and I could almost feel his eyes boring into Conroy's computer screen. "How do you see this, Skip?"

"It seems that the Department of Defense is going to do the same thing Synco Systems is doing with *our* security system. Right now, while we're installing the system, things are a little loose. As soon as we activate the controls and Synco changes all the codes, it will be very hard to get into this facility." I sat back in the chair, rereading the first page.

"And when Synco Systems gets the codes for the Defense Department computer system, things will be a little loose over at the DOD." James was tapping his fingers on the desk again. "Then, when Synco finishes the install, the department will change all the codes and it will be next to impossible to break into their computer system, right?"

"Right."

"We waltzed in here tonight because things are loose."

I couldn't help but smile. "Only temporarily, James. But you're right. They're very loose."

"So someone could conceivably waltz into the Defense Department during that lapse between security systems."

"They could. Their computer system will be vulnerable."

"How about Feng? Chen?"

"You think—"

I jumped when I heard the sharp rap on the door.

"What?"

James bolted from behind the desk and had the door open in two seconds.

"A car pulled up. Yellow Lotus or something very fancy." Em's eyes were opened wide and she was short of breath.

"It's Conroy. What the hell is he doing here at this hour of the morning?"

"What the hell are *we* doing here?"

"Em, is he coming in?"

"Skip, I don't think he pulled into the lot to stargaze."

I hit the shutdown button and watched the flickering light go dark. This time I was thankful for the blackout.

"Where do we go, amigo?"

I grabbed my laptop, and the three of us walked out of the office, carefully closing the door behind us.

"The rear hallway, behind the offices. It leads to an emergency exit. We can hide back there."

"If he—"

"He won't. There's no reason for him to go back there." My heart was racing as I led the way.

"If it's an exit, why don't we—"

"Because I don't have the code."

Em put her hand on my arm. "What happens if we just push it open and walk out? Do you need a code to exit?"

I thought about it for a second. "I don't know. But if we try that," I glanced over my shoulder as we hustled toward the rear of the building, no sign yet of anyone entering the building, "there's a good chance that an alarm would go off."

"We don't need that to happen on top of everything else." James shook his head.

"Right here. He'll never come back this far."

"You're sure?"

"Won't happen."

We were quiet, the only noise that I could hear was that of the air-conditioning system and our heavy breathing.

Then came the footsteps, slapping on the tile floor. More than one person. And laughter. A woman's high-pitched giggle.

In a whisper James said, "Sarah's with him."

I considered the possibilities. Conroy had forgotten something from his office and Sarah had been with him when he remembered. Or maybe they had a room here. Maybe one of the offices I hadn't seen yet. A love nest. At this level of money and power, anything was possible.

Their muffled conversation echoed as they entered the work area. And then as if someone flipped a switch, their voices were crystal clear.

"So I had the one kid in here tonight." Conroy's voice. "That smoke detector they put in my office went off for no reason. Scared the crap out of me. Thing must have had a short in it or something. It wasn't his fault, but I chewed his ass out anyway. This whole project has got me on edge."

I waited for a response, but no one else spoke. Maybe he was on his cell phone, telling someone else the story.

He started again. "If DOD hadn't demanded the system be updated, we wouldn't have to worry about these bozos. They're idiots. The other kid runs into the parking lot thinking he's got a bomb in his hands? What was with that?"

Then the female voice. "They'll be out of here in two days. And when this all comes down, they'll be part of the confusion. They won't have a clue, but they'll be up to their necks in this. Trust me. This will work."

James frowned, looking at me as we pressed our backs to the wall. He shook his head back and forth, and I knew exactly what he was getting at. Conroy wasn't with Sarah. The woman's voice belonged to his wife, Carol Conroy.

CHAPTER FORTY-TWO

"I have a bad feeling about those two."

"If you hadn't had Feng put the GPS unit under their truck, nothing would have happened."

The room was cool, but there was a cold sweat on my forehead. I wiped it with my hand, and listened intently to the movement of the voices. I was guessing they were now in Conroy's office with the door open. Maybe only twenty feet from where we stood, but around the corner and inside the office. We could still make out the conversation, but it was more distant now.

"He didn't trust them."

"He didn't trust *me* either. Trying to put a GPS on my car in the middle of Miami." She laughed again. "He almost got caught."

"Yeah. And what were you doing with the kid? At some dive like the Red Derby?"

"Setting him up, Sandy. I told you. When it all shakes out, you're going to be very pleased. Just get the codes, get the passwords, and get out of the way."

"Setting him up?"

"I don't know how to say this any other way. Get out of the way and just do your job. Understood? After everything you've done, I don't think I have to explain myself to you."

Silence. I figured they walked out of hearing range. Then Conroy spoke up. "You've got it all worked out with Chen and his group?"

"Honey, stay out of the way."

"Your dad is not going to go down easy."

"My father isn't going to know what hit him."

"Carol, tell me there won't be anymore like Ralph Walters or Tony Quatman."

Everything was still, and I wiped my brow again. Em just stood there, bathed in the eerie security lights, and James was chewing on his bottom lip.

"There's over seventy-five million dollars at stake here, Sandy. I'm not promising anything."

I saw James whip his head around and stare in my direction. Almost as if he thought I knew about the money. I'd never in my life heard figures like that being tossed around. $75,000,000?

"Babe, I've got this feeling that the two kids —" He paused, and I knew he was talking about James and me. "Those two punks are keeping an eye on me."

"You're imagining things." She was quick with the come-back. Almost too quick.

"Am I?"

"They're not bright enough to keep an eye on anybody. And after what happened to them tonight, I don't think they're going to give us any trouble."

"What happened?"

"There was a little warning."

"Oh, man. What kind of warning?"

"Trust me, they're going to go about their business very quietly from this point on. They'll finish the installation, and we won't hear from them again. When the entire plan unfolds, they'll appear to be right in the thick of it. Just drop it, okay? All I want you to worry about is getting those damned codes. I trust you haven't told anyone anything they didn't need to know?"

"For your eyes only kind of stuff, yeah. Feng is the only one, and since he's our main contact—"

"And sweet little Sarah? She's none the wiser?"

Now the voices were traveling, more and more distant and muffled as if they were headed for the exit.

"She knows there's a bonus and that I'm taking her away from all of this."

"You were a fool to ever get involved."

"We've been through this—"

"I know. But I'm not going to forget that it happened. I will never forgive you for that. Never. Regardless, your Sarah will be the easiest one to take a fall. I wish I could—I wish *we* could be here to see it."

I was straining to hear their words.

"The damndest part of this is we're ready to start making the software, and we can have it installed within two weeks. Two weeks, Carol. If it wasn't for Jason Riley and the government watchdogs, we never would have had to put in this useless security system. By the time they actually activate it, we won't even need it."

"We never needed it. But the two boys play right into our strategy. I told you, don't worry about it."

Just before we lost their conversation altogether I heard Conroy say, "If Sarah is the easiest one to take down, who's the second easiest to take a fall?"

Carol Conroy's harsh laugh rolled down the hallway.

CHAPTER FORTY-THREE

We waited a good two minutes. If they were still in the building there was no sign of it. "I think we can give the all-clear sign."

"Jesus."

"Being the religious man that you are, James, you can say a prayer of thanks that we didn't get caught."

"The Lord's will, Skip. It was the Lord's will." This time I think he meant it, and I wasn't going to argue with him.

"Obviously, you guys know a whole lot more about this than you've told me." Em was miffed. Big time. "Maybe we should share a little bit more."

She's a turn-on even when she's mad. None of us spoke again until we were in the truck and rolling home.

"I'm not sure we know enough to piece it all together." James kept his eyes straight ahead, staring into the inky blackness as the potholes in the asphalt jolted our truck's suspension system, shaking us down to our molars.

"Em, we really don't know what's going on."

"Well, I can tell you something about that conversation back there. Carol Conroy is high maintenance and a total control freak. What a bitch." Em could certainly call them.

We bounced out of a hole or crack and it felt like the bottom had dropped from the truck.

"I don't want to believe that Carol Conroy orchestrated the death of Walters, but Sandy hinted that—"

"James. There were a lot of things I don't want to believe about that conversation. They're going to try to surprise her father—"

"And not in a good way."

"They're going to take down Sarah."

"And somehow implicate us? And we're still not sure what we're going to be implicated in." I needed a beer. Or a deep sleep.

"You keep saying *they*." Em rested her hand gently on my thigh. "Skip, it's not *they*."

James gave her a brief look, a frown visible by the dashboard lights. "There were two of them in the building, Em. I was there."

"There were two of them James, but you and I must have heard two different conversations."

"Okay," he gripped the steering wheel, "you tell me your version."

"Sandy Conroy said 'those two punks are keeping an eye on me.'"

How were we ever going to forget that statement?

"So far we heard the same conversation."

"And Carol Conroy responded with 'You're imagining things. They're not bright enough to keep an eye on anyone.'"

"A slam. We heard it, Em."

"Don't you get it James? Skip? She's the one who asked you to spy on him. And then she gives him that answer?"

"And your point is?"

"She's telling him that you're not bright enough to pull it off.

She jumped right in and said it could never happen. After she *knew* it had already happened. She has the proof. She has the transcript you took off the computer card."

"You're right." James was shaking his head up and down.

"Why would she say that? Why wouldn't she tell him that you had put up the bogus smoke detector? I don't think *they* are going to take down Sarah. *They* are not going to surprise her father. *They* are not going to involve you guys."

"She said they were. Why would she say that?"

"She lied to him, Skip. Don't you get it? She's planning on pulling something off by herself. She's going to do the dirty work. She's not going to involve him."

"Why not? Why not involve Sandler Conroy? The philandering husband? What's going to happen to him? Is he going to be left out in the cold?"

"When he said 'please tell me there won't be anymore like Ralph Walters or Tony Quatman,' do you remember what she said?"

I did. I'd practically memorized that short conversation. "She said she couldn't promise that. There was seventy-five million dollars at stake."

"I definitely remember the seventy-five million dollars." We had James's attention. "What could be worth that kind of money?"

"Well, if it was murder, if somebody killed Ralph Walters or maybe Tony Quatman, too, the next person to be murdered isn't going to be Carol Conroy."

James braked for the stoplight. At this hour of the morning, there was no one except us on the street, and with our bad brakes he should have just coasted through the intersection. The screech of brakes grinding metal on metal sent shivers through my body.

"The whole reason we're involved in this spy thing is because Carol Conroy is concerned for her life." She'd told me that at the Red Derby.

"That's what she told you. But think about the conversation you just heard."

Damn. Em was right. After what we'd heard tonight, it all made perfect sense. "It's going to be Sandy Conroy. That's what you're getting at isn't it? She's setting him up to be killed. It has to be him. He knows too much."

"My guess." There was a self–satisfied tone in her voice. Almost like a vocal smirk.

"Too much about what?" James pulled into our parking lot and his headlights hit the plywood window covers of our apartment. "What information does Conroy have? We don't have a clue, do we?"

"It has to do with codes and passwords. It has to do with Feng and Chen. It has to do with Walters and Conroy and Sarah and Carol Conroy. That's what it's about." I was suddenly very tired, and very pissed off. This entire day seemed like a really bad dream.

"Want to spend what's left of the night together?" I put my arm around her, half hoping she'd say yes, and half hoping she'd say no.

Em gave me a brief hug, then pushed off. "No offense, but this isn't the safest place to be right now. I think I'll just drive home."

I totally understood. I wasn't sure even James and I should be sleeping here tonight. Somewhere nearby there was a shooter on the loose. "Be careful." I kissed her.

"*You* be careful."

"We'll be fine." Bluff and bravado. Always trying to be a little more macho than I really felt.

"Skip," she leaned in again and gave me one more tight hug, "I'm serious. Watch yourself because I seriously think that lady may be planning on taking care of you and James, too."

She didn't have to explain what *taking care of* meant.

CHAPTER FORTY-FOUR

"We'll clean up the broken glass in the morning, pard."

The we would be me. Splinters of sharp-edged glass littered the cheap gray carpet and vinyl kitchen floor, and I didn't want to think about it.

"Do you think Carol Conroy is a killer?" James opened the refrigerator.

"They're all gone." We'd finished the last cold beer before our little adventure. "We're going to have to drink it warm, man."

He reached down into the case I'd just purchased and pulled out two bottles. Pitching one to me he popped the top on his and took a long swallow. "Warm, cold, it's still better than water."

"What the hell was that all about tonight? It's like we should be calling the cops, but we don't know what to tell them. Is Carol Conroy a killer? That's not possible."

"Compadre, you told your girlfriend that you thought Mrs. Conroy might kill Sandy Conroy. Your girlfriend thinks Mrs. C. may be out to kill us."

"There's that."

The pounding on the door made me almost drop my beer. I

glanced at James and he shrugged his shoulders. Three in the morning. Nobody stops by for a social visit at three a.m. Well, in college you stopped by twenty-four hours a day. For a cigarette, a beer, or a shoulder to lean on. But in the adult world —

James pulled the door open and I half expected someone with a gun. Or a cop. Or maybe Carol Conroy. Or Em.

"Hi, guys. Sorry to bother you so late, but I couldn't sleep and I thought I should share some information with you." Jim Jobs, in his boxer shorts and a sleeveless undershirt, walked into our apartment.

"Watch your feet, dude." James was looking at the floor where J.J.'s bare feet were walking through the slivers of window glass and pieces of blown-up computer.

"I saw the car."

"You want a beer?" James stood by the cardboard case, ready to serve my beverages at this ungodly hour of the morning.

"Sure."

"It's warm."

"Still better than water."

James tossed him a bottle.

I couldn't believe it. Better than water? "You saw what car? You mean the truck?"

"No. *The* car. The two guys pulled in, parked across the lot, and took four shots at your apartment. I saw it."

It occurred to me that I'd seen a car pull in just before the shots. The one with no headlights. "Did you see what kind it was?"

"I did. Couldn't make out the two characters inside, but there's no doubt they stuck a rifle out the window and took those shots." For the first time he started looking around. "Man, they really messed your place up."

"Have a seat," James said. The three of us straddled our three kitchen table chairs and we proceeded to take deep swallows — of warm, bitter beer.

"Skip," J.J. never looked at me, just stroked his bottle and looked at the floor, "I questioned you the other day about that smoke detector. It wasn't that I was trying to run the show—I mean, God knows I'm grateful to you for the job."

And he should have been.

"But there are a lot of strange things going on in that place."

James gulped his next swallow. He could drain a bottle in two swallows if he put his mind to it. Finally, he caught his breath and said, "More than you know, Jim. More than you know."

"Well, I think I've got it figured out."

A little magic, a little sleight of hand. James, Em, and I had been working on it hands-on, and this presumptuous bastard thought he'd figured it out?

"Why don't you tell us what you think is happening?" James had a look of genuine curiosity on his face.

"Could be wrong, boys. Could be wrong." He scratched himself through his shorts and I had to look away. "These guys at Synco Systems are putting in your security system to protect their secrets, right?"

I didn't want to be cynical, but I couldn't help myself. "It's usually the reason people put in security systems."

"But there's some secrets that aren't normal. That head of security guy—Feng. He's sneaking out to the parking lot and talking to another Asian guy. Sometimes two and three times a day."

I hadn't noticed that.

"And the president, that Conroy fellow, he's got Feng in his office ten times a day. It's not like there's a big leak in the security around there. So I say to myself, why all this secret stuff? What's the big deal?"

James nodded. "So what did you come up with?"

"Well, Synco Systems is working on a security system for the Department of Defense, right?"

I was somewhat taken back. "How do you know that?"

J.J. put the beer down on our coffee table and rubbed his hands together. "They got maybe forty, fifty people working there. You can't keep a secret from forty or fifty people. Gossip is thick in that place."

This little guy was just a runner. And in the short span of three days he'd been promoted to temporary operation director by Andy Wireman, he'd questioned my decision to put in a smoke detector, and he'd picked up on the DOD, plus he'd listened in on plant gossip. He put James and me to shame.

"What was the gossip?"

"Like I said. This project that they're working on is being delivered to the Department of Defense. The department in charge of defense of the entire United States of America. The defense of our country, Skip. Now come on. That's pretty heavy stuff. Am I right?"

Actually, it was pretty heavy stuff. "And?" I didn't think he had a clue.

"And? Listen to me, Mr. Moore. When a Chinese guy — two Chinese guys — get together and have secret parking lot meetings, when one of those guys is working on a top secret project for the Department of Defense, I get worried."

"And what do you think they're talking about? What do you think these meetings are about?" James, Em, and I had all waltzed around the idea. But we'd never committed. This little weasel, this handyman who'd threatened me after I got him his job, this guy was going to lay it all out for us? I couldn't believe it.

"You need security codes to put in a computer system."

"And?" I didn't want him to say it. I didn't want this to be true. I wanted my money from Synco Systems, from Sarah, and from Carol Conroy. Whoever shot up our apartment, it was all a mistake. The Feng and Chen connection, just a coincidence. The conversation we'd heard earlier tonight, totally out of context. Everything was going to be fine when we got up in, in about four hours.

"And? Are you kidding me? The Department of Defense is going to have to give security codes to Synco Systems so Synco can install the software. And when they do, the Chinese guys can steal every frigging secret in the entire system."

James stood up, walked to the case, and pulled three more warm beers. He distributed them to us, then straddled his chair again. "Every frigging secret?"

"Every secret. About nuclear weapons. About new technology. About battle plans, spy networks, and whatever else the Department of Defense deals with."

"Jesus." James put the bottle to his mouth, closed his eyes, and we were all silent for about twenty seconds as he drained the beer.

"You know this? For a fact?" I so didn't want this to be the truth.

"No. No. Hey, settle down. I could be wrong."

James's eyes rolled, possibly because of J.J.'s accusation, possibly because the beer was overwhelming his brain. "Our government isn't that dumb. Do you understand me? The Chi Mak thing, the guy who stole missile secrets, that was because a trusted engineer was able to steal stuff he was inventing. It's not the same, J.J."

Jim Jobs gave him a blank stare. He obviously had never heard of Chi Mak or the stolen documents case.

"Our government isn't going to just give up all their secrets to some stranger. Or the enemy. We're not going to make that mistake again. We learned our lesson. I'm convinced of it."

"James, it happens."

"But not like this. They don't just open up their systems to somebody without a safety check. Do they?"

"It happens every day." J.J. took a short swallow of beer. There was a tremor in his hands and I thought he might spill his drink. "There was a story the other day, *Wall Street Journal*, some hotshot from DOD was storing some of the department's sensitive information on his home computer."

"Home computer?"

"Yep. Let me tell you something else. I used to work for a subcontractor for the Rocky Flats plant outside Denver. They make nuclear weapons."

"What does that have to do with computer codes?" James was obviously agitated.

"I'll tell you what it has to do with security. One of the laptop computers with serious information went missing while I was there."

"And?"

J.J. stood up, tugging on the boxer shorts. "I'm trying to tell you. I was accused of stealing the computer, and trying to steal government secrets."

"You?" I couldn't believe it. This strange neighbor whom I didn't trust at all was telling us that he'd been implicated in a major government scandal.

"Me. They couldn't find any evidence, and eventually I was cleared. Fired from the job, but cleared." From a nuclear spy to neighborhood handyman. Someday I wanted to explore that journey.

"Do you know who stole the computer?" Still not certain this guy was giving me the truth, I wanted some closure to the story.

"Ended up being three computers. Eventually four. By the time the third one went missing, they decided not to prosecute anyone. It was too damned embarrassing. Our government can't keep anything a secret. So don't assume that the Department of Defense won't open up their entire system to Synco Systems.

And if they do, it could be the single biggest security breach in the history of the United States."

There it was. A real possibility.

"Jim, this really happened to you?" James was staring at him, wide eyed.

"I could never make up a story like that. And do I know who stole the computers? Everyone knew. Even the guys investigating the crime. But it's all political. And if we had called *them* in on it, *they* would call us in on our thefts. And we're stealing information from countries all over the world. It's a treacherous game we play, boys. Treacherous."

"So you're telling me that this happens all the time?"

J.J. took the last swallow of beer. Scratching himself again, he moved toward the door. "I'm a simple handyman. I never stole a thing in my life—except a pack of lifesavers when I was seven. That's all I know for sure. But what's happening at Synco Systems is damned suspicious."

I watched as he turned the door handle and pushed the door open. "J.J., wait."

"What's that?" He turned.

"You saw the car? The one with the shooter who shot our windows out?"

"I did."

"Well, what was it?"

"It was a Honda Accord, Skip. Same kind that Feng drives."

CHAPTER FORTY-FIVE

I fell asleep sitting on the sofa with the beer in my hand. It had happened before, but usually because I'd had too many beers in my hand in the preceding hours. Now, it was because I was exhausted.

I woke up to Springsteen singing "Born in the U.S.A." I flipped open my cell phone and I'm sure the word I answered with was something like 'lo.

"Is this Water Connection Plumbing?"

"Huh?" I checked out my watch, and in the dark, with fog covering my eyes I think it said 4:30.

"This isn't Water Connection Plumbing?"

"No, this is . . . yes. Yes it is." They'd seen us. It came back fast. Someone had seen the truck and was checking up on us. Now what was I going to say? Got a problem? We'll be there in a jiffy. We'll have that toilet clog cleaned out in no time. And then I wondered if it was someone who knew me. Conroy? Feng? And would they recognize my voice and know that I wasn't a plumber? I had that sinking feeling that I might be caught. I

knew the feeling well. It had been coming about every two or
three hours for the last three days.

Once again. "This *is* Water Connection Plumbing?"

"Yeah. It sure is." I spoke a little deeper. Growling. Maybe
they wouldn't know it was me.

There was a long silence on the other end, and I closed my
eyes. This plumbing thing had been a bad idea from the beginning. Finally, "Well, your truck is about four doors down from
our apartment and we've got a leaking faucet that's kept me up
most of the night. Is there any chance that you could —"

I closed the phone, unlocked the front door, walked outside,
and stripped the vinyl magnetic banners from both sides of the
truck. Rolling them up, I threw them in the driver's side, and
stomped back into our condo.

James was snoring peacefully as I shoved open his door. The
catch had never worked on the cheap hollow piece of pressed
wood and it crashed against the wall. He kept on snoring.

"James." I shouted out his name as his snoring drowned me
out.

Walking to his bed, a metal frame, mattress, and cheap box
springs, I shook him.

"Um." He sputtered.

"Wake up."

"Mmm?"

"Wake up."

"What? Are the cops here?"

"No. Someone just called and asked about Water
Connection Plumbing."

"Mmmm?"

"Get up. We need to talk."

James struggled with the top sheet, twisting it, and finally
freeing himself. He staggered to his feet, standing there in his

boxer shorts, looking like a taller version of Jim Jobs. "What's all this about, Skip?"

"First of all, people thinking we're plumbers. Not a good idea."

He just did an elaborate nod, not fully awake.

"Second of all," I was wide awake and ready to take some action, "we need to review that smoke detector camera card."

"Oh yeah?"

"Oh yeah. There were some things said that don't match the conversation we heard tonight between Carol Conroy and Sandy."

"So am I being paid overtime?"

"You're the one who started this spy stuff, so don't give me any crap about overtime. Okay?"

James staggered to the doorway, walking out into the living area. "Okay. Let's view the movie, amigo."

I'd thought about it. Carol Conroy couldn't involve us with any degree of evidence. She had nothing. There were no witnesses at the Red Derby, no one had taped my conversations with Sarah — at least I didn't think they had — and the rapport that James and I had was very private. What kind of evidence did Mrs. Conroy have that would implicate us in any of this sordid mess?

"The movie, Skip."

I unfolded the computer and turned it on, clicking on the icon for the small video disk.

Not available. Disk missing

I tried it again.

Not available. Disk missing.

"Hold on, James." I pushed on the slot where the disk was, hoping it would pop out. There was nothing.

"What's going on, pal?"

"You know that digital card from the smoke detector?"

"Sure. You got it back when Conroy told you to take the smoke detector and leave, right?"

"That's the one."

So what's your problem?"

"Well, it only plays back when you have it in the computer."

"So play it."

"James, did you take it out?"

"Absolutely not."

"For any reason at all?"

"Skip, I did not touch it."

I'd picked up the detector about thirteen hours ago. The card was in it. I'd seen it myself. I rubbed my eyes, thinking.

"Kemo Sabe, if it was in the smoke detector, we might try looking there."

Of course. Breathing a sigh of relief, I walked into the kitchen and flipped over the two plastic pieces of the detector. I hadn't moved them since I walked in and found Carol Conroy in our restroom. I held the loaded side up and looked inside. The card was gone.

CHAPTER FORTY-SIX

"Carol Conroy. It's got to be." James was talking softly, not wanting to bother the neighbors. Although the gunfire, the construction company nailing plywood on our windows, our all-night visitors, and our on-again, off-again plumbing business had probably bothered them already. He puffed on a cigarette and drank an RC Cola from the can. "It just makes sense, Skip. You came in and mentioned the camera. Remember? She walked out and said 'You had a camera?' first thing."

As we sat in the gloom on our cheap lawn chairs, we could hear birds waking in the distance, and I sniffed the air, smelling someone's rotting garbage in a can down the way. Our back porch. Love it or leave it.

"She's got the proof."

"She wasn't the only one in there tonight, James." It had been like Grand Central Station. "Think about it. J.J. was there."

"Point taken. He didn't want you to put up the smoke alarm. Maybe he knew it was a camera and he lifted the card."

I glanced down at Jim Jobs's rear door, hanging by one

hinge. "The guy seems to know a lot about what's apparently going on."

"He does."

"And the three cops. Those two guys who interviewed us and the one who checked the parking lot and interviewed the neighbors. All three were in the apartment."

James shook his head, leaning back and drinking his RC. "And," he belched quietly, "Em."

"Em?"

"She's on the list of visitors tonight, pard."

"Em didn't take the card."

"She knew where it was. That's all I'm saying."

"Two guys from Twenty-Four Seven. Both those guys were inside when they boarded up the windows."

"Man, we had a boatload of company tonight. That makes eight people, Skip."

We both sat there, listening to the noise of people waking up. A car with a noisy muffler started out front and the squeaking of bedsprings and a frame was playing in rhythm about two apartments to our right through an open window.

"Somebody's starting the day off with a bang." James tossed the empty can at our trash container. Of course, he missed.

"So what do we do, James? If Carol Conroy wants to involve us down the road, she's got the card. If she can prove that we installed the smoke detector, we're screwed."

"We're probably screwed for a lot of other reasons as well," he said.

"Give me a cigarette."

"What? You don't smoke anymore."

"Give me a damned cigarette." It had been a rough twenty-four hours.

James pulled the crumpled pack from his pants pocket and

shook out a forlorn looking smoke. He handed me his matches.

"I don't want the matches." I stuck the cigarette in my mouth and sucked on the filter.

"They're close, James. Threatening us, stealing the card, all the other stuff going on, I think they're getting the codes soon. Maybe today."

"And then what happens?"

"My guess, okay? Synco sends two installers to the Department of Defense. They tell the bigwigs there that they need to get into the computers and get them ready for this new software. The minute they enter the codes, they start downloading. They know exactly what they're looking for, and by Monday there are no more secrets. It's all in the hands of Chen or Feng or whoever is paying seventy-five million dollars."

"You're crazy. This is the United States Government. They're a little more sophisticated than that." My roommate was usually the cynic. This time he was taking the side of the government. My rebellious roommate who hated the cops and any other form of authority. He was backing the Department of Defense. The thought actually depressed me.

In the early gray morning, James stood up and gave me a cold, hard look. "There may be something going on, Skip, but you don't just walk into a government agency and steal them blind."

"Have you been listening, man? You've heard the same stories I heard tonight, James. J.J. and the briefcases. Chi Mak, who just e-mailed the secrets to his home computer. It was that simple. We've read stories about missing uranium, government secrets, the KGB—I mean there must be hundreds of other stories. Security is a joke. Look how easy it's been for us to walk through Synco. Hell, we opened up Conroy's computer, James. And we didn't even know what we were doing. Installed a smoke detector that doubled as a camera. Compromising these agencies, these groups, is just too easy. Think about it. I mean, two complete idiots like us, we're accidentally able to identify a national security issue. How safe is that?" I'd raised my voice and he raised his eyebrows. "And Synco Systems is a company that has a contract with the federal government. I can't even get my mind around this. You and I just strolled in and walked out with some very scary information. You know I'm right."

He walked to the concrete wall and slammed his fist against it. "Ouch."

"James, we've got to go to work."

"Knowing that Feng tried to kill us last night. Do you think it's safe to ever go back there?"

"He's not going to kill us at work."

"Skip, I wouldn't be surprised at anything that happened after last night." He spit on the concrete and opened the door.

"Born in the U.S.A." blared from my phone. I didn't even look at the number. Anyone who called was probably trouble.

"Skip, are you there?"

"Yeah, Michael. What's up." I felt whatever energy I had start to drain.

"Listen, Skip, we've got a bit of a problem."

I wanted to tell him he had no idea how big our problem was, but I waited for him to tell me his "bit of a problem."

"Top guy says no-go on the hookup until we get our money."

I'd seen it coming. I wasn't totally ready for it, thinking that maybe there would be a last minute save, but I'd seen it coming. "You haven't gotten the down payment, right? She was supposed to send it, Michael."

"That's why you're my top guy, Skip." Sarcasm was creeping into his voice. "You're so good at figuring these things out."

I wanted to go right through the phone and strangle him. "I'm going in to Sandy Conroy's office this morning, Michael. I'll confront him and get at least half the money. Can we turn it on for half the money?"

"You get half and I'll see what I can do, Skip. I'll see, okay?" He waited for an answer I never gave him.

I flipped the phone closed. Conroy didn't know what we knew. He didn't have a clue. He was still playing it straight up, like everything was okay. Maybe he'd give me the down payment. Maybe he'd give me the entire amount. Sure, this was doable. Sandy Conroy wanted everyone to assume that it was business as usual. He wanted to be the upstanding businessman. Therefore he'd pay the bill. If he paid the bill, then everything would appear to be all right. And right now, just before all hell broke loose, Conroy needed things to appear to be all right. Right? This was going to work out. I was convinced. For that moment.

"I'm going in for the money, James." James was no longer there. He'd gone inside to take a shower, get dressed for work, take a powder. Whatever it was, he'd left me on the porch by myself. "I'm going to walk into Conroy's office and walk out with a check," I yelled through the back door. Damn the neighbors. I was working my ass off, almost getting killed in the process, and somebody was going to pay me for my time.

CHAPTER FORTY-SEVEN

James drove the truck. Minus the Water Connection signs. We'd left early enough that last night's caller was probably unaware I'd stripped the signs from the doors. James just shrugged his shoulder and tossed the rolled up vinyl on the floor.

"What are you going to say, pard?"

"That we've done the work and haven't been paid."

"Sarah was supposed to —"

"Forget Sarah. Remember? She's going to be the first one they throw under the bus." I had no idea where that statement started, but it seemed to fit.

"We could tell her."

"Yeah. That's exactly what we want to do. Tell the hooker that she's going to be betrayed. Listen, James, I want my money. We're — I'm walking a very thin line here. *I* still stand to make a lot of money. I'm not giving up on that dream. You, James, you screw it up and I'll make your life miserable."

"Screw it up?"

"Yeah. Get a moment of moral superiority and tell Sarah? Or mention this to someone else."

"Amigo —"

"Don't amigo me."

"You're my roommate, Skip."

"Yeah?"

"My best friend."

"Thanks, man." I softened.

"No, what I'm saying is that you hired me for this job."

"I did."

"You got me into this mess."

I had no comeback.

"And ever since we've been working for Synco Systems, my life has *been* miserable, so how is this going to change things?"

I refrained from slugging him.

We arrived fifteen minutes early. I didn't see the yellow sports car, but then again I'd never seen it any other morning. Maybe he parked it in a private spot.

"There's one good thing about today, pard."

"Name one thing, James. I'd love to hear it."

"It's Friday."

"Yeah?"

"Date night."

"Ah, yes, the lovely Eden Callahan."

"Who knows, man?"

"I hope she doesn't bring the tear gas and the gun."

"Handcuffs maybe." He grinned. We got out of the truck.

Sarah met us at the door in a short, silver skirt and scarlet blouse. "He's not in a good mood, guys." She wore a fragile frown.

"Something we did?"

"Something about a smoke detector? And it appears that someone hacked his computer last night."

My chest tightened up, and I had trouble catching the next breath. I just didn't think that was going to happen.

"How do you do that?" James asked. His nervousness was apparent. "How would anyone hack Mr. Conroy's computer?"

"Well, I'm not sure, but I know that he called me in this morning, and—" I detected the tremor in her voice, "and he showed me the screen. He said there was a record of the sites that were visited and he asked me if I'd been—" she sniffed and I knew right away she was going to cry. "Oh, God, Skip. I wouldn't know how to hack anyone's computer." Tears rolled down her cheeks, and I felt about as low as I could. Not low enough to admit that I'd hacked it, but almost that low.

"Hey, I'm sorry. The guy can apparently be a jerk, huh?" I took a tentative step toward her and gave her a hug, feeling her softness press into me. At that moment she felt very tender and frail.

"You know who I think used his computer?" Wiping her face with her hand, she pushed off me and stared into my eyes. Then she shifted to James.

"Maybe we don't want to know."

"Oh, I think you should know." She sniffed, and with her delicate condition it was hard to picture this creature as a call girl.

"Sarah, this isn't any of our business." James took a step back.

My dream of getting paid today was fading fast. Conroy was not a happy camper. We'd missed something last night. Some way to erase our activity on his computer. Sooner or later he'd figure it out. Sooner or later he'd realize that I had access last night. And there wasn't any feeble excuse I could think of to lie my way out of this. "Okay, who do you think used his computer?"

"The bitch. His high-and-mighty wife."

"Why do you say that?"

"Somebody saw her here last night. Early this morning."

Oh, man. If they saw her they probably saw us. "Who?"

"Follow me, Skip."

"Where are we going?"

"No. Follow my story. Sandy came in this morning and said his computer had been hacked."

"Okay."

"He tried to figure out who had access, and for some reason he thought of me. Me, Skip. And he knows how I feel about him."

"And you just told me you'd never do that."

"That's right. And he said if it wasn't me, then maybe it was Carol. He drove by last night and thought he saw her walking by the building."

"What?" James was giving her a very strange look. I tried to ward him off, giving him a "safe" sign with my hands.

"Maybe she went into the building and got into his computer. I think she did."

I felt certain that Carol Conroy was setting Sandy and Sarah up for a hard landing. She was planning on getting $75,000,000 and leaving the two of them and Feng to take the fall. I couldn't even fathom the depth of deception. But here was Sandy Conroy trying to blame his wife for rifling through his files.

"Sarah, do you think he's right? I mean, she's his wife."

I wanted him to shut up. Let the "bitch" suffer the consequences. It was okay with me, because I didn't want any blame.

Sarah shrugged her shoulders. "Anyway," she said, "the wicked witch is in his office right now, and I'm sure it's not pleasant." Sarah wiped her eyes, reached out and squeezed my hand, then walked back to her office. I stood there with my mouth hanging open.

"Dude, deception is the point! Any man can counter strength. But now he has to counter what he can't see." I thought he was done as he paused, but I was wrong. "And fear what he doesn't know." He rocked back and forth on the balls of his feet.

I stared at him. "What the hell are you saying?"

"It's from *The 13th Warrior*, Skip."

"Yeah?"

"I love that quote."

"What does it mean?"

James squinted and stroked his chin. "Doesn't it sort of fit this situation?"

"I asked you before, what does it mean?"

"I have no idea, Skip. No idea. I've just been waiting for an excuse to use it."

Walking past him, I headed for Conroy's door, full of bluff and bravado. I didn't believe I could actually pull it off, but if I didn't confront him now, I'd never get it done.

Feng appeared from nowhere, holding up his hand like a Gestapo officer, and stopped me as I entered the work area.

"Mr. Moore." He put his hand on my arm, and I shook him off.

"Don't touch me, Feng."

Giving me a wry smile he took a step back. "Speaking of touch, you're a little touchy today yourself."

"Somebody fires a gun into your home, you tend to be a little off your game."

"Someone fired a gun into your home?"

"I feel certain you know about that incident."

"As a matter of fact, I don't. But let me assure you, if you proceed to Mr. Conroy's office, your situation won't get any better." He crossed his arms, and puffed out his chest. "Whatever you think happened, things could be a lot worse."

I wasn't going to talk about it. Play it cool. But I was building a head of steam and this little guy was just the beginning. "How could they get worse, Feng? When someone in a car that looks like yours tried to kill me?"

Feng's eyes shifted, over my shoulder. "A car that looked like mine?"

"Where were you last night, Feng?" I was way off course. Just get the money, just get the money.

"Mr. Moore, Mr. Conroy is busy. Whatever your problem, it will have to wait."

"I'm going to see Conroy right now."

"Oh?"

"If your company doesn't pay my company the money you owe us, you'll never get your system turned on." I was in charge. The Person in Charge of the Project. No one seemed to respect that position.

"You're threatening to halt the project?"

I hadn't exactly talked to Wireman about it yet, but Michael had threatened me. I was just passing on the information. Person in charge and all that. "You heard me."

"Let me understand this." Feng hooked his thumbs in his belt. "You were shot at last night?"

"I was."

"And on an unrelated note, you feel someone owes you money?"

I was breathing fast and heavy. "I do. My company does."

"And you are threatening us with not completing the job if someone doesn't pay you?"

"You're brighter than I gave you credit for, Feng."

"I really am. You'd be surprised."

I thought of the little guy chasing around a UPS truck with our GPS unit under it.

"The accuracy of the shooter must have been poor."

"What does that mean?" He was back to the sniper.

"The next time, the assassin who planned your execution should hire someone who has a higher degree of accuracy."

Feng had pretty much told me that the intent was to kill me. I didn't know how to deal with that. I brushed past him, half expecting him to draw the pistol from his belt holster. Reaching

271

Conroy's door, I rapped on the solid wood. Once, twice, three times. The son of a bitch wasn't in. Or, he wasn't answering.

I glanced behind me and Feng stood there, his right hand now resting on the butt of his gun.

"Mr. Conroy," I shouted.

"Mr. Moore, I'm asking you to move." Feng was seething.

Once again I pounded on the door, finally slapping it with the heel of my hand. There was going to be a bruise there tomorrow. The door flew open and I took a big step back, staggering as Carol Conroy rushed out, looking neither right or left. Spinning around, she stared back into the office and calmly said, "Oh, you'll give them to me. Yes, you will. Today. Or so help me God, I will bury you." She blew by me like a hurricane, and before I could think, she was through the work area and into the hall on her way out.

We had already decided she was going to bury him. Now she was making it public. It sounded to me like Sandy Conroy had the codes, and if he did, this thing was going to go down quickly. If James and I were right, Carol Conroy was going to sabotage her daddy's company and take Sarah and possibly her husband down with it.

When I stepped into the doorway, Sandy Conroy was standing behind his desk, pointing his finger directly at me.

"Get the hell out of here, kid. Now." Fire shot from his eyes, but couldn't melt the cold, icy tone of his voice.

I ran back past a table of lab-coated technicians, past James who was standing in the hall with his mouth wide open, and into the lobby where Carol Conroy was exiting the building. Feng had magically disappeared.

I almost ran over Eden Callahan, who started to say something to me, and I pushed open a glass door. She'd only exited seconds ago, but there was no sign of Carol Conroy. There was no sign of a living person in the parking lot. No people, no traffic this morning, just the desolation that is always Carol City. Eerie, depressingly quiet. And then I saw her.

Her head was bobbing, five, six rows away. Her Lexus must be up ahead. I yelled. "Mrs. Conroy." She never looked up.

I heard an engine roar, breaking the solitude, and saw the car come out of nowhere, streaking down the strip of pavement. As I ran down across the asphalt, between the parked cars I heard the sickening thump and watched her body fly into the air, up over the hood and bounce off the top of the car. I kept running, my lungs burning like the fires in hell.

Now I was in the lane as she rolled on the pavement, and I hoped it wasn't too late. Her body lay in a crazy, twisted heap. Up ahead the automobile had braked to a screeching halt, the driver realizing that he, she, had hit the woman. I stopped, leaned against a Dodge Viper, and gulped in large mouthfuls of air.

It was then I saw the tail lights flash on and the car went into reverse, gaining speed by the millisecond. I jogged toward the broken body as the auto streaked toward me. At the last second, I dropped, banging my shoulder and feeling the hot asphalt burn my bare arms and face. Rolling hard to my right, I ended up under the nearest vehicle, a Chevy Silverado. I worried about my heart as it banged in my chest, trying to get out. It was the second time I'd been under a vehicle in this same parking lot in the last week. It was the tenth time, twentieth time, thirtieth time my heart had scared me almost to death.

I wish I'd been blinded to the view of what happened, but I wasn't. I stared out as the gray Honda Accord, swerving back and forth in reverse gear, hit Carol Conroy's lifeless frame with a bump, crushing her legs and chest. Rolling over the cadaver, the Accord switched gears, and roared out of the parking lot. Everything went silent, and it was as if life went on. Only it didn't.

I shuddered, rolling out and running back to the building, bursting in and gasping for air.

"Call nine one one. Now. Carol Conroy's been in a serious accident." Serious accident? "She's been killed."

The girl behind the desk, Daliah or something like that, dropped the magazine she'd been reading, and punched in a number as I grabbed the reception counter and tried to catch my breath. She spoke briefly as I huffed and puffed. Serious huffing and very serious puffing.

"Moore."

I looked up and Feng was standing there. "Suppose you tell me what happened."

Between gasps I said, "Suppose you tell *me* what happened."

"You told Daliah to call nine one one?"

I couldn't talk. There wasn't enough oxygen in the room, hell, not enough oxygen in the world, to fill my lungs. Breathing heavily, I leaned against the receptionist's counter.

"Moore. Tell me what happened."

"I," gasping, "just," taking two huge lungfuls of air "saw you."

"You saw me?"

"I saw you," breath, breath, breath, "run over Carol Conroy with your car."

CHAPTER FORTY-EIGHT

James was in office five, splicing a wire connection.

"Drop it pal. This project isn't going anywhere right now."

"Bro, I've got about ten minutes here and I'll have the —"

"Drop it." I screamed at him, and he stepped down from the ladder. Without looking back, I strode from the room, knowing he was right behind me. I was the person in charge of this project and people had better start paying attention.

Through the work area, through the hallway, and into the lobby. Daliah was on the phone, talking fast and furiously. "Yes. Her body is still there. No. Wait, there's another call. Hello? Yes. We're off of a Hundred Seventy-Second Street. Please hold. Hello? No, she's," Daliah paused, "she's dead."

I turned and James was right behind me.

"We're out of here?" He asked me so innocently.

"Yeah. We're out of here. In another minute the cops are going to be here asking me all kinds of questions."

I heard him, quietly behind me. "See you tonight. Eight sharp. And, I'm looking forward to it."

The response was equally soft. "James, be careful. Take

care of yourself." Eden Callahan was praying for the date to still be on.

Son of a bitch was still in there working it. If we had a Friday night, my roommate was set. If we *had* a Friday night.

No other words were spoken. James came up by my side as we exited the building, and he looked the other way when we walked by the blanketed body and the three paramedics who were lifting her onto the stretcher. What was left of *her*.

He didn't say a word as we approached the truck. James pretty much knew what I was thinking and I knew that he did. It was scary how close we were. Em and I shared a very close relationship. Not as close as I wanted, but damned close. James and I — it went beyond understanding.

He opened the door of the truck and started the engine. The traditional cough, the belching of black smoke, and he put it into drive. "Where are we going?"

"Remember the day care center?"

"The one we visited on that first GPS excursion?"

"Tiny Tots Academy. The same."

"I remember."

"There was a reason Feng stopped there."

"And the locked building?"

"No one there to ask, but we can ask someone at the school."

He pulled out of the parking lot, and as we glanced out of the windows, we could see the emergency vehicle parked by the body of Carol Conroy. It was hard to fathom, hard to understand. Here was a lady who was supposedly scared for her life, a lady who had asked for our help, and a lady who had led us down a very dark path. Here lay a lady who had betrayed her husband and me. Me. I wasn't getting a check from this lady. I know it sounds very selfish, but when you think of the time, effort, and expense we'd gone through, I had a reason to be slightly upset. Somebody had to pay for the smoke detector/camera.

"Why the day care center, Bro?"

"I want to see who works there, James."

"Very strange."

Ten minutes later James pulled into Tiny Tots Academy. Somewhat shaken and battered by the ride, we stepped from the truck. I opened the front door and walked in. A policeman greeted us right inside.

"What can I do for you two gentlemen today?"

The uniform caught me off guard. "Is there trouble here?"

"No. Why?"

"You're a policeman—" And, I thought, a murder just happened fifteen minutes ago. The victim was a lady who carried a pencil from this place and—

"Off duty. Off-duty policeman. This is my day job. Security for—"

"Can I ask you a question?"

"Certainly."

"You have a professional staff here?"

"Of course. The instructors. I believe most of them have certificates. You guys surely aren't here to check licenses." He looked me up and down. Jeans, the bruise on my arm, a ripped T-shirt.

James looked at me, still not sure where all this was going.

"No. I don't check licenses. But you also probably have volunteers, am I right?"

"We do."

"Do you know any of them?"

"Most."

"Is there a volunteer named Carol Conroy?"

"There was. She worked one or two days a week."

Yes. Finally a good piece of spying. I was proud of myself. "She worked?" Past tense.

"I understand that she's no longer with us."

I nodded. "Did she ever have a visitor? Maybe an Asian gentleman in a security uniform. Drove a Honda Accord."

The cop studied me for a second. "No. Not that I ever saw."

Maybe he was lying to me. I'd had this thing half figured out, but if he never saw a visitor—

"Now, Mr. Chen, he drives a Honda."

"Mr. Chen. The guy who owns the laundry?"

"Yep. The same. He stopped by most days she was here and they had little meetings out by the playground."

I grabbed James by his shoulder. "Thanks." I spun around and walked out the door.

"What the hell was that all about?"

"I don't know for sure. But Chen has the same car that Feng has. I think we put a GPS unit on Chen's Honda, not Feng's. Chen has been meeting with Feng in the parking lot at Synco daily."

"Yeah. That's what J.J. said."

"James, it was Chen's voice that I heard while I was hiding under the Honda in the parking lot. After I put the GPS on the car, those two guys walked up and it was Chen, the guy with the scuffed shoes, that was talking to Feng."

"Okay. So why is he visiting this school?"

"Don't you get it? To meet Carol Conroy. She probably volunteered so they could have a safe place to meet. Think about it. They could walk outside, talk, pass information, and kids don't gossip."

"We know Chen wants those codes. But Chen and Carol Conroy?"

"I don't have all the answers. I mean, this thing is going faster than I can keep up with it. My guess is that Chen was working with Carol Conroy. Chen was pushing Sandy Conroy and Feng to get the codes from the Department of Defense. He and Carol were planning all along to take the money and split."

"So Chen was the Chinese connection and Carol was the Synco Systems connection. And Ralph. The deceased Ralph? Didn't we hear that he was supposed to be getting the codes?"

Somehow I knew that Ralph had never known Sandy, Feng, Chen, and Carol were going to steal defense secrets for the Chinese. Ralph looked at the software order as a great sale. That's probably all it was to him. The others were plotting on how they could make $75,000,000 off the government. And if Ralph Walters did find out that they were plotting the dastardly deed, that was probably the reason he'd been killed.

"As soon as Synco Systems got the codes and passed them on to the Chinese, the Chinese could start downloading the computers. Chen would get the seventy-five million from the Chinese government for all the secrets, and Carol Conroy would let the whole thing blow up in Sandy's face. They would lay all the blame on her husband."

"And it would blow up in Sarah's face, and Feng's face."

"And ours. We both heard her say that."

James took a left, ran a stop sign, and tromped on the gas. "So it was going to be Chen and Carol Conroy?"

I'd only gotten so far with my logic. If you can call it logic. "When she hired us, we thought *she* was the victim."

"Right. She told you she was afraid of being killed."

"So she fooled us. She sucked us in and made us a part of the game. We'd naturally think that Sandy and Feng were the bad guys. And her husband Sandy thought he'd been *somewhat* for-given with the Sarah infidelity thing, and that Carol was going to share the money with him and pin the crime on Sarah, Feng, and you and me."

"The other night when they were in the building, she sure made it sound like it was going to be just the two of them. She was good at manipulating people, Skip. There's a talent there."

"Was good."

"And Sandy thought he was the chosen one."

"He did."

"But it was Chen."

"And once the codes were passed down and Chen had the money, once all the groundwork had been laid by Carol Conroy, she was expendable."

"So why did *Feng* kill her in the parking lot?"

He still didn't get it. "Feng and Chen both had gray Honda Accords."

"Yeah."

"It had to be *Chen* that hit Carol Conroy with his car. He probably assumed no one was around to witness the hit-and-run, and even if someone saw it he could blame it on Feng. Same car."

"Clean the car, fix up the dents, and go on his merry way."

"Seventy-five million dollars richer."

"And what about Sandy Conroy?"

I'd considered that. Carol Conroy would have planted some deep evidence that he was guilty of stealing secrets. And he was. If she didn't kill him, the evidence would.

He hit a pothole and the truck veered to the right.

"By now, Sandy's probably figured out that he's one of the scapegoats."

"What about us?"

I didn't want to tell him what I thought about us, but I figured he needed to know. "I believe that Sandy Conroy knows we were the ones who hacked his computer. He admitted to Carol that he thought we were spying on him."

"So he's after us?"

"By now, I'd bet on it. He's going to do everything in his power to cover his tracks."

"What about Chen?"

"Chen's already tried to kill us. I think he'll continue to try."

"Oh, my God. So Chen is the one who shot at us. Not Feng?"

"He is. It was his gray Honda that J.J. saw. I'll stake my entire pay on it." I was quickly realizing that was a hollow stake.

"So what do we do now?"

"Call Jason Riley."

James pulled into our apartment complex, slamming the tires against the sidewalk as he came to a stop. I know that one day he's going to go up over the walk and right into the building.

"Who, pray tell, is Jason Riley?"

"Department of Defense contact. Remember? His name was on Sandy's list when we broke into his computer."

We stepped from the truck and walked up to the door. Someone had left a note in an envelope, shoved inside the screen door.

"Skip, we can't trust anybody at this point. You just made that case. And how can you be so certain that the codes have been passed?"

"Carol Conroy was run down by Chen's Honda. He doesn't need her anymore. Which means —"

"He's going to take out as many of us as he can."

That was my thought.

"And what are you going to tell this Riley? Assuming he's straight and not on the take."

I unlocked the door and walked in, tossing the sealed envelope on the small kitchen table. "I'm going to make the case as fast as possible and tell him to either stop any access to their computers or change the codes immediately."

"Jesus, Skip. If you're right, the fate of our entire country's defense is in your hands."

That's something you just never expect to hear. I mean ever. But I suppose he was right.

CHAPTER FORTY-NINE

I'll admit it. I didn't have a shred of evidence to present. I'd heard conversations, we'd found a GPS on the truck, and attached it to a UPS surrogate. We had the smoke detector video of Conroy's conversation, and it disappeared. I'd had two face–to–face conversations with a dead woman, but no actual proof that we'd ever met. I'd attached a GPS unit to a gray Honda, and now I wasn't even sure whose Honda it was. But I still had to make a call to Jason Riley. Without a shred of evidence, without any idea of how codes work at the U.S. government level, I had to explain to this guy that someone was trying to steal all the information stored in the Department of Defense computer system.

"As I pointed out, pard, this guy may be part of the problem. He may hear you spout your suppositions, your hypothesis, and he might be the next guy in line to take you out. *Us* out.

I pointed at my laptop. "Can you get online and find a phone number for the Department of Defense?"

"I'm sure they have a main number where people like us can just give them a jingle anytime we feel like it."

"James. Try it." There were times when I wanted to choke him.

He clacked away at the keyboard, occasionally giving me a dirty look. I walked to the refrigerator and grabbed two cold beers. Popping the top on both, I took him one and got a half smile.

"Son of a bitch." He obviously wasn't happy that I'd been right. "Here's the number." I looked at the screen. 1 (703) 428-0711 +1.

Sometimes a free beer does the trick. I dialed the number, glancing at the time digitally displayed on my cell phone. If they ran the department like a business, they should still be open. Their phone rang three times and then an automated attendant answered. I waited, two minutes, and finally the robotic voice gave me directions. Three minutes later—a lifetime when national security is at risk—I was connected to a live operator.

"How can I help you?"

"It's a matter of national security that I speak to Jason Riley."

"National security?" I heard a snicker in her voice. Obviously this was not the line that terror threats came in on.

"Lady, this could be the most important call you'll ever take in your life. Please tell me how I can reach Jason Riley."

It was obvious that she had no idea who Riley was. Neither did I.

"Let me check that name, *sir*." Very brusque.

Quiet. There was nothing on the line. After thirty seconds, I thought there had been a disconnect. Finally, she answered. "He happens to be in his office and will take your call." She sounded surprised. My guess was that no one was ever in their office. Every employee at the Department of Defense had voice mail and every employee used it. I waited about thirty seconds.

"Hello. This is Jason Riley. How can I help you?"

"Mr. Riley," sounded like a young guy. If he was part of the problem, I was just digging us in deeper. If he was a good guy, then we were still in a lot of trouble. "This is Skip Moore and I need to tell you a story you are not going to believe."

"I've heard stories like that before. Someday I'll write a book. Go ahead, Mr. Moore. Tell me your story."

I did. Passionately laying out a half-brained plan that had only been hatched in the last two or three hours. But it flowed. Better than when I talked to James. And I saw my best friend, my roommate, nodding enthusiastically as he picked up the unopened envelope on the table.

"Mr. Riley, stop any access to your computer system. Don't let anyone from Synco Systems have access to your system." James tore open the side of the envelope and pulled out a sheet of paper.

There was a dead silence on the other end of the line.

"Mr. Riley?"

"Mr. Moore, do you seriously think that we pass out computer codes to every vendor that we do business with?"

"I hope not."

"I appreciate your concern, but I can tell you, there's no one who has access to any codes. I'm not sure where you got your information, but whatever you've heard regarding that is nonsense."

"Mr. Riley, have you ever heard of Chi Mak? Stole missile secrets from the government? How about the DOD employee that kept defense secrets on his home computer?"

"That was something that—"

"Oh, and finally, do you remember how many laptop computers went missing at the Rocky Flats project outside of Denver? The place where they make the bombs? I think it was four or five computers. So, Mr. Riley, don't tell me that the United States government doesn't just give away secrets on a regular basis. I'd say it happens a lot."

"Mr. Moore, give me your phone number and I'll have someone get back to you."

I knew damned well he already had my phone number. By now he probably knew that I'd graduated from Samuel and Davidson college, that I worked for Jaystone Security, and that Em and I were dating. I was easy to track. They were all spies, every one of them.

"Mr. Moore?"

James was waving the paper in my face.

"Look, Riley, I can't stress to you enough how serious I am. I am positive that the codes for your computers are going to be used to steal defense secrets. If you don't take that warning seriously, we're all going to be in some deep trouble."

"Thank you, Mr. Moore. The department appreciates your concern. Now, if you'll give me your phone number —"

James waved the paper in front of my face.

I said a silent prayer, and flipped the phone closed. If Riley didn't take me seriously, we were all in a world of hurt. If he did, well, I'd been known to be wrong before.

"It's Em." He handed me the paper.

I saw her signature at the bottom of the sheet. My eyes drifted to the top.

Mr. Moore,

I knew that wasn't the salutation I'd expect from her.

> *Your girlfriend is in our custody for the moment. We expect you to deliver the video/computer card to the following address or she will be killed. Don't take this to the authorities. Don't call anyone for help. You'll hear from us by phone.*

The letter was signed by Em.

285

"I am so sorry, pard. Whatever we need to do, I'm here."

"Jesus, James, say a prayer." My phone rang and I grabbed it.

"Mr. Moore?"

"Where is she?"

"Safe."

"You son of a bitch."

"Well now, Mr. Moore," I was getting very tired of the Mr. Moore crap, "with that attitude I can't guarantee her safety for much longer." I listened carefully to the muffled voice, trying to place it. It sounded as if someone was talking through a sweat sock.

"I'm sorry. How can I get her back?" James sat in the kitchen chair straining to hear every word from the other end of the line.

"Sandy Conroy says that you have to bring the video card."

"Where? When?"

"Thirteen twenty-five Waterview Lane." When I finally caught my breath, I thought it out. The locked up building. The two-story cement-block structure that had shown up on the GPS tracking device. They wanted me to deliver the card to that address. The biggest problem was, I didn't have that card. Someone had taken it. And Em's life was on the line. I'd been in some tough situations, but this one was the worst.

"When do you want it?"

"Now."

"Now?"

"Be here in one hour, Mr. Moore. And bring Mr. Lessor with you. I'd feel better knowing where the two of you are at the same time."

"We'll be there."

"Mr. Moore, one more thing."

"Yes?"

"Bring the white truck."

"Okay."

"Not the brown one." And he was gone.

James was leaning in, picking up the conversation. "Didn't seem to appreciate the UPS truck diversion, did he?"

"Nope. What are we going to do, James?"

"J.J. is home." He'd walked to the door and looked outside.

"I don't care about J.J. We've got to get that card."

"Listen, amigo. You may not agree with this, but Jim Jobs turns out to be a pretty good tech guy. Hell, he worked with nuclear bombs. Look how he took charge of your project."

I didn't need to be reminded.

"If we can lay this out for him, maybe he can help us."

"Jim Jobs? Have you lost your mind?" He was already walking down to J.J.'s door.

CHAPTER FIFTY

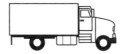

"Closed the place down, boys. Feng comes out and says 'everybody go home.' And then he and the Gestapo stood there by the front door and checked everyone before we left."

"And the cops?"

"Oh, they got all of the names and contact information." J.J. sat on the well-worn green cloth couch, his wrinkled T-shirt proudly announcing *Age and Treachery Will Win Out Every Time Over Youth and Skill*. I hoped that wasn't true.

"Guys, we don't have time to sit here and discuss this. Em is in serious trouble."

"Em?" J.J. gave me a puzzled look.

I laid it out as fast as I could, and it still took me over four minutes.

"You don't have this card, correct?" He smiled and I could see his tongue through the missing front teeth.

"No. And if I don't produce this card, this blue —"

J.J. scratched himself, let out a long breath and stood up. He turned the corner at the hallway, a mirror opposite of our apartment, and disappeared from view.

"James, Em is in serious trouble and we're dealing with a—"

"Here you go." J.J. had the identical card between his thumb and index finger. "It's blank, with a lot of static on it. Now, if you give this to them, it's probably enough. If they want to check it out to see if it's the genuine card from the smoke detector," he glanced at me, then held me with his eyes, "that one I told you was going to be trouble. Do you remember?"

I nodded.

"Well, it will have static. You tell them that it was run through a magnetic field. You got on an airplane or went through a metal detector somewhere."

"That erases the card?"

"No. But chances are these guys don't know that. We haven't got time to develop much of a plan at all. Go with what you've got."

I couldn't believe this guy actually had a plan at all. "We'll use it. Thanks so much, man."

"You mentioned, briefly, that you had other detection equipment?"

"Well," James started to do his shuffle, possibly because a spring from his chair seemed exposed and was possibly painful. "We used a GPS unit and something called The Sound Max. It's a—"

"Hey, I know The Sound Max."

I remember rolling my eyes at James. "I doubt that you—"

"Long wand, picks up conversations from almost anywhere."

Damn.

"This building, it's got two stories?"

"Yeah."

"Get there early."

Early was now.

"Set that puppy up on the roof and record the entire transaction."

"Thanks, man."

"It's the best I can do on short notice." He picked up a toothpick from the end table by the couch and started working in his mouth. James and I bolted for the door, and sixty seconds later we were on the road.

"For a ten-minute talk, it's not a bad plan, Pancho."

I had to admit it.

"Damn Sandy Conroy."

"James, it's not Conroy."

"Guy on the phone said it was." James ground the brakes at the stoplight, looking right and left, then driving through the red.

"Doesn't make any difference. Chen is the only one who knows about the card."

"How do you figure?"

"We were in the building the night Sandy Conroy asked Carol about us spying on him. She didn't volunteer the information about the smoke detector, did she?"

"No. It never came up."

"But she thought Chen was her partner. Chen was meeting with her at the Tiny Tots Academy. She told him about it. Chen knew about the card."

"Why didn't she give it to him. It pretty much incriminated Sandy Conroy."

"I would guess, just a guess, that she kept the card as a bargaining tool. She had evidence on Sandy with the card. Chen may not know what's on it, but he knows it has some evidence of the codes."

"So you're pretty sure Chen has Em?"

It rang in my ears. Chen has Em. Chen has Em. Chen has Em. "I'd bet on it. And he's blaming it on Sandy Conroy, just in case we tell anyone."

The brakes ground as he stopped at a light. It flashed green and James tromped on the gas as the truck eased ahead, slowly.

"James, if anything happens to Em, I will never, ever forgive myself."

"I won't forgive myself, amigo. But you know what? We're going to get her back. I promise you."

We were both quiet for sixty seconds. Then I could see the building, two blocks away, the gaudy graffiti splashed all over the outside. "I'd give my life for her, James."

"Hey, you won't have to."

"I would. I really would. I just know that." At that moment there was no question. If I had to die to save her, I'd do it. I just didn't know it would come to that.

CHAPTER FIFTY-ONE

"Where do we park the truck?" James wheeled into the small parking area. I watched as the black and red whirls and swirls blended and spread out on the white stucco surface of the building. The artist had almost effected motion in his spray-painted tableau.

"Pull around back."

You could ask James just about anything, but don't ask him to back up. Without a rearview mirror—using only side mirrors— he was a basket case. But pulling around back was within his capabilities.

And there it was. As if by magic, a metal ladder ran to the roof of the second floor, bolted to the graffitied surface of the structure.

"You son of a gun. I've been around you all my life, Kemo Sabe, and I've never seen you get so lucky."

I jumped from the truck and jogged to the rear, opened the sliding door and pulled out The Sound Max.

I checked my cell phone. We had about twenty minutes before I had to turn over J.J.'s bogus card. Pulling the box with the wand and recording unit out, I walked to the ladder, and, cradling the equipment in one arm, I started the climb. Two stories. Not a big deal.

"You'll be all right, compadre," James yelled up after me. He knew I was somewhat apprehensive when it came to heights.

Another step, and don't look down. And another, and another. You can make fun, laugh if you will, but once anyone steps off ground zero, things get a little iffy. By the time I passed story one, I was breathing hard. Partly from the exercise, partly from the fear. I finally reached the top, looking down at James in the truck and wanting to throw up.

Pulling myself up on the roof, I refrained from looking down again. I dropped the bundle, then set the folding tripod in place. Lowering it to almost surface level, I mounted the wand onto the tripod. "James, can you see the wand?" I never looked down. Just shouted out loud.

"I see nothing, pardner."

Plug in the wire, to the wand, then to the recorder. That should do it. The battery pack still showed two hours of life. If anything was said in the parking lot, we should be able to capture it. The word capture gave me a chill.

"Get down here, pal. They may be coming any minute."

"Without an armload of spy ware, the descent was considerably easier. And, I was headed for the ground, where I belonged.

"Quick, let's drive around front."

James shifted into drive and pulled around front, parking next to the door with the rusty padlock.

"Number one thing is to get her back. That's all. That thing on the roof, it's not the most important thing here, James."

"Settle down, pard. Courage."

"I don't feel so courageous. I just want her back."

"We're the only ones who can do it. Cops aren't any help."

293

The bitterness was in his voice. "You know, whatever we say down here, right now, will be on the recording up there."

"Yeah."

So we both shut up for five minutes. The occasional car drove by, a couple of box trucks similar to ours. Even a police car cruised by. Nobody gave us a glance. The workingman's vehicle, a used Chevy box truck. It was like walking into a business with a tie on and a clipboard in your hand. I'd heard that you could go just about anywhere with a clipboard. You looked official and nobody would question you. And I agreed with James that you could drive a box truck just about anywhere as well. It just seemed to fit.

Three blocks away a gray Honda turned the corner. "Heads up, amigo."

"We've got to get her back, James."

"It's the Lord's will. I mean it."

The car pulled up and the driver's door opened. An Asian man stepped out. Dark hair, good build, square jaw, and a sharp crease in his trousers. Professionally ironed, I would guess.

"Mr. Moore, I don't believe we've met." He didn't offer his hand. "Do you have the card?"

I looked down at his feet. The black shoes were scuffed. "I have the card, Mr. Chen. Where's Emily?"

"Safe."

"Where?"

"I'm going to take you to her. Let me see the card."

The Sound Max was up there picking it all up. I needed to make sure there was no mistake as to what was going on. "Once I give you this card, you'll release Emily?"

He glanced around the parking lot. Walking to the truck, he unlatched the rear door and looked inside. Finally he walked back to me. "Yeah. I'll release the girl."

That was what I needed to hear.

"Lean against the car, hands on the door."

I did as he ran his hands over my sides and front. I would have been hard-pressed to conceal a recorder in my jeans and T-shirt. He had James do the same thing.

"I assume this is the card," he said as he pulled an envelope from my rear pocket.

I hesitated. This was the moment I'd dreaded. If he didn't believe it was the real thing, I could probably say good-bye to Em.

"Get in the car."

James took a step back.

"You. You drive the truck and follow us."

Chen opened the passenger door, and I glanced at the hood before sliding in. A dent on the left side looked like a body might have done the damage. Shuddering, I closed the door. James got in the truck.

Chen was quiet as he started the car.

There were so many things I wanted to say. So many questions I wanted to ask, but if this guy knew what I thought *we* knew, he'd never let any of us go. I'd pretty much figured out he was behind Ralph Walters's death and possibly those of Tony Quatman and his wife. I knew he'd killed Carol Conroy. This guy had nothing left to lose, except the rumored $75,000,000 from the Chinese. I think LeBron James got a contract with Nike Shoes for $99,000,000 and he never had to kill anyone. Just rough them up on the basketball court.

We drove a familiar path. I'd been heading that way for several days now, and I was pretty certain that Synco Systems was our final destination. This was the time where Chen should admit what had been going on. Telling me that he had a private plane taking him to an unknown location, and we'd never hear from him again. But he didn't. This was the place in a good movie where I would say, "You know, you'll never get away with this. The Department of Defense has all the information on you, and they're freezing all their codes." But I didn't.

I was pretty certain that the DOD had blown me off. And this was the time I should have leaned over, looked him in the eyes as he drove, and said, "If anything has happened to her, I'll hunt you down and kill you." But I didn't. Nothing was said as we pulled into the parking lot, James driving in behind us.

Chen got out of the vehicle and looked back at the truck. "I didn't think that thing could make it this far."

He opened his trunk, and motioned to James and me. We gathered around and he pointed to a large package in the well. "It's heavy. Pick it up and take it inside."

We looked at each other, an uneasy frown on James's face. Together we picked up the box, about the size and weight of a case of beer. It was wrapped in several layers of plain brown paper. I wondered how much $75,000,000 in cash would weigh. Probably more than this, but I certainly had no frame of reference.

"Go." A man of few words.

Three cars were in the lot. Em's new blue BMW wasn't one of them. Neither was Sandy's yellow sports car. There was Carol Conroy's Lexus, a new Cadillac, and another gray Honda Accord. I could only guess who was left in the building.

"Work room. Set it on a table." We put it on a worktable next to a computer station and stepped back.

"Office one." Chen pointed. No gun, no force, just the fact that he had Em and we didn't.

I opened the office door and there they were. On the floor, side by side, tied with white plastic rope. Sandy Conroy, Feng, and Emily. And sitting on the desk, pistol in hand was Sarah Crumbly.

"Skip. I'm really sorry you had to get involved." She nodded at me, a grim smile on her face.

"Gotta go where the money is, right, Sarah?"

"It's just too sweet a deal to pass up, Skip. Just too sweet."

CHAPTER FIFTY-TWO

I'd never seen it coming. But then, I'm not sure she did either. Sarah Crumbly was a hooker. For sale to the highest bidder. When someone made her a better offer, she took it. It was as simple as that. It made sense.

"Can we untie Emily now. You've got your card." James froze his stare.

"It's not quite that easy." Chen glanced around the room. "We're taking the girl with us."

"Hold on, you promised me that—" I glanced at Em. A rag was stuffed in her mouth, and her eyes were full of fire.

"We're leaving her at the abandoned building. If you leave this building, or this office, within the next half hour, we'll kill her."

I turned my attention to Sarah. Hooking was one thing. Killing was something else. She never met my gaze, just held onto the pistol, waving it back and forth at the trio on the floor.

"Are we understood?"

I wanted to jump this guy. He was about five eleven, in good shape, but I knew James and I could have taken him. And why we didn't, I don't know. I don't think that Sarah had the courage or desire to fire the pistol, but I couldn't take the chance.

Chen leaned down and picked up Em, dragging her toward the door. "I'm closing this office door. And then I'm going to stand here and wait. I can't tell you how long. If you open that door, I'll shoot the girl, and I'll shoot you. Do you understand?"

I nodded.

"You can pick the girl up at the building in an hour." Cold, menacing.

Sarah jumped off the desk and followed Chen out the door. I didn't hold out much hope that she'd survive this ordeal either, but you could never tell. She pushed the door shut and James and I stood there, not knowing what to say. Em was still in a lot of trouble.

There was a gurgle from the floor and Sandy Conroy scooted on his back and gave me a pleading look. Feng stared up as well.

"I don't see any reason to help these two, do you?" James nodded to the two men.

"No. James, we should call the cops."

"You should *never* call the cops, Skip." The day they hauled his father off to prison was the end of any trust James had for officers of the law.

"But, man —"

"Bro, you call, they go after Chen, he kills Em."

And, of course, he was right.

"What do you think was in the box?" The thought was in my mind too.

"I thought it might be money."

"Yeah." James sat down on the edge of the desk. "Lots of money."

"James, do you think they'll leave Em off at the building?"

"Skip, I can't figure out why they left us all here. I mean this guy has apparently killed anyone who got in his way. So why leave us all alive to tell the authorities what happened?"

"Makes no sense."

We were quiet for a minute. I glanced at my cell phone and saw that five minutes had passed. Sandy and Feng lay on the ground, obviously very pissed off at us.

"Do you think they're out there? Ready to shoot if we open that door?"

"No." I didn't. I figure Chen was buying time. He was long gone.

"Care to take a peak?"

I thought about it. Em's life would be in danger. I walked to the door and twisted the handle. "I'll just tell 'em I had to go to the bathroom."

I opened the door just a crack. Couldn't see much. A little wider and I froze. There she was, lying on a worktable next to the brown box. I cringed, waiting for a gunshot. Nothing. I opened the door just a little farther, and saw the raw fear in Em's eyes. Quickly glancing around the room I saw they were gone. And then it hit me.

I bolted out of the room. "James. Down. On the floor." I grabbed the box, heavy, bulky like a case of beer, and I bolted for the doors. Down the hall, past the reception area, my legs pumping, my arms aching. The flames in my lungs leaped into my throat and my mouth as I hit the door. It opened and I ran into the parking lot, thinking that I'd seen this play out once before. Ten steps into the lot, I heaved the box, fell to the ground, and buried my head under my arms. I think I heard the roar of the explosion. But I'm not sure. I was dead.

CHAPTER FIFTY-THREE

If you donate your organs, they like to harvest them when they're fresh. And when the body is still functioning, but there's no brain activity, the organs are fresh. I never signed the paper to donate my organs. Probably a good idea, considering.

They call it neurologic shock. There's no brain activity and your brain is swelling from the concussion. As far as I'm concerned, when your brain quits working, you're dead. And that's what the doctor told me.

They can drill holes in your head to give the brain room to swell. James would have had a field day with that solution. But I think it was a drug, Mannitol, that takes fluid from the brain so it goes back into your bloodstream, that saved me. That and a bunch of very good doctors. I've got to thank the team of Drs. Bob and Pat Gussin, James Kahn, Praveen Malhotra, and Anne Gideon. I'm pretty sure I wouldn't be around if it hadn't been for them.

"You saved us, pally."

"Yeah. But died in the process."

James grabbed my arm and squeezed. Very hard. I thought

there were tears in his eyes, but this was my buddy James. I'm sure I was mistaken.

"Visiting time is over." The surly nurse escorted him out. Five minutes at a time. They said they just wanted to keep me alive this time. I appreciated the effort.

"Two weeks. And it seems like two minutes."

"Hey, you slept most of the time." Em looked great, fresh, hair hanging down around her shoulders, a light summer dress. She stroked my cheek. "You're getting a little shaggy, Skip."

"When you sleep twenty-four-seven there isn't much time to shave." I was sitting in a chair. An hour a day now.

"I kind of like a beard on you."

"So, you've been quiet about current events."

Em sat on the edge of the hospital bed. "They caught Chen. He never got out of Miami."

"You know the thing about Sarah is that she's a —"

"I know. James told me. She wasn't with him when the cops took Chen in."

"You don't think he killed her?"

"Personally, we don't think there was time. James is scanning the escort services. He says she'll show up sooner or later."

"They know that Chen killed Carol Conroy?"

"Evidence was all over his car. He never got it fixed."

"And Sandy? Feng? How can they still be walking around?"

She reached out and put her hand on mine. "No evidence. They didn't do anything wrong."

"You and I both know that's bullshit."

"Can't prove it, babe. That video card hasn't turned up. If there's any evidence on that, it's disappeared." She stroked my hand. "You saved their lives."

I couldn't help but smile. "I did. I did. Didn't really care about their lives."

"You saved mine. You saved James."

"Yeah. Come to think of it —"

Ellen DeGeneres was on the flat-screen television. No sound. I could look out the window and see two stories below. There were three box trucks clustered by a construction site where workmen were building an expansion to the hospital. "The truck's gone, right?"

"Yeah. James found another one. Not quite as good, but it's the same model. He's trying to pull some money together —"

"He's nuts."

"He's your best friend."

"Other than you."

The phone rang and I flipped it open. "Yeah."

"Amigo. I'd be there today, but I'm working two shifts at Cap'n Crab. Got to make some extra money for a new truck."

"Yeah, well, I'm sorry I blew up your old one."

"Could have been me, Skip. I owe you so much, I'll never, ever be able to pay you back for this one."

"You know, you showed me how to dispose of a bomb. I just didn't think I'd ever have to use your example."

He chuckled. "Called Riley at DOD, pard. He's not there."

"Like, not in?"

"Like, doesn't work there."

"James, I talked to him. Tried to get him to cancel the codes."

"Very hush-hush. I don't know if they downloaded from the computers or not."

Em smiled at me. Beaming. She'd had that smile since she walked in.

"What about the money? Did Chen have the millions?"

"I get the impression, no. But no one's talking." James and I would probably never hear all the details.

"And Synco Systems?"

"Closed. I don't know what's going to happen." I did. They weren't going to pay the bill. Carol Conroy couldn't pay the bill, and the best I could hope for with Sarah was to take it out in trade. And with Em in my corner, that wasn't ever going to happen.

"Hey, James, did you thank J.J.? I mean, he gave us the plan."

"He did. Cops took the sound card from The Sound Max and they're going to use it as part of the case against Chen. They've got him on explosive charges, attempted murder, kidnapping—"

"But no stealing codes. International espionage or whatever it's called?"

"No proof."

"Anyway, thank J.J."

"Never got a chance, Kemo Sabe. He moved out a couple days after you died."

"So tell me, James, did the date with Eden ever happen?"

"Number three coming up this weekend. And number three is the magic one, right pally?"

"Good luck, James."

"Good looks and charm, Skip. That's all you need."

I suddenly felt tired. Not sleepy, but like at the end of a long workday, or at the end of a long vacation where you partied just a little too hard. I said good-bye to James and closed my eyes.

"Hey, I'm going to stay awhile. If you want to sleep—"

"Maybe." I opened my eyes again. "Do I still have a job?" Flowers from Michael were on the desk. I think he bought them in the discount bin at Wal-Mart.

"I think so. Obviously things are a little crazy at Jaystone right now."

I smiled. I hoped I had a job. I needed the money. I owed Jody Stacy for a smoke detector, GPS unit, and The Sound Max. The cops were keeping that as evidence. Jody apparently had called Em several times. Checking up on me, probably checking up on when he'd be paid, and I'm certain he was checking up on Em. Another reason to bust out of this joint as soon as possible.

"So no one is looking into the fact that secrets were stolen? That the DOD was compromised?" I gazed at her. God, she looked good.

"Oh, I think they're looking into it every minute. I think the government is scared out of their minds right now. I think, because of you — because of you —" she started crying. "Because of you, Skip Moore, I'm alive."

"Hey."

"No. Let me say this. I didn't make this up, someone said it before me, but I mean this so much. So much." She wiped the tears from her eyes. "To be your friend was all I ever wanted. To be your lover was all I ever dreamed." She hugged me and hugged me and hugged me, and I hugged her back.

Damn. Now Emily was doing obscure quotes and I had nothing to give her back.